MW00491761

The Other Tenant

The Other Tenant

Lesley Kara

bantam

TRANSWORLD PUBLISHERS
Penguin Random House, One Embassy Gardens,
8 Viaduct Gardens, London SW11 7BW
www.penguin.co.uk

Transworld is part of the Penguin Random House group of companies
whose addresses can be found at global.penguinrandomhouse.com

Penguin
Random House
UK

First published in Great Britain in 2024 by Bantam
an imprint of Transworld Publishers

A CIP catalogue record for this book
is available from the British Library.

ISBNs
9781787636125 (hb)
9781787636132 (tpb)

Typeset in 12.5/17pt ITC Giovanni Std by Jouve (UK), Milton Keynes
Printed and bound in Great Britain by Clays Ltd, Elcograf S.p.A.

The authorized representative in the EEA is Penguin Random House Ireland,
Morrison Chambers, 32 Nassau Street, Dublin D02 YH68.

Penguin Random House is committed to a sustainable future
for our business, our readers and our planet. This book is made
from Forest Stewardship Council® certified paper.

To Phoenix Heath, Milo Max and Theodora Moon

DO YOU HAVE WHAT IT TAKES TO BE
A PROPERTY GUARDIAN?

We have vacancies all over London starting from £50 a week and are looking for tenants with a difference – responsible people willing to act as property guardians.

You would occupy a shared living space (although solo occupancies are sometimes available) under a non-exclusive licence agreement, and would be required to look after the property in accordance with the property guardian guidelines.

Please note, your live-in presence would act as a deterrent for antisocial behaviour common to unoccupied buildings, e.g. squatting or asset-stripping, but in no circumstances would you be required to intervene in or prevent criminal activity.

You must be 18+, employed, and with no live-in dependents or pets.

Please email Harry Kiernan at hkiernan@guardianangelsinc. com for an informal discussion.

Hayley

This place gives me the creeps. Pools aren't supposed to be empty. They're meant to be full of water. Blue and inviting. Silky-smooth against the skin.

It isn't just the air of neglect, or the dated, institutional vibe; there's something about the shape of it I find unsettling. The hard, unforgiving angles of the exposed rectangular basin. The dramatically sharp slope to the deep end. Then there are the clinical white tiles with black mould in the grouting, like food stuck between teeth. And the metal ladders, flat against the sides.

I walk as far from the edge of the pool as I can possibly get, convinced I can still smell chlorine, still hear the echo of shrill voices, the splashing as young bodies propel themselves through the water. Every time my trainers squeak against the tiled floor, I flinch.

The tiered seating area to my left is shadowy in the fading light. I force myself to swivel my head, braced for the sight of a lone spectator watching my every move, even though I know I'm quite alone in here. I've been observing it from outside for ages, and no one has come in or gone out. If only my rational brain would communicate that fact to my heart, which is beating fit to burst through my chest.

When I've satisfied myself that there's nothing of interest to be found in the immediate vicinity of the pool, I climb the stairs to the spectator area, letting my gaze travel along each row of seats. Then I look under the seats, but apart from old sweet wrappers there's nothing there. I go back down to the pool and into the changing rooms, where a thorough search reveals nothing more exciting than a couple of slimy old swim caps and a pair of dirty knickers left scrunched up in a locker.

Feeling much calmer now that I can no longer see the exposed shell of the swimming pool, I explore the rest of the building. The door to the pump room stands open, and I can see all the equipment inside. The bank of switches on the wall. The maze of pipework and valves, that looks like the back of a giant washing machine. The massive filtration cylinder and circulation pump.

Even with everything turned off and disconnected, it feels dangerous to be standing so close to it all. For a moment I think I hear a ticking noise, like a radiator warming up. I stand perfectly still and listen intently. No, the only sounds I can hear are my own breath and the beating of my heart.

I reach out my hand and touch the cylinder with the very tips of my fingers. Stone cold. Of course it is. This pool has lain empty and unused ever since the school closed down two years ago.

I'm about to leave and do a quick check of the toilets when I hear footsteps coming from further down the corridor. The brisk, echoey slap of shoes on linoleum. I freeze. I'm definitely not hearing things this time.

Panicking, I look around for somewhere to hide.

I push the pump-room door till it's almost closed, then tuck myself behind the filtration cylinder. I crouch down on the floor and hold my breath as the steps draw nearer. I hear a door opening and closing, and the footsteps stop. I can't be sure, but I think they've just gone into the changing rooms.

Shit! I left my tote bag on one of the benches while I was searching the lockers. My phone is in that bag. What if it starts ringing?

My knees are stiff from crouching down, and I shift position. Further along the corridor, a door swings shut. I hold my breath, too petrified to move a muscle. *Please God, don't let them have found it. Please God, don't let anyone call me until they've gone.* The footsteps start up again, only now they sound like they're heading away from the pump room and back towards the exit that leads to the playground.

I rock back on my haunches, relief flooding through me. I must be crazy doing this. I should have got the hell out of here days ago. Slowly, gingerly, I stand up.

And that's when I see it, tucked behind one of the pipes that run horizontally along the wall about four inches from the floor. Suddenly, I know exactly what's going on here. I know what this is all about.

The tap on my shoulder makes me gasp. If this is who I think it is . . .

I turn my head reluctantly, desperately trying to think of a good reason for why I'm here, a reason that will reassure them I'm not—

'Oh! It's you!' I almost laugh out loud. 'Thank God.'

Then I see the look on their face and register what they're holding. But . . . but surely that's for something else. It can't be . . .

My mouth goes dry. I've got it wrong. So very, very wrong.

'I won't tell,' I say, my voice little more than a squeak.

The loud rasp of the gaffer tape as it peels away from the reel makes my stomach contract.

'I promise I won't—'

I

Marlow

The agency is supposed to give me a month's notice, and to be fair, they usually do. But not this time. I've got less than a week to pack up my stuff and find somewhere else to live, before the developers move in and turn this place – my home for the last ten months – into two swanky apartments, the likes of which I'll never in a million years be able to afford.

I look into the eyes of the angel in the stained-glass window, and a small part of me hopes for divine intervention.

'Come on, Angie.' My voice echoes in the rafters. 'Prove you're not a figment of the collective imagination and bloody well *do* something. Save me. Please.'

For one split second, I think I see a flicker in Angie's

glassy eyes, but of course it's just a trick of the light. I squint up at the benevolent figure in the blue robe. Perhaps he isn't keen on being called Angie, although it's a bit late to give him a new name now.

From somewhere outside comes the sound of a fire engine. It cuts straight through me like a jolt of electricity, and I find myself waiting, as I always do, breath suspended in my lungs, to see if the sound gets closer or recedes. Today, thankfully, it recedes. My shoulders soften and I exhale.

I turn away from the window and face the empty pews. My invisible congregation.

'Right then, you lot, we've got work to do.'

When I first spotted the old chapel on the agency's website, I knew straight away that I'd be happy here. It was just a feeling I had. An inexplicable sense that, out of all the possible places I could choose to live, this one would suit me best. I guessed it would be draughty, and it is. But the cold keeps me sharp, makes me feel alive. In any case, the beauty of the building, its *history*, more than makes up for its chilly interior.

There was another, more compelling reason why I was so keen to move in. It was a solo occupancy, and that alone made it an attractive option, never mind the Gothic architecture or the way the light shines through the stained-glass window. Never mind the solidity of the thick stone walls and the sturdy, double-planked door with its iron studs and bands to repel intruders.

8

When I draw the heavy bolt across each night, I feel an overwhelming sense of peace and security. Now though, everything's up in the air again. If the agency can't find me another suitable vacancy, I'll be homeless. There's always Dev's place, of course. I won't exactly be on the streets, but even so . . .

In the tiny vestry, I retrieve my large, framed rucksack. It's the most useful thing I've ever bought. One of the most expensive too, apart from my camera. As I lift it clear of the hook on the wall, the backs of my eyeballs start to tingle. I screw up my face and shake my head till the sensation passes. Tears are no use to me – they won't change anything. I've always known this day was coming. Everything in life is temporary. Provisional. At least, it is in mine. But it's the life I've chosen, so I can't really complain.

I plonk the rucksack on the vestry table and unzip its various compartments, running my hands inside each and every one to check they're empty. Once, I found a tenner folded up small and caught in one of the seams. I love it when that happens – it's like an unexpected victory. No such luck today though.

Half an hour later, I've made a good start and packed my underwear, my second pair of jeans, and the few T-shirts and jumpers I still possess. I've also packed my sturdy walking shoes – I had to scrape the dried mud off the soles first and give them a good clean – plus the waxed jacket with the fur-lined collar I found on a bus. Yes, I know I should have handed it to the driver so he could take it back to the depot as lost property, but I really needed a coat, and it's my size and a good make, and somehow I found myself putting it on and getting off at my usual stop, casual as anything but with my heart thumping wildly. It's not quite the same as stealing, is it?

My phone vibrates in my pocket, and I pull it out. It's Harry from the agency.

'You're in luck,' he says. 'I've found you another place, but you're going to have to make your mind up quick. It won't hang about. Not this one.'

My heart soars. When he called me with the bad news earlier this morning, he offered me a room in an empty office block in North Acton, and I turned it down. He wasn't best pleased. I'd heard what he was thinking in his voice: *beggars can't be choosers*. But that's where he's wrong. I'd rather doss with Dev for a few weeks than shack up on the floor with a load of other people snoring and farting on the other side of a flimsy partition wall. I've lived in an office block before, and it was a dismal experience. Almost as bad as working in one.

Sometimes, being a property guardian feels like a brave, exciting thing to do. I'm an adventurer, living on the edge, spurning the tedium of a humdrum existence. A non-conformer. A *bohemian*. Other times, it feels sordid and sad. Not much better than being a squatter, as my dad would say. As he *has* said, on more than one occasion.

'Sounds promising,' I tell Harry. 'What is it?'

'A school in North London. You'd have a whole class-room to yourself in a nice old Victorian building. We've already got a small team installed there, but one of them's had to leave at short notice.' I hear him sigh. 'I'm really annoyed with her, actually,' he drawls in that bored-sounding, public-school voice of his. 'She was adamant she wanted this licence. I turned down several good, reliable applicants on the strength of that.'

I don't say what I'm thinking: that it's a bit rich of the agency to expect 100 per cent commitment from their guardians, when long-term security is the very last thing they offer us. Harry's given me hardly any notice to vacate the chapel, and I wouldn't mind betting I'm as good and reliable a guardian as any on his books.

'I can whizz the details over to you in a sec,' he says. 'But it won't be available for much longer.' He pauses. 'I've got at least six other people interested in this one.'

'I'll take it.'

'Sure you don't want to look at the details first?'

I hesitate, but only for a second. A whole classroom to myself, and the architecture in some of those Victorian schools is stunning. If I wait till he sends the details over, someone else is bound to beat me to it. Harry always makes out he's on my side and that he's doing me a big favour by letting me see the best places first, but all he really cares about is bums on floors. Whether it's my bum or someone else's won't matter a jot to him.

'I'll take it,' I say again.

When the email comes through a few minutes later and I click on the link, my legs start to wobble, and I have to sit down. I assumed it would be an old primary school. They're always being sold off and turned into luxury flats.

But this is a secondary school. And not just any old secondary school. It's *my* old secondary school.

I stare at my phone in shock, the old panicky feeling rising up through my body, swelling like a wave. I'll have to call him back and tell him I've changed my mind, tell him the accommodation isn't suitable after all. Of all the places to be offered . . . I've spent the last eighteen years trying to expunge McKinleys from my memory. I can't go back. I can't.

I shake my head and try to blank out the images that blaze through my mind because if I don't, the physical sensations will surely follow: the tight chest, the racing heart, the sweating. But it's too late – they're already happening. I'm burning up. Even my eyes have started to sting.

I get up so fast I knock the chair backwards. It lands with a crash on the stone floor, but I don't stop to pick it up. I leave the vestry and go back into the nave. *Think of something else, quick. Look at this place. Just look at it. Focus on what you can see. Right here. Right now. Focus, and breathe.*

Eventually, the mindfulness techniques I've perfected over the years begin to work and the panic recedes. In the late afternoon sun, the chapel is more beautiful than ever. I press the camera icon on my phone and line up another shot of the window. I'll miss it so much; the way the light refracts through the stained glass, the way it lends everything it touches a heavenly glow. I've taken hundreds of pictures since I've been here, and no two are identical. It's like watching the sea every day from the same position on the shore. The light changes everything.

I post the picture on Instagram, then stuff my phone back in my pocket and lie down on my favourite pew, the one I've draped with scarves and covered with scatter cushions. I gaze up at the vaulted ceiling and reflect on my situation. If I turn down this offer, I'll almost certainly end up in that ghastly office block. I'll have to get rid of half my stuff or ask Dev to store some for me. All my lovely finds.

A whole classroom though . . . now that would be something. It might even be good for me, seeing the place empty and unused. Consigned to history. It might even, in some weird, masochistic way, be healing. Exposure therapy, isn't that what it's called? Facing your fears head on. Extinguishing them one by one.

I look up at the window. 'What should I do?'

Angie stares down at me, as he always does. Silent. Benign. Do I honestly expect him to give me an answer?

'Please, Angie, give me a sign if you think I should go. A wink or something.' My voice rings out in the silence. Pleading. Almost childlike. A *wink*? Am I mad?

I'm about to fish my phone out of my pocket and read Harry's email again, when an arrow of light falls across the pew and makes me start. I squint up at the window. It looks like a laser beam is coming straight out of Angie's left eye. In all the time I've been here, I've never seen the light do that. Not once.

It's a fluke, that's all. A freaky coincidence. To interpret it as a sign would be absurd.

And yet . . .

I must have watched this clip on Twitter (or X or whatever it's called now) a hundred times or more, yet each time it gets better. First, a slim guy dressed in black saunters up to a car parked on one of the driveways. It's night-time in a typical suburban street on the outskirts of London. He tries the handle, and for a second it looks like he's one of those opportunist car thieves. But then, in one swift, practised manoeuvre, he's done something to the lock and got the door open.

As he steps away and out of view, another man, also dressed in black, enters the frame, chucks something on to the front seat, and sprints away. Within seconds, the car goes up in flames. The speed is astonishing. Exhilarating.

Then comes the voiceover from the person filming. His voice is low but jubilant. 'And that, my friends, is what happens when you spout a load of shit on the internet.'

I add my comment to the ever-growing list under the video.

'Pity he wasn't in the car when they torched it.'

Someone immediately pounces on me. Someone called @Sue5Dilby. 'What's wrong with you people? Why do you have to be so hateful?'

So hateful? Is that the best she can come up with? I'm about to respond, when the familiar clang of the letter box and the thump of what sounds like a heap of post landing on the hall floor drags me away from my screen.

I go downstairs and scoop it up. None of it's for me – it hardly ever is – but I take it back to my room anyway. My housemates have been pissing me off lately, always going on about how I don't clean up after myself in the kitchen. Just because I left a couple of dirty cereal bowls in the sink one time and got curry stains on someone's best tea towel. Christ Almighty. Talk about uptight. And who the hell has a best tea towel?

I spend a little time reading their post. Then I drop it into the fireplace grate and put a match to it all. I'd lay a proper fire in here if I could, but we're under strict instructions from the landlord not to use any of the old fireplaces in the house because the chimneys haven't been swept. Fucking tightwad. Bet he's got one of those poncy woodburners in his own house.

There's something mesmerizing about fire, isn't there? Watching the flames dance in the air. Listening to the distinct-ive crackling and popping sounds. There's nothing like it. It's such a destructive force. The speed that car went up – it was incredible.

After I've swept the ash out of the grate and put it in my waste-paper bin, I return to my scrolling. Maybe it's time I had a break from watching that video. I have a quick look at

@Sue5Dilby's timeline, but honestly, she's so boring I'm not even sure I can be arsed to wind her up. And she's hardly ever online. Where's the fun in that? I follow her anyway, just in case. From a different username. Obvs.

I know, I'll have another pop at some of those lifestyle twats on Instagram. I haven't done that in a while and they really crease me up. I've been following a few new ones lately. Like this one who calls herself Boho Birdie and goes on about all the beautiful vintage pieces she's found. She's got ten thousand followers, would you believe? Ten thousand followers who drool over her photos and say things like '@bohobirdie, you are SUCH an inspiration!'

Excuse me while I puke. She doesn't say where she lives, only that it's a renovation project in London that she's been working on for the last couple of years. To be fair, it is rather beautiful. Looks like it could have been a church in a former life.

I'd love to know what she looks like, but unfortunately, she never does selfies. She posts the odd story, but she's always behind the camera, never in front of it. Same with her reels. Her stupid fucking reels that everyone seems to love but which make me cringe. Why don't these saddos realize how embarrassing they are?

Every so often there's a glimpse of one of her hands, or a foot. Once, she posed in front of a full-length mirror, but the way she took the photo you couldn't see her face. She jokes that nobody wants to see her 'ugly mug' and that anyway, 'it's all about the interiors'.

Now come on, Birdie, tell the truth. It's not all about the interiors, is it, love? It's all about YOU!

I think about that video. What a buzz it gave me, seeing that dickhead's car get torched. Imagining his reaction when he looked out of his bedroom window.

You see, people think we're harmless in real life. They think we're sad, pathetic creatures who wouldn't say boo to a goose, but we're not. Not all of us, anyway. Some of us don't mind taking things offline once in a while. Some of us actually relish the chance.

2

Marlow

It's Sunday, two days after my conversation with Harry Kiernan, and I'm ready to go. I could have stayed on for a few more days, but there's no point in hanging about and prolonging the agony. I walk round the outside of the chapel to make sure it's secure and that there are no signs of forced entry, no fresh graffiti on the walls or litter in the tiny, overgrown graveyard. I've followed the same routine every single day for the past ten months as part of my duties, and I've come to enjoy the ritual. The silent communion with the dead.

Earlier this year, during the peak of the heatwave, I found a smouldering disposable barbecue tray someone had tossed into the bin. People are so stupid, so thoughtless. I shudder to think what might have happened if I hadn't sensed something was wrong and gone out to investigate. One spark flying out on to the tinder-dry grass, and the whole graveyard could have been set alight.

That kind of thing happens to me sometimes. Dev says it's nothing more than good, old-fashioned intuition, and laughs when I tell him I'm sure it's a form of psychic ability. I mean, there was no *way* I could have known about it. There was no smell or noise, not inside the chapel.

Fire. My worst fear. I screw my eyes shut. Refuse to think of it.

There's a nip in the air today, a reminder that autumn is on its way. The leaves have already started to change colour and fall, and for a moment I stand among the ancient gravestones, mulch sticking to my trainers, and let the sadness wash over me. If it weren't for Dev parked on a double yellow line at the front of the chapel, I'd stay even longer.

When I finally tear myself away and join him on the street, he's hoisting the last of my bags into the back of his white van, a grubby Ford Transit.

'Don't know what I'd do without you,' I say.

It's the first time I've said anything like that to him, but lately I've sensed a slight shift in our friendship, as if something has come loose, some vital connection that might suddenly and irrevocably sever.

'Sure you mean me and not the van?' he says.

He's grinning, but something about his eyes isn't right. I plant a kiss on his stubbly left cheek.

'We are OK, aren't we, Dev?'

'What do you mean?'

'I dunno. You seem . . . different.'

He gives me a level stare. 'You think?'

'Dev, you *can* talk to me, you know, if something's bothering you. We're mates, aren't we?'

Dev laughs, but there's an edge to it. 'Yeah, course we are.'

He shuts the doors at the back of the van and walks round to the driver's side, opens the door and climbs in. I get into the passenger side. I've got a bad feeling about this.

He points at the satnav stuck to his windscreen. 'Stick the address in, will you?'

'Shit! I've left my Rubik's cube on the altar table.'

Dev sighs. 'Don't tell me you're going to go through the rigmarole of unlocking and locking that fucking door again for a piece of old tat?'

But I'm out of the van before he can say another word. I've had that cube all my life and it's coming with me. One of these days, I might even manage to solve it.

Ten minutes later, the cube safely on my lap, I tap the postcode into the satnav and settle back as Dev starts the engine and pulls away. Anyone else would probably turn around to take one last look at the chapel, but not me. When one part of your life is over, it's over, and that's that. *Finito.* Jobs, lovers, homes, childhood. There's no point revisiting any of them. No point at all.

So why the hell am I going back to my old school?

Because I've run out of options, that's why. And because

Angie told me to. In his own, inimitable way. At least, that's what I'm telling myself.

'Guess I won't see you much if you're living on the other side of town,' Dev says.

'You can see as much of me as you like.' I glance at the side of his face. 'Stay over tonight if you want.'

We've shared a bed before, usually when Dev's had a drink and can't drive home, but we've never actually done more than cuddle up for a while and fall asleep. I get the feeling he'd like more, but he's never tried it on. Not once.

My words hang in the air between us, and I'm horribly aware that they sound like an invitation.

His left hand lands on my knee and gives it a brief squeeze. There's something apologetic about it. 'Cheers, but no. I've got an early start tomorrow.'

'Oh yeah? Where you off to?'

I didn't particularly want him to stay over, not on the first night in a new place, but now that he's said no, I feel snubbed. Rejected. How stupid is that?

'Bristol. Then it's Birmingham the day after.'

I nod. All the kids are starting uni. Dev and his van are in demand. 'I suppose you could have done without me adding to your workload.'

Dev shrugs. 'It's what mates are for, innit?'

He puts the radio on, and for the rest of the journey, neither of us speaks much. It's not exactly awkward – we've known each other too long for that. But it's not entirely comfortable either. I uncross my legs and roll my neck, first in one direction, then the other. I hear it pop and do it again. I think of what another friend, another 'mate', once said. *You could do a lot worse than Dev, you know.*

Even now, months later, that comment still rankles. It was the underlying assumption that I probably don't have much hope of doing any better. Or worse still, that settling for Dev is better than being on my own. It sounds like the sort of thing my mum would say, if she were ever to meet him. Not that there's anything wrong with him. Dev's cool. Dev's a laugh. Well, normally he is.

Who am I kidding? Dev's so much more than that. Dev is my best friend and I've taken him for granted, assumed that what suits me suits him too. I meant what I said earlier. I don't know what I'd do without him.

We've reached the outskirts of Belsize Park now, with its tree-lined streets and wide pavements, its trendy boutiques and cafes. With Camden to one side and Hampstead to the other, it's a world away from Woolwich. As a property guardian, I've lived on both sides of the river, but I've grown to prefer the south. It doesn't take itself quite so seriously. And yet here I am, moving north again.

I shift position in my seat, forcing my gaze on to the windscreen and the road ahead. We're passing through a more residential area now. I'm holding myself so stiffly, my neck and shoulders have begun to ache.

'Bet these places cost a bomb,' Dev says, more to himself than me. The disapproval in his voice is unmistakable.

I check out the grey plantation shutters on my parents' bedroom window. Not that it *is* their bedroom window. Not since they sold up and moved into a fancy apartment in Montpellier. But apart from the shutters and two different cars on the driveway, the house looks exactly the same as it did when I lived there.

'Yeah,' I say. 'I bet they do.'

We're almost at the school now. It looks both familiar and eerily different. Like one of those weird dreams where you think you recognize where you are, but it's not quite the same as you remember, and you're lost and unsettled.

Dev peers at it through the windscreen. 'Looks like it must have been a private school.'

If I told him what the yearly fees were and that I used to be a pupil here, he'd never believe me. There are times when I hardly believe it myself. He'd be furious, too, that I've been lying to him all this time, pretending to be something I'm not. Our shared 'working-class' background and disdain for the privileged elite is what drew us together in the first place, what binds us still.

The stupid thing is, if I'd told him to start with, we might still have become friends. I'd probably have had to work a bit harder to earn his respect, but once he got to know the real me, it would have been fine. I know it would. But it's too late for all that. Our whole friendship is based on a lie. To come clean now would ruin everything between us. It's why I can't even contemplate a romantic relationship with him.

The perimeter fencing is higher than before, with large, strategically placed notices that state: *This property is protected by live-in guardians.* But that hasn't stopped someone from scrawling graffiti across one of the fence panels where the property developers have fixed their logo. Big letters in red paint spell out the word 'SHAME'.

'I guess it makes a change from "Fuck Off",' Dev says, and even though I make an amused exhalation in response, I feel shaken by it. Where the paint has run it looks like blood, and there's something about that solitary word that's more unnerving than the usual obscenities. Shame about what?

'Take this side road on the right,' I tell Dev. If Harry's instructions are correct, the East Gate – at the entrance to the original school building – is the only way in and out of the campus, now that it's been secured by the agency.

The old tightness in my chest returns. The Monday-morning dread that used to start at about four o'clock on a Sunday afternoon. But it's more than that this time. I can feel it in my gut too. As if I'm shivering from the inside out. What on earth was I thinking, agreeing to move here of all places? Why the hell did I take any notice of a stupid angel? Correction: a decorative window. I must be mad.

Dev parks up, and I get out to press the button marked 'Reception'. After several long minutes, when I'm on the verge of getting back in the van and telling Dev I've changed my mind, a male voice answers.

'Hello? Who is it?'

'Marlow. Marlow Cairns. I'm moving in today.' The words don't sound real. Surely I'm not doing this?

There is a brief silence. Then the buzzer goes, and the gate slides open with a low whirring sound. I walk through and gesture to Dev to follow me in, tell him where to park the van. As I look up at the words carved into the stone lintel above the entrance – 'McKinleys School for Girls' – the gates click shut behind us and something in my stomach curdles.

This is a terrible mistake.

3

Marlow

The first time I stood here, aged eleven, I was flanked by
my parents. I remember gazing at the imposing red-brick
building covered in creeping ivy, its high arched windows
and bell-tower, and thinking it looked more like a church
than a school. Dad launched into one of his many lec-
tures, explaining all about Victorian Gothic architecture
and how it was expressly designed to draw the eye upward,
towards God. I was more than a little apprehensive, but
something of their confidence and pride must have rubbed
off on me that day, because I was excited, too. I was going
to be a McKinleys girl.

Now, as my eyes travel up to the finials on the roof once
again, my overriding sensation is queasiness. Why did I
ever think this was a good idea?

A lanky guy in his thirties steps out to meet me. There are old acne scars on his cheeks, and he wears a pair of tortoiseshell glasses. He pushes them up his nose with his middle finger and walks towards me.

'I was expecting you earlier,' he says. His eyes are small and sharp. Pink-rimmed, like a rodent's.

I stick my hand out towards him. 'Hi, how you doing?'

When someone is rude, I always weigh in with extra courtesy to make a point. But as soon as I touch his clammy palm, I really wish I hadn't.

'My friend is here to help me move my stuff in,' I say, trying to rub my hand on my jeans as discreetly as I can.

The two men grunt at each other.

'His name is Dev,' I say. Why are men so hopeless at this sort of thing? 'And you are?'

'Sorry, yeah, I'm Rob. Rob Hornby. I'm the HG.'

'What's that stand for?'

'Head Guardian. Follow me. I'll show you to your room.'

As soon as I step into the darkened interior of the school and catch sight of the old hall, I feel like a schoolgirl again. Eighteen years might have passed since I was last here, but it feels like yesterday. I keep expecting to hear the strident tones of Miss Latham, the headmistress, ringing out from the stage.

We pass the old office. There's just one computer now, rigged up to security cameras, and a typing chair on wheels with a torn cushion. A Bombay Bad Boy Pot Noodle with steam rising from it has been left on the one remaining desk.

27

'Looks like we've interrupted your lunch.'

Rob shrugs. 'It's too hot anyway.'

'The clue's in the name,' I say, immediately wishing I hadn't. I always make stupid jokes when I'm nervous. It makes me look like a pillock.

'This way,' he says. 'I'll give you the full tour once you've brought all your stuff in. You'll meet the rest of the squad later. I've arranged a meeting at seven o'clock. In the drama block.'

I almost groan out loud. After ten months of doing my own thing in the chapel, of not having to answer to anyone else, I've walked straight into my worst nightmare. I'm part of a squad.

'Where am I then? Which classroom?'

'You're in Block C, across the playground. Unit 9. Top floor. The lift's not working, I'm afraid.'

I stare at him, dismayed. Having one of the rooms in the beautiful old *Instagrammable* part of the school with the lovely arched windows was the only reason I agreed to come here in the first place. The only thing that made this decision seem slightly less crazy than it clearly is.

'But Harry said I'd be in the old building.'

Rob blinks behind his glasses. 'I'm afraid there's a bad leak in the room that's just been vacated. It's unlikely to be fixed for a while.'

'Oh, I don't mind about that. I've put up with a lot worse—'

'Sorry,' Rob says. 'You don't have a choice.'

I bite my lip. I want to tell him that I *do* have a choice. I can turn around and walk away from here right now. Go back to Dev's place and wait for something else to come up. I could even call my parents and blag the fare to Montpellier. They've been on at me to go over and visit them for ages, even though we all know we'll be sick of each other after a couple of days.

No. Weird and uncomfortable though it is being back at McKinleys, it can't be as bad as living with Mum and Dad again, listening to them go on and on about how I'm wasting my life and how it's not too late to turn things around.

I can still remember the shock on their faces when my A Level results came through. And when I refused to resit them and insisted on getting an ordinary job, the sort of job they didn't want a daughter of theirs to do, the shock turned to anger. I was the investment that didn't pay out.

Rob sets off across the hall towards the door to the playground. 'This room's actually better,' he says over his shoulder. 'No one's ever lived in there before, so you'll be starting with a clean slate.'

'Why don't we go back to the van first and get some of your stuff?' Dev says. 'Seems daft walking all the way over there empty-handed.'

'No,' Rob says. 'She has to check the unit first, and sign and date the inventory form and the declaration before she can start moving in.'

Dev pulls a face. 'Well, she can still do that, can't she? We'll leave the bags outside till she's signed the form.'

Rob shakes his head and keeps walking. 'We don't do it that way. Sorry. We have a system.'

I exchange a glance with Dev behind Rob's back. The 'Head Guardian' title has clearly gone to this guy's head. All the talk of squads and systems is making me uneasy. It's like being back at . . .

I laugh under my breath at the absurdity of it all. It isn't *like* being back at school. I *am* back at school, and in September too. Just like the start of a new school year.

A great heaviness fills me. I'd thought seeing it like this, empty and abandoned, would be good for me, but already I'm regretting it. The old feelings are coming back. Not that they've ever gone away.

We're halfway across the playground before I risk a glance at the enclosed garden on the left – Lottie's garden – and am shocked to see that the sculptures have been removed. All three of them.

Rob sees me looking and stops.

'There used to be an art studio there, but it was demolished after a fire.'

It's a common joke as a child, to say you wished your school would burn down. I bet most kids have said it, or thought it, at one time or another, but you never really mean it. When that fire started, it was terrifying. I only have to smell a whiff of smoke now and it all comes back.

'They said it was probably accidental,' Rob says. 'Something to do with batteries exploding, apparently. Although they couldn't entirely rule out the possibility of it being deliberate.' He starts walking again. 'One of the pupils died,' he adds, almost as an afterthought.

I stare at the back of his shoulders, appalled at the matter-of-fact way he says this, as if Lottie Lansdowne's tragic death wasn't the most awful, shocking thing to have happened. She was my closest friend. McKinleys was never the same again. How could it have been? The events of that terrible day cast a pall over everything. They're why I flunked my exams, and I wouldn't mind betting they were one of the main reasons why the governing body eventually chose to merge with another school and sell the premises, burying the name McKinleys and all that dreadful history for ever.

'The family have started a local petition to keep the memorial garden on site and incorporate it into the new development,' Rob says. 'There's a lot of support for them locally. It's turned into a real campaign.'

He carries on walking. 'The owner's in negotiations with them over it, but between you and me, I doubt he's going to give in. He strikes me as the sort of man who always gets his own way. Which means it's only a matter of time before this whole playground, including the garden, becomes a residents' car park.'

Rob ushers us into Block C, his last words about a car park reverberating in my head. The graffiti on the fence makes sense now. Lottie's parents must be devastated, although I can't imagine they'd condone vandalism. But before I can fully digest everything Rob has told me, he's introducing me to two people who are coming down the stairs as we go in. A young woman with auburn hair cut in a sharp, chin-length bob, and a man with short Afro hair shaved at the sides.

'This is Craig and Elle,' he says. 'They're in Unit 8, two floors down from you.' He nods in my direction. 'And this is Marlow. She's replacing Hayley.'

'*Replacing* her?' Elle's face looks pinched with worry. 'Has Hayley gone then? She never said anything.'

"Fraid so,' Rob says. 'Family emergency.'

Elle turns to Craig. 'Did you know she'd gone?' Her face isn't pretty, but it's interesting. Attractive. Rob seems to think so too. He can't take his eyes off her.

Craig shakes his head. 'I had no idea. What kind of emergency? Did she say?'

'No. And even if she did, I wouldn't be allowed to tell you because of confidentiality.'

Craig rolls his eyes at Dev and me. 'No, of course you wouldn't.'

Later, when Rob's shown me the room and gone through all the paperwork, he finally gives me the go-ahead to start moving in. Dev is already outside, unlocking the van. As I go to join him, I can't resist glancing at one of the classrooms that lead off the main hall. I can't see inside because the window in the door has been covered with a piece of cardboard on which someone has written 'WET FLOOR – DO NOT ENTER'.

Curious, I try the handle, but the door is locked. I wonder why Hayley was allowed to live in there with a leak and yet I can't. Unless the leak was only discovered after she'd gone. I try to unpick the tape from one corner of the cardboard.

'Marlow? Are you coming or what?' Dev is standing by the main entrance, a frustrated expression on his face, and I hurry over to join him. As I'm carrying the first of my boxes across the hall and past Hayley's room a few minutes later, I have the same sensation in my gut I had when I first arrived. An internal trembling. A dread.

I swallow hard and increase my pace until I'm outside and the fresh air blows the feeling away. It must be all the negative energy associated with this school and its tragic past.

So why do I feel like it's more than that?

4

Rob

Rob makes up a new folder for Marlow Cairns and puts her signed inventory and induction papers inside it, lining them up carefully and paperclipping them in place. He opens the bottom drawer of the filing cabinet to the side of his desk and inserts the folder into the hanging file marked 'Licensees', making sure that it is positioned exactly in the centre so that there is an equal amount of green cardboard showing at either side. Then he closes the drawer, picks up his spoon, and starts shovelling the remains of the cold Pot Noodle into his mouth.

At least she didn't make a fuss when he told her about the room. She's fed up about it – he can usually recognize that emotion in others now – but she's accepted it. That's the main thing. She has a plain face, he thinks, and her nose is on the large side, but she looks clean. He doesn't like her two-tone hair though. Why would anyone want a purple fringe?

He wipes his mouth with the back of his hand, and carries the empty container and the spoon out to the kitchen. The day has turned gloomy all of a sudden, and he flicks on one of the wall switches, hearing the familiar low-level buzz of the fluorescent strip lights overhead. Instinctively, he heads for his favourite sink, the one he singled out for use on first arriving at the site, back in those glorious days when he was the only one here and had the full run of the place.

He rinses the container under the cold tap, then disposes of it in the recycling bin. Not for the first time, it occurs to him how much like a mortuary the kitchen looks, with its bank of stainless-steel equipment, now dulled with time, its clinical shelving units and metal tables on wheels.

A disturbing image flashes into his mind, but he forces himself to think of something else. For a second, he thinks he sees her in the corner of his eye. An apparition. He spins round, but there is nothing there. Of course there isn't.

On his way back to the office, he finds himself whistling one of his made-up tunes. But as he passes Hayley's old room, the anxiety returns, and he stops. The palms of his hands have begun to sweat.

Just when he thinks he is on the verge of understanding people, they go and do something monumentally stupid. His mouth sets in a grim little line. The sooner he stops thinking about her, the better.

5

Marlow

When Dev's gone, and I'm back in Unit 9 with all my belongings piled up on the floor, I take stock of my new surroundings. The room is bland and functional with ugly vertical pipework running up one of the walls. It's only when I look more closely at the ghosts of algebraic equations on the whiteboard that I recognize the handwriting. Of course. This floor is where the maths department used to be. This is Mrs Barrie's old classroom.

It's not what I was expecting, but I suppose it will have to do. That's the thing about being a property guardian. You learn how to transform the strangest of places into a home. All it takes is a little thought and imagination. A touch of creative flair. I could use the board as the base for some sort of collage. I could even make a feature out of this old flipchart stand in the corner, and attach some of my black-and-white photographs to it.

I run my hand over the last remaining sheet of paper. There's a faint imprint from a page long since torn off. It looks like the beginning of one of those logic puzzles. I squint at the words. *Bryony and Dave have been seeing each other for five weeks and four days.* Thankfully, that's the only part of the question I can make out. If I knew the rest, I'd be tempted to stop everything and work out the answer. I've always loved puzzles. They force me to focus and take me away from any worries, giving me a break from my incessant internal monologue.

I wander over to the windows. What they lack in aesthetics, they more than make up for with their view of the school campus and the city beyond. I never fully appreciated it when I was at school here. I took it for granted, that skyline. But a view like this comes at a premium. Whoever's bought this site is going to make an absolute killing.

The original vertical blinds are still in place, but they're old and unsightly. Broken, too, by the looks of them. I gaze down at Lottie's garden and, for a couple of seconds, the building that once stood there shimmers like a mirage in my mind's eye. A fissure of panic opens up inside me, and I have to press my hands on to the windowsill and breathe deeply till it passes.

Everything passes. Eventually. The acrid smell of smoke. The screams. The terror. But the embers remain. They never entirely go out.

I focus on a sun-catcher sticker stuck on one of the

windows. It's designed to look like a stained-glass tulip but, having lived with the real thing for the past ten months, I think it looks a bit naff and am about to peel it off. Then I have an idea. I pin the blinds out of the way with my elbow and take a stream of photos of the view, filtered through it. It's like an itch, this compulsion to take pictures, to view the world through a frame.

I resize the best of the images, pleased with the result.

'OK, tulip, you can stay.'

I put the picture on Instagram, and the likes come in almost immediately. The hit of dopamine I so desperately need right now. It's only as I'm turning away from the window that I catch a glimpse of something on the far end of the windowsill, partially hidden by one of the tatty blind slats. A pair of binoculars in a case and a small flask. That's odd. Neither of these objects were on the inventory Rob made me sign, which makes me think he doesn't know about them.

I unscrew the top of the flask, expecting to see grey mould, but when I gingerly peer inside, it's neither mouldy nor empty. There's an inch of milky brown liquid at the bottom. I give it a tentative sniff. The milk is starting to turn, but only just. Whoever left this here must have done so very recently. And yet, according to Rob, no one has been living in here.

I take the binoculars out of their case, instinctively drawing them up to my eyes and fiddling with the focus, although it's pretty sharp already. I can see directly into one of the classrooms on the first floor of the drama block opposite. A figure comes into view – a young woman wearing only her underwear, fair hair in a messy topknot – and I hastily put them down. Has one of the other guardians been coming in here to spy on her? I doubt very much they've been using these things for birdwatching. Not the feathered kind, anyway.

A sharp tap at the door makes me jump. I slide the binoculars further back behind the blinds. Maybe this is their owner right now. They've just realized the room is going to be occupied and are coming to retrieve them. Although won't that be tantamount to a confession that they're a Peeping Tom?

I open the door and see Rob, armed with a clipboard. 'Ready for the tour?' he asks.

'Tell me about the other tenants,' I say, as we head back across the playground towards the older part of the school.

Rob holds the door to the main hall open for me. 'We're not tenants,' he says. 'We're licensees. A tenant is someone who has a legally binding right to—'

'Yes, I know. I've been a property guardian before, remember? It's just that "tenant" is quicker and easier to say.'

Rob frowns. He pauses to remove his glasses, and gives them a quick clean with the hem of his jumper. 'There are three of us in this building,' he says. 'I'm in the old staffroom next door to the office, and Mags and Lou are further down the corridor.' He points in the direction of what used to be the English department. 'Don't get on the wrong side of Lou,' he says. 'She can be a bit . . . fierce.'

We're level with Hayley's old room now, and I wonder if Rob's noticed where I tried to unpick the gaffer tape from the cardboard notice on the window earlier. I might be imagining it, but I sense him stiffening as we pass. 'You're better off in Block C,' he says, even though I haven't said a word. 'It's much better equipped.'

He opens the door to the girls' toilets to prove his point. 'They're pretty rank now, as you can see. The ones in the newer part of the campus are more modern, plus the buildings are better insulated, and you've got the benefit of the showers in the drama and PE blocks.'

'I suppose you use the old staff loos then.'

'Yes. And a shower pod's been installed in what used to be the caretaker's cupboard.'

He's leading me into the kitchen now. I've only ever glimpsed it from the other side of the shuttered serving hatch that opens into the hall, which used to double as our refectory. I try to imagine the place full of red-faced cooks and dinner ladies, steam rising from pans, and for a moment, I fancy I hear the echoes of clanking plates and the lunchtime chatter of girls queuing up at the hatch, the imagined smell of school dinners connecting me to the past in an instant. Why, oh why, did I ever agree to this?

Rob points out the safety leaflets for each appliance and urges me to read them at my leisure. Now we're heading for the part of the corridor that turns right towards the science block and the old chemistry labs. A barrier blocks our access.

'You mustn't go beyond this point,' Rob says. 'It's one of the no-go areas.'

'Why's that?'

He shrugs. 'I guess it's possible there might be traces of hazardous materials somewhere. There's lots of junk still in the store cupboards.'

I raise my eyebrows. 'So you've had a look, have you?'

A slight flush creeps into Rob's cheeks. 'Certainly not. It's a no-go area. I thought I just told you that. Same goes for the bell-tower. The stairs aren't safe.'

He turns on his heel and marches back the way we've come. 'Just the drama and PE blocks now,' he says, as we emerge into the playground once more. 'Then we'll do a circuit of the grounds.'

The old gym smells the same as it always did, of rubber and stale sweat. The markings on the floor are faded now and most of the equipment has gone, but there's a torn leather pommel horse pushed up against the wall in the corner. Even in its current dilapidated state, it brings back unpleasant memories. The dreaded run towards it, knowing full well that there was no way on earth I was going to vault gracefully over it like the other girls, and that with every second I was getting nearer and nearer the ritual humiliation of having to clamber over, bare legs scrabbling to clear the leather, heart pounding from the effort, ears ringing with shame.

'Some of the squad play badminton in here, or use it to work out,' Rob says. 'Lou and Mags, mainly. And Big Dave. You'll meet them at the meeting this evening. Dave's always on the lookout for a badminton partner, so if that's your bag . . .'

'It isn't.'

Rob makes an approving noise. 'You and me both.'

'The only sport I was ever good at was swimming,' I say.

'Hah! You'd have liked being at school here then. They had their own pool. It's drained now, of course.'

Art and swimming – my two favourite lessons. The only things that made my life here bearable, until Lottie died and nothing about this place was ever the same again. Although, according to my parents, losing a friend in a school fire which also destroyed every last component of my A Level coursework was merely 'an obstacle to overcome'. A terrible obstacle, admittedly, Dad said. A tragic one, Mum added. But not something I should let *derail* me from my future.

My stomach tightens. They were of the opinion that I should have buckled down and spent every waking moment redoing my coursework, and doing it even better than before, not to mention all the other revision I still had to do for my academic subjects.

They thought having something to focus on was the best way through. The only way through. But it wasn't. Not for me. As if any of that exam shit mattered after what happened to Lottie. If good, kind people like her could die like that, in such a horrible, horrible way, what was the point in striving for anything?

Now though, and it pains me to admit this, I'm starting

to wonder if perhaps they were right. I can't keep living this itinerant lifestyle for ever.

Rob sets off again.

'Hang on, aren't we going to look at the pool?'

He shakes his head. 'Why would you want to look at an empty, dirty old pool?'

I can hardly say it's for old times' sake, so I settle for another, less revealing truth. 'I like architecture and design. I take photos of interesting places.'

Rob frowns at me as if I've just admitted to torturing small animals for pleasure. 'I'm afraid that part of the school is strictly out of bounds. The pool, the pump room. It's too dangerous.'

'I only want to look at it. I'm not intending to dive in.'

He shoots me a stern look, as if diving in is something I've seriously considered. 'You can't, it's been drained.'

I sigh. Rob Hornby is hard work.

'Besides which, it's structurally unsound. The whole building is going to be demolished at some point. Come on,' he says, striding ahead of me. 'I'll show you where the showers are, and then we'll head over to the drama studio so you know where to go for the meeting.'

As I'm following him inside, I catch sight of something green and gold and shiny glinting up at me from the ground, and I stoop to pick it up. It's a rather beautiful Art Deco drop earring. The sort of item I always gravitate towards at vintage-market stalls. The screw back is missing, and the post has what looks like dried blood on it – *eugh* – but all it needs is a nice soak in warm, soapy water. Sometimes I like to wear a drop earring in one ear and a plain gold stud in the other, although I should probably ask at the meeting if anyone's lost it before adding it to my collection. I wrap it in a piece of old tissue and slip it inside my pocket.

Rob is droning on about low water pressure in the showers now, but I'm only half listening. A plan is already forming in my mind. An empty pool will make a great picture. I could enter that competition with it, the one I saw advertised the other day. The first prize is £1,000, a top-quality Nikon camera, and the chance to have some of my work published in a reputable photographic journal. Or I could start that portfolio I keep thinking about. I can't spend the rest of my life taking pictures of weddings and babies for a living, and putting all my good stuff on Instagram for free.

I'll get into that pool somehow.

6

Elle

As soon as she opens the door to their room, Elle wrinkles her nose. It smells even stuffier than usual. Craig's trainers aren't helping. She's going to bloody well have to buy those odour eaters herself. She's dropped enough hints.

She opens a window and leans out, wishing that instead of this overgrown playing field and the row of houses backing on to it, she was at home with her family in the Suffolk countryside. She closes her eyes and pictures the view from her childhood bedroom. Rolling fields and haystacks as far as her eye could see. Not another house in sight.

She opens her eyes again and sighs. This place is doing her head in. She's had enough of living like this. She's had enough of Craig.

Behind her, she hears him flinging himself down on the ratty old sofa.

'Keep doing that and the springs'll give out,' she says, not looking round. She's trying not to nag him, she really is, but he'd try the patience of a saint. They say you never know what someone's really like until you live with them, and Elle, who thought she knew Craig pretty well before they moved in together, realizes that actually, she didn't.

'It's a piece of shit anyway,' he says. 'What's the point of being houseproud in this place?'

Elle looks at him over her shoulder. 'Isn't it time you got ready for work? Those shelves won't stack themselves, you know.'

Craig eases himself off the sofa and comes up behind her, resting his chin on her shoulder. She shrugs him off.

'It won't be for much longer, OK?' he says. 'We'll be out of here soon.'

'You reckon?'

'Yup. I can feel it in my water.'

Elle pulls a face. She hates this expression.

'And don't forget,' Craig says, 'it wasn't that long ago you were standing on street corners with the wind blowing up your jacksie. This is a step in the right direction.'

Elle rolls her eyes. She doesn't need reminding of some of the things she's done in the past. And why does everything that comes out of his mouth these days sound like a line from a bad film?

Rob and the new girl come into sight. They're standing

at the edge of the playing field and Rob is pointing at something.

'So Hayley's gone,' Elle says.

'Just as well. She was becoming a liability.'

'Yes, but what if—'

'Elle, stop it.'

The silence between them lengthens. 'You're going to miss her, aren't you?' she says at last.

He gives her a curious look. 'What makes you say that?'

Elle raises her eyebrows at him. He must take her for a fool if he thinks she doesn't notice these things, doesn't watch him sometimes from the corner of her eye.

'Don't tell me you didn't fancy her.' As soon as the words are out, she wants to take them back. She doesn't want him thinking she's jealous.

Craig laughs. 'How could I fancy Hayley when I've got a girlfriend as gorgeous as you?'

Elle rolls her eyes. He's got an answer for everything. 'It is a bit weird though, isn't it? That she's just taken off like that?'

'It's that kind of life, isn't it? People take off all the time.'

Elle wishes she could take off, too. Get the hell out of this awful place as fast as her legs can carry her.

'I just hope she's all right, that's all.'

Craig zips up the black-and-lime-green fleece he detests. Elle is looking forward to being on her own, but at the same time she feels guilty. He's got a long, tedious night ahead of him.

'She'll be fine,' he says.

But when he's gone, Elle is still worrying.

7

Marlow

Rob's tour finally finishes, and I make a start on my room. But I only have time to sort out my bed and unpack a few essentials before it's time to head over to the drama studio for the meeting.

It's exactly as I remember it. Black walls and ceiling. Black curtains. Grey carpet tiles and moulded plastic seats stacked up on each side. A set of ground rules has been written on an old whiteboard on wheels tucked into one of the corners. I've got as far as 'No parties' by the time Rob appears at my side. The writing gets smaller and more squashed the further down the board it goes, and I have to lean in close to read it.

- No barbecues or bonfires
- No candles in rooms

'We had to revisit these a while back,' Rob says, 'to refresh certain people's memories.'

Not about the bonfires and candles, I hope. The last thing this place needs is another fire. The sudden roar of a motorbike screeching to a halt outside makes us both jump.

Rob sighs, noisily. 'That'll be Big Dave. I've asked him not to drive across the playground, but he never takes any notice.'

The door swings open and Big Dave steps inside, removing his leather gloves and then his helmet. He is both tall and broad: a solid, large-bellied man with muscular arms and a bushy black beard. What little hair he still has on top of his head is closely cropped, but what strikes me the most about him is his eyes. Dark brown. Kind. With a mischievous glint. There's no way you could call him handsome, but he is kind of sexy.

'This is Marlow,' Rob says. 'She's just moved in.'

'So it's true?' Big Dave says. His forehead pleats in a puzzled frown. 'About Hayley? She's really cleared out without saying goodbye?'

I frown. Another one who seems surprised by Hayley's sudden departure.

'Yup.'

Big Dave shakes his head. 'You think you know people.'

He turns his attention to me. 'Marlow. That's an unusual name. Nice to meet you. I think you'll find we're all one big, happy family here.'

'Yeah, so happy that one of us pisses off without even saying goodbye.'

It's Craig, one half of the couple I met earlier. He's wearing an Asda uniform and he's with two women, neither of whom is Elle. One of them has short, spiky hair, dyed a vivid shade of red. The other's in a paramedic's uniform and has blonde hair scraped back into a long ponytail.

'I'm Mags,' the blonde one says. She gestures to her companion. 'And this is Lou.'

So this is the couple who live in the old part of the school with Rob. The part Harry implied *I* would be living in.

'Hi, I'm—'

'Marlow, yeah, we know,' Lou says.

Ouch. Rude.

Mags looks embarrassed.

'How long's this going to take, Rob?' Craig says. 'Only I'm on nights, remember, so I need to get going soon. Elle's not coming, by the way. She's not very well.'

Rob is staring, trance-like, into the middle distance, almost as if he's seen a ghost.

Big Dave looks confused. 'How long's *what* going to take?'

'The meeting,' Rob says, snapping back to attention. Big Dave widens his eyes in mock horror. 'The one that's been posted on the noticeboard since Friday. To say hello to Marlow.'

'Oh, well, if that's all it's about, I guess I can leave now,' Craig says. 'Seeing as we already said our hellos earlier.' He clears his throat. 'No offence, Marlow.'

'None taken,' I say.

Three more people stroll in. One of them, a slim, fair-haired woman who looks to be in her early twenties, is carrying a bottle of wine in a silver cooler sleeve. She waves it in the air and gives me a curious glance. I'm pretty sure it's the same woman I saw from my window, when I was using the binoculars. The woman in her bra and knickers. The other two, a man and a woman, also have a bottle carrier that clinks as they set it down.

Craig eyes the wine, clearly torn between leaving and staying. In the end, he leaves, muttering something about shift work ruining his life.

Big Dave takes it upon himself to start unstacking chairs and arranging them in a circle. Some of the others help him, while Mags goes off to fetch glasses. I notice that Lou's just plonked herself down and taken out her phone.

When Mags returns, the meeting begins.

'I thought it would be nice for us all to say hello to our newest member,' Rob says, raising his glass of orange juice aloft. 'So I'd like to welcome Marlow Cairns to the site, and make sure she knows everyone's names and feels secure here.'

Rob means well, that much is obvious, and I appreciate the gesture, even if it does feel a little odd, sitting in a circle of chairs in my old drama studio as if we're about to start workshopping a scene from a play.

'Right,' Rob says. 'Shall we go round the circle and introduce ourselves?'

Oh no. I take it all back. Not the dreaded ice-breaker.

The young woman who waved the bottle of wine in the air exchanges an amused glance with me.

'I'll start, shall I? I'm Bryony and I'm an alcoholic.'

Everyone laughs, Big Dave louder and longer than everyone else. 'Oops,' she says. 'Wrong meeting.'

Bryony. Where have I heard that name recently? Then I remember. I haven't heard it anywhere. I've *seen* it. It was the imprint of a maths puzzle on the last remaining sheet of flipchart paper in my room. Or what I assumed was a maths puzzle. *Bryony and Dave have been seeing each other for five weeks and four days.* That can't possibly be a coincidence, can it? If it had been 'Susan and Dave', or some other girl's name, I wouldn't have thought twice about it, but Bryony isn't exactly a common name. I think of those binoculars I found on the windowsill and my mind starts ticking over.

Bryony continues speaking. 'I live in this block. Upstairs, room at the end. I work for British Gas. In customer services.'

She pulls a business card out of her bag and hands it to me. 'I also design and make my own greeting cards. I sell from Facebook and TikTok, if you're interested. And Instagram.'

I nod politely, take the card, and slip it into my top pocket. I've lost count of the number of property guardians I've met who have some kind of artistic side hustle. It takes a certain type of person to embrace this precarious lifestyle, and creatives often seem to fit the bill. Probably because most of us are skint.

The woman sitting beside her goes next. She's dressed in denim dungarees and tatty old pumps, and wears a bright yellow bandana on her head. 'I'm Gilly. Gilly with a "G".

I'm doing a PhD at Birkbeck.' She speaks in a soft Scottish accent. 'And this is my partner, Nikhil.'

Nikhil, who's been staring at his knees, jerks his head up at the mention of his name and looks caught out, as if he hasn't been listening to a word anyone's said. He wears a slim-fit navy suit and a thin purple tie. His hair is jet black and thinning on top, like Dev's. He has the same tall, lanky physique as well.

'Yeah, that's right. But you can call me Nik. Most people do. I have a very tedious job in insurance, but I'm writing a screenplay.'

'Isn't everyone?' I say, but he doesn't laugh and nor does anyone else. *Read the room, Marlow.*

Gilly gives me a sidelong glance. 'It's very good,' she says.

I smile awkwardly. It's always so much harder joining an established community like this, where everyone already knows each other and has formed bonds. It's a bit like being the new girl at school. Which is, I guess, exactly what I am.

It's my turn to speak now. 'I'm Marlow, and I'm a photographer. I work at a commercial studio. Babies and weddings, mainly. And headshots for actors. I mean, that's the bread-and-butter work.'

A few years after leaving school and working in a series of dead-end jobs, I managed to put myself through an online photography course. Not quite the same as the degree from Central Saint Martins or Chelsea College of Arts which Lottie and I had both dreamed of, but at least

I did it, and what's more, I did it without my parents' help. Without their money.

'So you're in Hayley's old room, yeah?' Mags says.

I open my mouth to answer her, but Rob beats me to it. 'No, there's a leak. She's in Block C.'

Bryony frowns. 'A leak? Since when?'

A flicker of irritation passes across Rob's face. 'Since all that rain a few days ago,' he snaps.

Lou looks up sharply, worry etched on her forehead. It's the first time she's taken her eyes off her phone since sitting down. 'Rain? What rain? We haven't had any rain for weeks.'

She's right. It's been one of the longest, hottest summers I can remember. I get that strange feeling in my stomach again. The one I had when I stood outside Hayley's room.

Rob must be lying.

8

Marlow

Rob glares at Lou. 'It rained during the night. Now, can we press on, please? It's your turn to introduce yourself.'

Lou raises her eyes to the ceiling, where the studio light rigging used to be, and keeps them there the whole time she is speaking. 'I'm Lou. I work for the council. I used to be in a rock band, but we were a bit shit so we split up.'

'Nonsense,' Mags says. 'You were *fantastic*! That's how we first met,' she tells me. 'They used to do sets at my local pub. The rest, as they say, is history.'

Lou looks at her and smiles, but the troubled look on her face is still there.

'Anyway,' Mags continues. 'It's obvious from my uniform what I do for a living. Best job in the world, being a paramedic, apart from when you're being vommed over. Nice to meet you, Marlow.'

'Likewise.'

Big Dave clears his throat and twiddles his beard into a point under his chin. 'I'm Dave and, as you've probably realized, I'm quite a big bloke, hence the highly original nickname "Big Dave".' He pauses for the expected laugh, but this time only Bryony obliges with a polite chuckle. 'I live in the unit opposite Bryony's.'

Bryony is staring at her feet. There's definitely something going on between these two. Something they don't want the others to know about. Except someone here obviously *does* know about it, because they wrote it down on a piece of flipchart paper in my room.

But why? Why would they do that?

'You haven't told Marlow what you do,' Rob says.

Dave sighs and lifts his jumper to reveal an HMV T-shirt pulled tight across his belly. A wide roll of flesh covered in dark, curly hairs is visible between the hem of his T-shirt and the waistband of his trousers. I clock Bryony staring at it, as if she's willing him to notice and tug his T-shirt down. 'Think this tells you all you need to know,' he says.

Rob leans forward. 'Thanks everyone. I suppose it's my turn now, although Marlow and I have already met, obviously.'

'Obviously,' Lou parrots.

I frown. Does she need to be quite so rude?

'I'm Rob Hornby and I'm the HG at this site, in charge

of coordinating rotas and liaising with the agency about any security breaches or areas of concern.'

He clears his throat, looking awkward all of a sudden. 'Talking of areas of concern, the owner wants the memorial garden kept padlocked from now on.'

Mags isn't the only one who looks put out. 'Why?'

'As a gesture of goodwill to the parents of the girl who died,' Rob says.

Lottie, I think. *Her name was Lottie.*

'They're still campaigning for the site to be made permanent, and in the meantime, they don't want people trampling over the plants.'

'Nobody tramples over the plants,' Mags says, crossly. 'Both Gilly and I have been looking after them.'

'It's true,' Gilly says. 'After the dry summer we've had, they'd be dead if we hadn't watered them. What kind of people do they think we are?'

'I'm just telling you what the owner has instructed,' Rob says. 'Now then, where was I?'

'You were giving us a list of your extensive duties,' Lou says, rather unkindly – not that Rob seems to notice.

'Ah yes, thank you, Lou. Although I think I'd finished that bit. So, when I'm not fulfilling my Head Guardian role, I work for a large college in the IT department.'

Lou claps her hands together and stands up. 'We done here?'

Once again, Mags looks embarrassed. 'Don't you want some more wine, Lou?'

Lou shakes her head and leaves without another word. I

know it's rude, but I've always rather envied people who can do that.

'Don't mind her,' Mag says. 'She's just upset that Hayley didn't say anything about leaving.'

Bryony nods. 'She's not the only one. I lent her some money last week. Seventy fucking quid! Don't suppose I'm going to see that again.'

Gilly pats her on the knee. 'Oh, I'm sure you will, Bry. It's not like Hayley to forget something like that.'

Bryony shrugs. 'It's not like her to piss off without saying goodbye to anyone either, but that's what she's done. And she isn't responding to any of my messages, so go figure. Rob, are you sure she didn't tell you why she was leaving?'

'A family emergency, that's what she said.'

'And she didn't leave any forwarding address?' Nikhil says. I notice the brief glance Gilly gives him. So, it seems, does Nikhil. 'I gave her my screenplay to look at,' he explains. 'She was going to give me some feedback.'

Gilly's face is neutral, but she's clearly hacked off.

She leans back in her chair and exhales through her nostrils. 'I thought that's what *I* was supposed to be doing.'

Uh-oh.

'You are, but she asked about it. Said she'd like to take a look.'

'And you didn't think to tell me about this?'

I look down at my lap. This is getting a bit uncomfortable now. The others look embarrassed too.

Nikhil pulls a pained expression. 'What's there to tell?

And anyway, you don't tell me about all the men you have coffee with at Birkbeck, do you?'

This is excruciating. Why are they washing their dirty linen for all to see? What's wrong with them?

'What men? What are you talking about? And what's coffee got to do with it? Are you saying you had coffee with Hayley now?'

Nikhil looks distinctly uncomfortable. 'Leave it out, Gilly.'

Mags stands up. 'Think Lou had the right idea. I'm going to wash up the glasses and head off. Nice to meet you, Marlow.'

Everyone else starts making moves to go as well. The meeting, such as it is, is over.

Rob presses a printed copy of a rota into my hand before I leave. I scan the list of jobs beside my name and see that he's put me down for the early-morning perimeter walk for the next two days. Yippee doodah.

'It's a good one to start with,' he says. 'You'll get more of a feel for the site. All you have to do is check for any damage to the fencing. And if you could take a bin bag with you, for any litter that's blown in or been lobbed over. You'll find them in the kitchen. Cupboard on the left under the sinks.'

It's dark when I finally cross the playground. Dark enough to see a scatter of stars against the night sky. As I pass the padlocked memorial garden, I think I see a shadow flit past the gate. I stop. If ever there was a place to see a ghost, it would be here, in this garden. Because this is the place where Lottie died, and something of her will always be here. Her spirit. Her soul.

I try to re-create the old art studio in my head. It was the only place at McKinleys where I ever felt truly happy. The place I slipped into during break times whenever I could, even though we weren't supposed to. I always felt safe in there, especially in our individual art pods upstairs. They were the perfect spaces for us to work in. Our own little zones where we could express our creativity and display our work.

Tears prick my eyes, because it was me who told Lottie how Ms Thompson sometimes left the door unlocked and how easy it was to get inside without her seeing. I used to do it all the time, but Lottie never did. She was too scared of being caught and reported to Miss Latham. Lottie never broke any rules. I might have found her too much of a goody-two-shoes if it weren't for our shared love of art, and the fact that she was one of the kindest, funniest girls I'd ever known.

But for some inexplicable reason, Lottie broke a rule that day. The day of the fire. My hands grip the top of the gate. She must have been terrified. If only the school had had the foresight to get a proper sprinkler system installed. If only Ms Thompson had been more vigilant.

But the awful truth is, if I hadn't put the idea into Lottie's head in the first place, she wouldn't have been in there that day. She wouldn't have died.

My breath judders in my throat. When the fire took

hold, before any of us knew there was someone still inside, all I could think about was my A Level coursework going up in flames. All my carefully composed photographs. And my sketchbook. My precious sketchbook that Ms Thompson had taken in for assessment. It was heartbreaking to think of it burning. I felt sick to the stomach. Hollowed out with the loss.

I wasn't the only one, of course. The whole of the A Level art group and all the GCSE students were bawling their eyes out, too. But when the registers were taken in the street and Lottie was missing, the heartbreak turned to horror. I can still remember us all screaming and crying, clinging to each other in shock. Teachers, too. The firefighters tried so hard to save her, but it was too late.

Breathing hard, I force myself to peer in over the gate, but there's no sign of whatever it was that cast the shadow. There are squarish patches of bare earth where the plinths for the bronze statues used to be. Without them it looks wrong, as if the garden has been ransacked, and once again, my anger at the new owner's plans to turn this beautiful, serene place into a car park returns.

Big Dave appears at my side. 'Can't believe we're not allowed in here any more. Fucking James Brampton!'

'Who's he, the owner?'

'Yup. James Brampton of Brampton Developments.' He pulls a packet of cigarettes from his pocket and offers me one, taking one himself when I decline. 'And don't think for a minute that this so-called goodwill gesture to the parents of the girl who died is motivated by anything other than self-interest. Bastards like him always put their profit margins first, don't they?'

I nod. I know all about property developers. My dad was one, before he retired early to live *la belle vie* in Montpellier.

Dave takes a deep draw on his cigarette and exhales a thin plume of smoke into the night air. 'Anyway, if you need help with anything, just let me know.'

'I will, thanks.' But I won't. I know I won't. Living with strangers is complicated. Once you start letting people help you with things and get close to you, sooner or later you find yourself with new friends. Friends you might lose, like Lottie, and never get over. Or friends who want things you can't always give them, like Dev. Sometimes it's easier to keep a distance.

A light comes on in one of the rooms above the drama studio – the same room I saw earlier through those binoculars – and we both look up to see Bryony standing at the window staring down at us. Dave raises his hand in a wave.

'Right then, I'm off,' Dave says. 'Hope you get settled in soon.'

'Cheers.'

I go back to my room and lock the door behind me. Without switching the light on, I walk over to the window-sill, where I left the Art Deco earring I found earlier sitting in a small bowl of soapy water. I stare at it in the deepening gloom, and am struck by a sudden and overwhelming feeling that this earring belongs to Hayley.

I lift it out between my finger and thumb, aware of a tightening in my chest. A rising and inexplicable panic that makes me hyper-aware of my breathing.

No, it's more than a feeling: I *know* it's hers. Just like I knew there was something dangerous happening in the graveyard that time, when I found the smouldering barbecue tray.

But is it *really* the same? Couldn't it have more to do with the fact that I've spent the last hour listening to the other guardians express their surprise and disappointment at her departure?

I drop the earring back into the water and stare out at the empty school playground. The light is still on in Bryony's room, and although she's now drawn the curtains, I can see two distinctive shapes moving about behind the thin fabric: Dave, tall and broad, and Bryony, sylph-like in comparison, her head barely reaching his shoulders. They are standing very close. Dave is lowering his head. Looks like they're about to kiss.

I avert my eyes, determined not to do this any more, but not before I catch a glimpse of the room below, where the curtains have yet to be drawn. Nikhil is attempting to embrace Gilly, but she's pushing him away. They are obviously shouting at each other. For a second, I think she's going to hit him, but then she walks off and I lose sight of her.

I stand there for a moment, transfixed by the little dramas unfolding before me. Maybe there's a good reason Hayley has upped and gone without saying goodbye to any of them. Maybe she just got sick of all the tensions simmering in the group and thought it best to cut her losses and move on. I'd do the same myself if I had some-where else to go.

But then why is Rob lying about that leak? I check the Met Office website and, sure enough, there hasn't been any rainfall in weeks. What possible motivation could he have for keeping her room locked?

Later, as I'm drifting off to sleep, moments from the day float in and out of my mind. But far from being lulled by the tide-like motion of my brain, it soon feels like I'm being pulled somewhere deep and dark and dangerous. The last thing I see before I lurch violently awake, heart pounding, is a girl struggling to tread water in a flooded classroom, her head thrown back as the water rises to the ceiling, two Art Deco earrings bobbing and glittering on the surface.

My housemates are back. I can hear them chatting downstairs. The stuck-up bitch who's got the room next door to mine is whinge-ing about her bank card not arriving, and how she's going to have to phone them again and end up waiting for ages in their stupid call system. I look at all the little bits of plastic lying in the ash at the bottom of my bin. I had to cut it up with scissors in the end because it wouldn't burn. Serves her right for making a stupid fuss about that tea towel.

I listen to them all for a while, but eventually my eyes are drawn back to my screen. @Sue5Dilby has just tweeted some-thing about a book she enjoyed reading which she highly recommends. I've never heard of it and I certainly haven't read it, but if @Sue5Dilby thinks it's good, then it's bound to be crap. I reply within seconds.

'Really? I thought it was a load of bollocks.' I make sure to tag the author.

Five minutes later, she's blocked me. Big mistake, sunshine. Big fucking mistake. I make a note to follow her tomorrow from one of my other accounts. Then I switch over to Instagram to see what Boho Birdie and the vintage-interiors gang are up to. I love how they view themselves as bohemian, when really they've got 'bougie' written all over them.

I notice Birdie still hasn't grasped the concept of common courtesy by following me back. Not that I expected her to. I scroll through her feed to find the right post to comment on. Some of them are hilarious. I mean, they're not meant to be. She obviously thinks she's doing us all a huge favour sharing snapshots from her fabulous home. Her fabulous life.

I 'like' a couple of her most recent pictures, adding a few saccharine comments, a few smiley face emojis and some pink hearts. They like their egos stroked, this lot. One image catches my attention as I scroll.

I zoom in on it and for a few seconds I can't quite believe what I'm seeing. Because it's not just the view I'm looking at that's caught my attention, it's what's framing it. The window itself. I peer at it again. I remember sitting next to that window regularly when I was in Year Ten. Mrs Barrie used to tell me off for staring out of it and daydreaming. She always had it in for me.

Curious, I google McKinleys School for Girls. After the fire I used to do this compulsively, hungry for information and pictures, for news, but it's been a long time since I've typed those words into the search bar. I'm surprised to discover that it merged with another private school a few years ago. Both schools have now relocated to a brand-new, state-of-the-art campus a few streets away. That explains it. The site must have been sold off for housing. Boho Birdie must have bought a place there.

Hang on a sec. It says here that McKinleys is currently awaiting redevelopment and that plans to turn it into a luxury housing complex have been delayed because of the pandemic, but that work is expected to start next autumn. There's a picture of it all boarded up.

I stare at the screen, confused. So how come she's living there? I don't understand.

I find the photo on her grid again and study it. Then I scroll, slowly and carefully, through her other posts, noticing the precise composition, what she chooses to focus on and what stays on the periphery, slightly out of focus. It's as if she doesn't want us to see what's just out of shot. Even the exterior photos are cropped in such a way that you can only see glimpses of brickwork, sections of roof and sky. You never get the whole picture. It could be anywhere. But that view. That window. There's no mistaking it.

My brain can't quite compute all of this. Is Boho Birdie squatting in my old school and passing it off as her amazing home? A small prickle of pleasure and excitement starts travelling up my spine.

Boho Birdie is a fraud. And now I know exactly where she lives.

9

Rob

The meeting went well, he thinks, as he walks back across the playground. As well as can be expected. Isn't that what people say? There were quite a few questions and comments about Hayley leaving, but he'd been anticipating those. He can't be 100 per cent sure, but he thinks Mags and Gilly were upset about the garden being padlocked. Although it was Lou who left early, without saying thank you for the drinks Bryony, Gilly and Nikhil had brought along, and without saying goodbye to anyone, not even to Mags.

And then there was that peculiar exchange between Gilly and Nikhil, which started off being about Hayley giving Nikhil feedback on his screenplay and then turned into something to do with coffee. What was all *that* about?

People mystify Rob. Life would be so much simpler if everyone was more like him. If people said what they actually thought, instead of speaking in riddles and questions. If people followed orders and obeyed rules.

Hayley's face flashes into his mind. Why did she go into the pool, when he expressly forbade it? His jaw tightens. Why didn't she listen to him?

If only Elle had been at the meeting tonight, her presence would have calmed him. Craig said she wasn't very well, which is odd because she looked absolutely fine earlier this afternoon when he passed her on the stairs. *More than fine*, he thinks. She must have deteriorated quickly since then.

Rob hopes she doesn't have a virus. He doesn't like to think of Elle poorly, lying all alone in her bed, with no one to look after her. Although actually, he'd rather she *was* on her own than being looked after by Craig. Rob clenches his fists. Craig doesn't deserve a girl like Elle. Sometimes Rob imagines what he would do to Craig if he ever caught him mistreating her.

He lets the fantasy play out in his mind, then palpates the glands in his neck and wonders if he might have caught the virus too. He and Elle have spent time together recently, behind Craig's back. He imagines the viral particles entering his airway from hers and is briefly alarmed. But then, he'd much prefer they came via Elle than anyone else.

He feels a stab of shame just thinking this.

He enters the hall, the tap-tap-tap of his shoes on the parquet floor ringing out in the silence, cold sweat pooling in the small of his back as he passes Hayley's room. His eyes stray to where someone has had a go at removing the tape from the notice. Rob clenches his jaw and presses it back down with his fingers. Then he hurries to his room, refusing to look into the shadows at the end of the corridor in case he sees her again. Her silent judgement of him is worse – far, far worse – than his own.

If that is even possible.

10

Marlow

The next morning is bright and sunny. I sit up and rub my eyes. I did, eventually, drop off to sleep again after that awful dream about Hayley drowning, but I don't feel refreshed at all. When I lived in the chapel, I slept really well, but I have a horrible feeling that now I'm here, my insomnia is about to return. I look up what dreams about drowning mean, and on one of the sites I check, it says they might signify that something needs to be saved.

Something or *someone*?

One way or another, I'm going to get into Hayley's room and see it for myself.

But not yet, because I have to do the early-morning perimeter walk. I don't want to fall foul of Rob Hornby's rota on my very first full day.

I get dressed quickly, tug a brush through my hair, and make my way to the toilet block at the end of the corridor. It's much chillier in here than in my room because the windows face north, over the playing field at the back of the school.

My toiletry bag and towel are still on the windowsill where I left them yesterday. I've lived in places before where you have to take your stuff with you each time you use the facilities, including loo roll and even a plug sometimes, but since I'm the only person living on this corridor, and Elle and Craig have their own toilets two floors down, I figured it was safe.

As I sit on the cold black toilet seat of the only cubicle that still has a door, I let my eyes wander over the schoolgirl graffiti. It's the usual eclectic mix of the profane and the innocent, and I'm immediately catapulted back to a time when I'd scour these little missives in case anyone had written something rude about me or someone I knew.

Genevieve is a stuck-up bitch; Leonie and Sam for ever; You don't have to be rich to come here, but it helps; Keep Calm and Have a Good Shit; Katy's sweet, Katy's keen, Katy loves her ketamine.

But then my eyes snag on one phrase in particular that jolts me back to the present. The words, written in small, neat capital letters and circled in red, read: *HG DEFINITELY INVOLVED.*

HG. Isn't that how Rob Hornby introduced himself to me when I first arrived? *I'm the HG,* he'd said, and then had to explain that it stood for Head Guardian. He said it again last night at the meeting, when it was his turn to speak. But surely this can't be anything to do with him. It's ancient graffiti. And why would someone have written it on the back of a toilet door in a corridor that, until my arrival, hasn't been occupied?

The initials must relate to a former pupil at the school. Perhaps it means Head Girl. That would make more sense.

Then again, someone's clearly been using my room for spying purposes, staying long enough to need a flask of coffee. Which means there's a good chance they would have used this toilet too.

I can't stop staring at the words. Graffiti is usually self-explanatory. Smutty phrases or character assassinations. Names of lovers in hearts. Crude doggerel or trite little sayings. But 'HG definitely involved' sounds more like a message of some kind. A message that would only make sense if a) you knew who HG was, and b) what they might be involved in. Otherwise, it's meaningless.

I examine the door to see if there's anything else that includes the initials HG, my eyes systematically roving from top to bottom, and left to right. It's a little like looking for a needle in a haystack, but at last, about a third of the way down, my gaze lands on another phrase in the same neat style of lettering. It too has been written and circled in red, and looks similarly out of place among all these childish scrawls in blue or black biro: *New SPG (HG?) – 2.13 a.m. in, 2.40 a.m. out.*

I stand and pull up my knickers and jeans, flush the chain. If I stay here much longer, my bum will freeze over.

These cryptic little messages were probably written years ago. I'm overthinking things as usual, making connections where none exist. It's always the same when I'm presented with a puzzle. I can't rest until I've solved it.

I walk across the playground towards the old school building, feeling almost as if I'm trespassing and that at any second Mr Piercy, the caretaker, will emerge from a doorway and ask me what on earth I think I'm doing here out of school hours.

What *am* I doing here? And why am I obsessing over a couple of bits of graffiti?

The door to the hall creaks as I open it. Light streams in through the tall windows, casting white oblongs on the dusty floor and stripes on the wooden honours boards; impressive lists of former students who graduated from Oxford or Cambridge, or excelled at some other note-worthy institution. All those ghosts from the past still proclaiming their achievements. I don't allow myself to look too closely for fear of seeing my own year group's board, because it won't be the names I *can* see that haunt me, but the two names I can't: mine and Lottie's.

Dust motes swim lazily in the air. They look other-worldly in the early-morning sunlight, and almost without thinking, I draw my phone out of my pocket and walk around for a bit until I find the perfect position. Then I adjust the exposure on the camera app settings and turn on the grid, play around with a couple of low-angle shots. iPhone photographs are never going to match those taken with a really good digital camera, but the results can still be amazing if you know what you're doing.

I only stop when the little hairs on the back of my neck stand up. Someone is behind me. I'm sure of it.

I spin round, but no one is there. The hall is still and silent, the air musty. I'm quite alone in here. I must be imagining things.

In the kitchen, I find several rolls of black bin bags in a cardboard box. I tear a couple off, trying to ignore the hunger pangs in my belly, but they're getting stronger and stronger. I open the large fridge, curious to see what's inside and whether there's anything I could take that won't be missed.

Frustratingly, there's hardly anything, apart from a lone energy bar on the top shelf which I can't bring myself to take. Presumably its owner will be well aware it's their last one.

I pull out one of the plastic drawer compartments at the bottom labelled 'LOU'S – DON'T TOUCH'. It contains an assortment of loose apples, carrots, one big old potato and a rubbery-looking aubergine. Meagre pickings indeed, but needs must, and surely she won't miss one apple. Not unless she's in the habit of counting them each day. I swipe one of her carrots as well and give it a quick wash under the cold tap. I can eat it while I walk round the school.

On my way out, I hear a rustling noise somewhere in the corner of the hall, where Mrs Judd's piano used to be.

I stand stock still and watch as a tiny brown shadow moves at high speed along the skirting board. Maybe that's what I sensed earlier. A mouse.

Outside, I make my way swiftly over to the caretaker's huts at the edge of the playground, unable to resist the temptation to peek in through the windows of one of them. It's full of buckets and brooms and old cans of paint, and stacked up on one side are more of those wooden honours boards. Really old ones, by the looks of them.

I slip behind the huts to the walkway that runs the length of the perimeter fencing. Once out of sight of the school buildings, I fish the carrot out of my pocket and start to munch away on it, my eyes peeled for litter. So far all I've seen is an empty crisp packet and a couple of crumpled cans of Special Brew. But as I reach down to pick them up, the hairs on the back of my neck stand to attention again, and once more, I have the strangest sensation that I'm not alone, that I'm being watched.

I straighten up slowly and swivel my head, first in one direction, then the other. I'm completely hidden from view here. There are thick bushes between me and the playground, and high fencing separating me from the street. Nobody can possibly see where I am at the moment, and yet the sensation is strong. Overwhelmingly so.

I shake out one of the bin bags as if I don't have a care in the world, drop the cans inside and walk on. It's being back here, that's all it is. It's prompted the old paranoia. Perhaps whoever it is that's been using my room as a lookout has now turned their attention to me. I'm the latest curiosity. The new girl.

I don't know what makes me look up. Some sixth sense, I suppose. And that's when I see it: the small camera at the top of the fence, pointing straight at me. Of course. There are security cameras positioned at strategic points all over the site. I remember seeing some of the images on Rob's computer screen yesterday.

I have a sudden urge to flash my tits at the camera. Not that I would. He'd probably insist on revisiting the ground rules to include a 'No baring of breasts in front of the cameras' clause.

I think of the graffiti on the back of the toilet door. *HG DEFINITELY INVOLVED.*

But involved in what?

11

Hayley

I wake with a violent jerk. Where am I? What's happening?

There is something stuck tight over my mouth. I'm numb with cold, but when I try to move my legs, I hear a horrible clanking sound. A jolt of fear ripples through me. There is something encircling each of my ankles and one of my wrists.

Chains. I am chained up, like an animal.

Jagged, sickening shards of memory splinter the black space behind my eyes. The empty pool. The pump room. Struggling with him in that enclosed space, my shoulders crashing into a tank. The rest is a blur.

My heart thuds painfully. I want to scream but can't open my mouth. Hot, panicky tears spring to my eyes, and I hear myself whimpering like a wounded dog. As my vision adjusts to the dark, I see that I'm in a small, dirty bathroom, shackled to a water pipe that runs horizontally along the wall. My left hand is free, but I've started shaking so much my fingers can't find the end of the tape across my mouth. It's stuck fast to my cheeks.

My nose is starting to block. I can't breathe. I can't *breathe*.

I scratch at the tape with my nails, and at last, I find a corner and rip it off. The sting is intense. I gulp air into my lungs and thank God I'm alive. I'm *alive*.

I force myself to take deep breaths, to slow my heartbeat. The chains are just long enough for me to reach the toilet and the sink. A tap is dripping.

It's not much, but it's something. I'm not going to die.

Not yet, anyway.

12

Marlow

For the rest of my walk, I take a special interest in the location of the security cameras. So far, I've counted five, and here's a sixth, positioned at the entrance to the swimming pool. If I want to get inside and take some photos for that competition, helping myself to the padlock key from the office isn't going to be an option. Not unless I want to be caught and frogmarched off the premises, my spotless record with the agency ruined.

I walk round the side and peer in through one of the few windows that hasn't been boarded up. As I do, a memory comes back to me. Mrs Piper, the swimming teacher, sending me to the walk-in store cupboard to collect some floats. I got the shock of my life when a door I didn't even know was there suddenly opened from the other side – the side adjoining the gym – and Mr Piercy, the caretaker, strolled in. Maybe I could access it that way.

'Gotcha!' says a voice from behind me.

I spin round, heart knocking madly, and come face to face with Craig. He must have just come off his night shift at Asda. His eyes look tired and bleary, but he's grinning at me.

'Sorry, didn't mean to make you jump.'

Yeah, right. That's why he crept up behind me and said 'Gotcha.'

'If you're thinking of going for a dip, think again,' he says. 'The pool was drained when the school relocated.' He sniffs loudly. 'Seems a shame, doesn't it? Mind you, they'd have charged us extra if we had a pool.'

I start walking in the direction of the main hall. Craig falls in step beside me, and I notice his eyes are trained on the ground, almost as if he's looking for something. Dev has a habit of doing that too, has done ever since the day he found two folded twenty-pound notes lying amid a collection of rubbish at the side of the pavement.

Craig points to the black bag swinging from my hand. 'Don't tell me, a couple of cans of Special Brew somehow found their way over the fence by the huts. It's the same place every morning. He's like a dog, marking his territory.'

'You know who it is then?'

'Yeah. Seen him doing it. Same old geezer who pisses in the bus shelter over the way.'

All of a sudden, Craig stoops down and plucks

something from the ground: a tiny scrap of gold sweet
wrapper. It's more or less in the same place I found that
Art Deco earring, and it crosses my mind that maybe
that's what Craig thought it was. But when he straightens
up, frowning, and gestures for me to open the black bag,
I realize he must have been actively looking for litter as
we walk, which is, of course, what I'm supposed to be
doing.

We've reached the section of the playground where
Craig, if he's going back to his room, will need to break
away and turn right, but he keeps on walking alongside
me, chatting away.

'Settling in OK, are you?'

'I've hardly had a chance to unpack yet,' I say. 'I'll feel a
lot better when I have.'

'What do you think the new owner will do with this
place? Raze it to the ground and start again?'

'Maybe. Not the old building though. It's too beautiful
to knock down.'

'Yeah, you're probably right. People pay a fortune for
period properties, don't they? Mind you, if I had the dosh
to buy my own place, I'd want a new-build. I wouldn't
want anything second-hand.'

It's the first time I've heard anyone refer to a property as
second-hand. He kicks a pebble with the toe of his boot
and sends it skidding across the tarmac. 'Not that I ever
will. Have the dosh, I mean. Not while I'm stuck in retail.
Anyway, nice talking to you. I'd better hit the sack before I
keel over. See you later, yeah?'

And with that, he turns on his heel and heads back in the direction of Block C.

I'm slightly baffled as to how he found me in the first place. If he came in via the East Gate entrance, he'd have had no need to walk round the side of the pool to reach his room. After a long night's work stacking shelves, surely getting to bed would have been his priority.

Maybe it was Craig who was watching me earlier. Is he the one who's been going into my room and spying on people? It would have been easy enough for him to get up there without being seen. After all, he only lives two floors below.

While I'm sorting out the rubbish in the refuse room next to the kitchen, my skin begins to prickle, and a creeping sense of dread makes me stop what I'm doing and freeze. I have the same feeling I had earlier: the sensation that I'm not alone, that someone is right behind me. Only this time it's accompanied by breathing. Unless it's my own I can hear?

I keep as still as I can and hold my breath. No, that sound isn't coming from me. Someone is standing just beyond the doorway that connects the kitchen to the refuse room. I turn my head as slowly as I can. This isn't my imagination – not this time.

At first, I can't see anyone. Then, just as I'm about to march out and confront them, a white face with thick black make-up round the eyes and hair the colour of bright red chilli peppers looms in at me. It's as much as I can do not to leap out of my skin.

'Fuck sake! You scared the shit out of me!'

'Did you take some of my food?' Lou's voice is accusatory, and I know that I only have a split second to decide how I'm going to respond and that my choice of answer will have a bearing on all future dealings with her.

I look her straight in the eye. 'Actually yes, I did. I was hungry and I haven't had time to go to the shops yet. Sorry about that.'

She walks into the refuse room and stands right in front of me. 'You can't read then?'

I take a breath to compose myself. If there's one thing I've learned from my years of being a property guardian, it's that you don't want to make enemies of the people you're living with, even if they're a piece of work.

'It was one apple, Lou. In fact, it was one apple and a carrot.'

Lou tilts her head back and looks down her nose at me. 'You could have asked me.'

'Yes, but you weren't there to ask, and I didn't want to knock on your door in case you were still asleep. I thought I'd be able to replace them before you even noticed they were missing.'

Lou stares at me through narrowed eyes. 'I don't like people rifling through my things.'

'As I said, I'll replace them. I'm going to the shops as soon as I've finished up here.'

I move towards the door, but Lou doesn't get out of the way. What is *wrong* with her? She has no reason to be so aggressive. Not for one poxy apple and a knobbly old carrot.

'Excuse me, I need to leave now.'

Reluctantly, Lou steps to one side. 'Make sure it's a Granny Smith,' she says. 'And those carrots were organic.'

Of course they were.

I'm halfway across the kitchen when she calls out to me again.

'What did the agency say exactly, when they offered you a room here?'

I stop and turn round, surprised by the sudden change of topic, the switch from belligerence to concern.

'Just that a room had become available at short notice. Why?'

But before she can answer me, the door swings open and Mags appears in running gear, her face covered in a fine sheen of sweat. She lifts her hand in a wave and grins.

'Hi there, Marlow. Recovered from your first squad meeting yet?'

I smile back at her. 'Just about.'

Lou stomps off and, once again, Mags looks embarrassed at her partner's behaviour. She refills her water bottle at the sink. 'Do you run?' she says.

I shake my head. 'Only for the bus.'

Mags laughs. 'Well, if you ever change your mind, let me know. I run most mornings when I'm on a late shift, and evenings when I'm on earlies. Bryony runs a couple of times a week too. We sometimes do circuits of the playing field. You're always welcome to join us.'

'Thanks,' I say, trying not to grimace. I've done enough

circuits of that bloody playing field to last me a lifetime, but I guess it's nice of her to ask me.

When Mags has gone, I tip the rest of my rubbish into the general-waste bin, but just as I'm about to bring the lid down on it and walk away, I notice something that doesn't belong in there. It's a book, and books can be recycled, or given to charity, or better still, read and then displayed on a bookshelf for ever. Especially *this* book, which is a beautiful old edition of *Rebecca* by Daphne du Maurier, the very same edition my mother had from the seventies, which I remember reading as a teenager.

I draw it out and open it up, noticing as I flick through to the title page that there are two inscriptions inside. The first, in elegant copperplate handwriting and clearly written with a blue fountain pen, says: *This book belongs to Esme Cartwright,* while underneath, in black biro and childish but still very neat handwriting, it says: *This book now belongs to the late Esme's granddaughter, Hayley Crompton.*

Unease flickers in my chest. Without stopping to think, I slip the book into my coat pocket and go back to my room. I don't know anything about Hayley Crompton, other than that she left this place unnaturally fast, but now I feel overwhelmingly certain of one thing. The sort of girl who takes the time to record her ownership of a book that once belonged to her grandmother is most unlikely to grow up into the sort of woman who would toss it into a bin like a piece of old rubbish.

13

Elle

Elle hears the swing of the fire door at the end of the corridor, followed by Craig's tuneless whistling. She leaps out of bed and pulls on her clothes in record time. His incessant whistling drives her mad, but this morning she has overslept and is glad of it.

When Craig opens the door, she is sitting on the side of the bed, putting on her socks and trainers, feeling slightly dizzy from the sudden exertion.

His shoulders sag theatrically. 'Don't tell me I've got to warm that bed up all on my own.'

"Fraid so,' she says, keeping her voice light and cheerful, because now is not the time for the conversation she has planned. The one where she tells him it's not working for her any more. None of it. Right now, he needs to sleep and she needs to get to work.

'That new girl was hanging about by the pool,' he says, kicking off his shoes. 'She's a photographer.'

Elle looks at him, and for a second or two they just stand there, eyes locked.

'Shit.' She runs a comb through her hair, then grabs her laptop and phone and puts them in her shoulder bag. She's at the door when she remembers and turns round.

'How did it go at the meeting last night? Anyone mention Hayley?'

'What do *you* think? Of *course* they did.'

Elle stares at him, hating him for being so terse. So hard. '*And?*'

Craig puts his hand in the air, palm side out. She knows he's shattered, but who the hell does he think he is, doing that? As if she's a child he's trying to shut up.

'She's gone,' he says. 'Period. Nobody knows a thing.'

'Yes, but *where* has she gone? You don't think . . .?'

She can't bring herself to say the words out loud. The guilt is killing her. She should have tried harder to warn Hayley off. She should have found a way.

Craig sighs and scratches his head. 'It's too late to do anything about it now. Keep your eyes on the prize.' His jaw hardens. 'It'll be payday soon enough.'

Elle wants to scream. She shuts the door behind her and practically runs along the corridor. She needs to get outside, on to the street. She can't stand it here another second. It's not worth it. None of it. It never has been, and it never will be. It's a mug's game and she wants to stop playing.

But she can't. Not yet. She's in too deep. She has to keep rolling the dice and moving forward. One square at a time. All the way to the finish.

14

Marlow

Later that evening, as I'm coming home from work on the bus, I call Dev. When he drove off yesterday, I made a resolution to be a better friend and not let the slight tension between us grow any worse.

He answers straight away. 'I'm in the van. How's it going?'

'OK – *ish*. But I've decided I'm going to ask Rob about that other room again.'

Dev gives a long, impatient sigh. 'You're not still on about that, are you?' There's a pause. 'Fucking idiot!' he bellows. 'Sorry, didn't mean you. Some lunatic just cut me up. Seriously though, it's only a room. The one you've got is fine.'

He obviously thinks this is because of my obsession

with architecture and aesthetics, which he's never really understood. As long as he's got a bed to sleep in and a settee to sprawl on and play his Xbox, Dev is fine.

'It's not what you think,' I explain. 'Some of the others can't believe that the girl who used to live in it – Hayley – would have left without saying goodbye. I get the impression it's totally out of character for her to do something like that.'

'So what are you saying? No, don't tell me, you think Rob's done away with her.' He laughs. 'You've been watching too many crime dramas. She'll have found somewhere else to live and cut her ties. It's what you do all the time, isn't it?'

'I've never cut my ties with you.'

There's an awkward silence. Dev fills it first. 'What are they like then, the others?'

'Too soon to tell. One of them's been really rude to me. A girl called Lou. All I did was eat one of her apples.'

Dev snorts. 'Not being funny, Marl, but that sounds like something a twelve-year-old would say.'

'Well, she's certainly behaving like a twelve-year-old. Mind you, she's worried about Hayley too. And wait till you hear this.' I lower my voice and tell him about the binoculars I found in my room, and the imprint I read on the flipchart pad, about Bryony and Dave. I also tell him about the possible Rob Hornby-related graffiti in the toilet and the discarded copy of *Rebecca* with the inscriptions inside.

There's a long pause before Dev responds. 'Have you considered whether living in a school is making you all regress to being kids again? Nicking each other's apples and writing messages on toilet doors.'

I'm about to call him a cheeky bastard when he says: 'And not everyone holds on to old books for years on end like you do. Sorry, Marl, I've got to go. I've just got back from Bristol, and now I'm about to drive two posh twats called Hamish and Xander and a load of climbing equipment to Heathrow. Catch up later, yeah, and Marlow . . .'

'What?'

'Don't get involved in other people's shit.'

It's almost 9 p.m. by the time I get back to McKinleys, the plastic handles of the bag of shopping I picked up from Tesco Express cutting into the palm of my hand. The light's still on in the office, but Rob isn't there. I put the shopping down and rap my knuckles on the door of the old staff-room, already tensing up in anticipation of his refusal and what it might mean.

The door opens a crack, and he peers out. When he sees it's me, he opens it a little wider. Wide enough for me to get a glimpse inside. I was expecting it to be messy, but it isn't. It's not exactly warm and cosy, but it's very well organized. It has a pared-back, minimal vibe. As far removed from the cluttered staffroom I remember peeking into in the past as it's possible to be.

'I've come to ask you about Hayley's room,' I say. 'I know it's got a leak, but I honestly don't mind about that. I can always put a bucket down until it's fixed. It's just that—'

Rob is already shaking his head. 'No. You can't. I told you yesterday. It's against health and safety regulations.'

I take a breath and make myself count to three. 'Really? Even if I sign something to say I don't mind?'

'What's wrong with the unit you've been allocated?'

'Nothing, it's just that . . . I really love old buildings like this. They've got so much character and history. I'd feel much happier over here. Safer too,' I add, biting my bottom lip for effect. Anything to convince him that my desire to get into the room is purely for my own benefit and nothing whatsoever to do with not believing him about the leak.

Rob frowns. 'Safer? Why, has something happened in Block C to make you feel *unsafe*?'

'No, not exactly, but I do have to do late shifts at the studio sometimes, and I feel a bit vulnerable walking across that dark playground late at night. I mean, I've got the torch function on my phone, but my battery doesn't last very long these days.'

Rob nods. 'I've got just the thing,' he says, and walks back into his room to open a cupboard.

'Here,' he says, pulling out a large torch. 'You're very welcome to borrow this whenever you like. You can leave it in the office when you go out, so it's always there for when you come back.'

'That's very kind of you, Rob, but I'd much prefer to live over here, if you don't mind. I don't expect any help with moving. I'll bring everything over myself.'

A muscle in his left cheek begins to twitch.

'I'm very sorry, Marlow, but it's just not possible. The agency is very particular about health and safety on site. The ceiling has got to be checked by a builder. The whole thing might come down on top of you.'

I keep on pushing. 'It must be a pretty bad leak then. Is that why Hayley left?'

He stares at me. 'No, she had a family emergency. I thought I'd already told you that.'

'Can I at least have a look at it?'

Rob shakes his head. 'No one can go in until the builder's been to assess the situation.'

'And when will that be?'

He shrugs. 'No idea. You know what builders are like. They keep to their own schedule. I'm going to have to go now, Marlow. There's something I need to watch on TV.' And with that, he closes the door in my face.

I stand there for a moment, unsure what to do next. It's quite clear that Rob isn't going to change his mind about this any time soon. The sound of his TV coming on reaches my ears, and before I know what I'm doing, I'm picking up my shopping and walking into the office next door, gazing around for evidence of keys. I need to satisfy myself that this leak actually exists, although I'm not entirely sure what I'll do if it doesn't.

My heart begins to pound. Being in here again is like being hurled back in time, and I imagine Miss Latham striding in after me, her voice dripping with icy disapproval: 'Marilyn DeVere-Cairns, what on *earth* do you think you're doing?'

Marilyn. It was by no means the poshest-sounding name at McKinleys – there were a fair few Octavias and Cosimas and Allegras – but I hated it just the same. Is it any wonder I dropped it the first chance I got? And as for DeVere . . .

I banish Miss Latham's ghostly presence from my mind and try the top drawer of the desk, but it's locked and there's no sign of the little key to open it. The other drawers are open, but all I find in them are sheets of typing paper and envelopes, some grubby unwrapped chewing-gum pellets, and an assortment of pens, paperclips and staples.

By the time I hear footsteps on the hall floor, it's too late to duck down and hide. I'm an *idiot* for not turning off the office light and searching by moonlight.

There's only one thing for it. I'll have to brazen it out.

I close the bottom drawer just as Elle pops her head round the door, a curious expression on her face. 'Hi, what are you up to in there?'

'I was looking for a torch.'

Elle looks dubious. 'Can't you use your phone?'

'It needs charging.'

She twists her mouth. 'I don't think I've ever seen a torch in here. Lou and Mags might have one though. They have everything.'

'Thanks, I'll ask tomorrow. In fact, come to think of it, I'll probably buy my own.'

Elle nods and moves aside as I leave the office, turning off the light as I go. Moonlight slants in from the lancet windows.

'You don't even need a torch tonight,' she says. 'You hardly ever do in London. It never gets properly dark. Not like it does in the countryside.' There's a wistful tone to her voice. 'Mind you, it's still creepy as hell in this place. I mean, just *look* at it. I keep expecting to see two little girls in blue dresses at the end of the corridor, like in *The Shining*. God, that was scary, wasn't it?'

I follow the direction of her gaze and wish I hadn't, because now all I can think of is the very same thing, and I know for a fact that now she's planted that image in my mind, it's all I'll ever be able to think of when I'm here alone at night. Maybe I *am* better off in Block C.

'Word of warning,' she says, under her breath. 'I'd keep my head down here, if I were you. Don't go snooping around too much.'

'Why do you say that?' I wonder if Craig's told her that he saw me by the pool this morning.

A flicker of something unreadable crosses her face. 'I dunno, some of the people are a bit . . . weird?'

'Really? Who?'

She gives a hopeless little shrug. 'Look, forget I said anything. I'm just sick of it here, that's all. I'm sick of being a property guardian, if I'm honest. It's no way to live, is it?'

'Seriously though, is there anyone I need to look out for?'

For a second or two, Elle looks like she's about to say something, but then her face changes and it's as though a shutter has come down. 'Ignore me,' she says. 'I'm tired and I'm fed up. Stay safe, yeah?' And with that, she heads off down the corridor.

I hurry across the playground to my room. What the hell was that about? More to the point, why was she heading towards the science block when it's supposed to be out of bounds?

15

Rob

Rob puts the torch he offered Marlow back into the cupboard. She is annoyingly persistent, but there is *no way* she
is having that room. She can badger him all she likes.

He switches his TV on and channel-surfs for a bit. Then
he turns it off again and begins to pace backwards and
forwards across the floor. He can't get her face out of his
mind. The way she just stood there. There is only one thing
that will calm him now. Only one thing guaranteed to
slow his racing heart.

He looks at his watch, but it is far too early. He flexes his
fingers.

Outside his room, he hears voices. It's her again. Who is
she speaking to? He presses his ear against the door, but
it's no good. He can't hear what she's saying. He opens his

door a fraction and peers out, but the corridor is empty. He takes a few steps into the hall, his eyes landing on the locked door of Hayley's room, the cardboard sign still covering the window.

But the hall is deathly silent. Marlow Cairns and whoever she was talking to have gone.

He stands there for a few minutes more, imagining the hall in a previous life. Full of girls. Rows and rows of them, fidgeting and whispering and giggling behind their hands. He turns back, towards his room and the sanctuary it offers. But something resolves out of the shadows at the end of the corridor. He doesn't want to look, but he *has* to, because he knows it's her.

'Rob?'

He looks up. He was mistaken. That is Elle's voice, he is sure of it. His heart soars when he sees her walking towards him, that strange little smile playing at the corners of her mouth. He tries to do the same thing with *his* mouth. He knows this is called *mirroring someone's body language* and that it's done to show empathy.

Elle's smile widens. She must be feeling better now. Maybe it wasn't a virus after all.

16

Marlow

The next morning, after another restless night not helped by Elle's ominously vague warning to keep my head down, I feel achy and unrefreshed. I make myself a mug of instant coffee, neck a couple of paracetamol, and wander over to the window. The sky looks amazing, all streaked with red, and now that I've seen it, my tiredness dissolves in the urge to capture the image in a photograph.

I rest my mug on the windowsill and study the vista before me. A red sky isn't exactly original, and it won't be as atmospheric as an abandoned old swimming pool, but with the right composition and shutter speed, and a long focal length so that the red parts of the sky occupy most of the frame, it could be a great addition to my portfolio. If I open the window, I could take a couple of shots from up here, then go outside and take more from the playing field.

When I reach for my coffee again and gaze down at the playground, I recoil in shock. Scalding coffee slops on to my hand and wrist, but the pain is lost in a surge of adrenaline. I take a step back, the palm of my hand pressed against my chest, my heartbeat fluttering beneath my fingers. Someone has written the words 'DON'T GET TOO COMFORTABLE' in white chalk on the grey tarmac.

The letters are huge. Unmissable. And what's more, they've been written this way round, so that they're facing Block C.

So that they're facing *me*.

Just then, I hear men's voices over by the drama block. It's Nikhil and Big Dave. Nikhil is pointing to the chalked message. Now they're walking over to it, talking as they go. I open one of my windows and lean out. The two men look up at me.

'Did you see who did this?' Nikhil calls out.

'No, I've only just looked out of the window.'

They're both standing near the letters now, gazing down at them.

Dave tugs the end of his beard. 'This'll be a warning to James Brampton. It must be from one of the campaigners.'

Nikhil nods in agreement. 'They must have got on site last night. Seems they're not content with spraying graffiti on the fence.'

My shoulders soften. The campaigners. Of course. That

makes more sense than it being some kind of personal threat.

I get dressed as fast as I can and stuff my feet into my trainers. By the time I get downstairs, Dave and Nikhil have been joined by Bryony and Gilly. Gilly is all zipped up in a long, quilted coat and Bryony is still in her dressing gown, a pair of beige Ugg boots on her feet.

'It's scare tactics, that's all,' Bryony says. 'I think we should wash it off and ignore it.'

'You're probably right,' Gilly says. 'But let's see what Rob has to say first. I'll go and get him.'

It isn't long before she and Rob emerge from the old school building, closely followed by Lou and Mags.

Mags is already in her uniform. She's twisting her hair into a ponytail and securing it with a band. 'Where are Elle and Craig?' she says. 'Shall I go and get them?'

'I wouldn't bother,' Nikhil says. 'Craig's probably asleep by now. He's on nights, isn't he?'

'We need to inform the agency about this,' Rob says.

'And the police,' Gilly adds. 'They can have a word with the campaign organizers, see if they know anything about it.'

Lou snorts. 'They're hardly likely to admit to breaking into a private site though, are they?'

'I didn't see anything on my run this morning,' Mags says.

Rob pulls out his phone and starts taking pictures of the message. 'I'll send these through to Harry and see what he has to say. Let's not wash it away yet.' He looks up. 'Who's down to do the perimeter walk this morning? It's you, isn't it, Marlow?'

For a moment, I stare at him, still flummoxed by what's happened. Then I remember. He put me down on the rota for two consecutive days.

I nod. 'I'll do it now. See how they might have got in.'

'I'll come with you,' Dave says. 'In case they're still on site.'

I shoot him a grateful glance. I'm not usually the sort of woman who takes kindly to men making assumptions that I need their help, but if whoever did this is still here, I'd rather not confront them alone. Dave comes across as a gentle giant, but his sheer size could be intimidating if you didn't know him.

'I'll come too,' Bryony says.

Dave raises his eyebrows at her. 'Thought you needed to get to work early today? Don't worry, I'm sure Marlow and I can manage perfectly well on our own.' There's a finality to his tone, as if he's confident in his power to affect Bryony's decision. It makes me like him a little less.

But it's as if she hasn't heard him. 'In fact, why don't we all go?' she says. 'Safety in numbers, yeah?'

Half an hour or so later, when we've done a complete circuit and a thorough check of the entire site, including the playing field, and found no obvious place where they could have broken in, we're back where we started, standing in a circle staring down at the chalked letters, as if simply by looking at them, we might glean some answers.

'I'll go and get some soapy water and a broom,' I say.

When I return, most of the others have started to drift back to their respective rooms. Only Bryony and Dave remain. Bryony's cheeks are pink with cold, and I get the feeling she'd like nothing more than to go inside and get ready for work, but she obviously can't quite bring herself to leave me alone with Dave. The two of them stay with me while I slosh soapy water over the chalked letters, and push the stiff-bristled broom back and forth until they disappear.

Except they haven't disappeared, because I can still see them in my mind's eye.

DON'T GET TOO COMFORTABLE.

Back in my room, when I'm getting ready for work, I can't help wondering if that message was an inside job. Wouldn't we have found signs of a break-in if someone from out-side had got in?

My eyes wander from the Art Deco earring, now dried and lying on a piece of tissue, to the well-thumbed copy of *Rebecca* I rescued from the bin. I think of that strange con-versation with Elle last night, and Rob's awkwardness when I questioned him about Hayley's room. Maybe I should get the hell out of here. It's bad enough being reminded of Lottie and the fire all the time without all this other weird stuff.

But whenever I've ignored my strange hunches in the past, I've regretted it, because they've invariably come true. Plus, I know every nook and cranny of this school. Who better to find out what's going on than me?

When I get off the bus opposite the school, the first thing I see is a poster stuck to the side of the bus shelter with the heading: SAVE CHARLOTTE LANSDOWNE'S MEMORIAL GARDEN. I go over and read the rest of it. It's a campaign organized by Miss Latham, our old headmistress. There's going to be a demonstration outside the school gates tomorrow morning.

Thank fuck I've come today then.

I look across the road at the school. My old alma mater. I remember walking out of those gates for the last time and giving the place the finger. It feels weird coming back.

The notices say that the site is being managed by a company called Guardian Angels Inc. I peer through a hole in the fencing, but all I can see are the bushes that border the playground. They've grown a lot bigger since I last saw them.

Wait a minute: a whole group of people have just come into view. Not sure what they're doing – it's hard to tell from this distance. *They seem to be walking around picking up litter. They must be the guardian angels, I suppose. If only I knew which one of them was Boho Birdie. Now I know why she never does selfies. Because she's a loser.*

I snigger. The thought of her having to collect litter each morning before she takes her daily photo and stage-manages it to make it look like she's living in a large, fancy property makes me want to laugh out loud. Except it's not funny. It's not funny at all. The nerve of the woman.

They're getting closer now. For a second or two, I think I recognize one of the women. She looks a bit like . . . No, it can't be, that's impossible. There's no way the likes of Marilyn DeVere-Cairns would be dossing in her old school. Her parents were loaded. She's probably living in Chelsea now, with a hedge-fund manager for a husband and a couple of spoilt brats at prep school. She used to fancy herself an artist. Painting over photographs, that was her thing. Taking pictures of weird stuff, and then printing them out in black and white and hand-colouring them. Sometimes she even added extra things. Things that weren't in the original photos. Working with mixed media, Ms Thompson called it.

I called it cheating. Barely one step up from tracing a drawing in a magazine and passing it off as your own. I challenged her about it once, and she just rolled her eyes at me and said, 'But I took the photos in the first place, you moron. I composed the shot. Honestly, Kat, you don't have the first idea about art.'

Moron, that's what she called me. And the name stuck. Some of the others heard her say it, and instead of Kat Morwood I became Kat Moron. It wasn't long before that became Fat Moron.

I move away from the fence and start walking back to the bus stop, my head full of memories I haven't had in ages. I suppose it's only natural that returning here after all this time is bringing back the misery and reminding me of old faces. The catty remarks and disdainful looks. The humiliation.

I used to think it was because I was on a scholarship and they looked down on me because I came from a poor family, but there were quite a few of us in similar circumstances and the others blended in just fine. It only seemed to be me who stuck out like a sore thumb.

Every now and then, I recognize one of those stuck-up bitches in a newspaper article or on TV, and I think to myself, I went to the same school you did. Breathed the same air. Was taught by the same teachers in the same rooms. And yet we might as well have been living on different planets for all the good it did me.

I pull them down a peg or two on social media whenever I can. Unsettle them. I've never managed to find Marilyn online, more's the pity.

My lip curls. It should have been her who died in the fire, not Lottie.

When I reach the bus shelter, I sit down on the red plastic bench and stare across the street. I can't afford to dwell on ancient history, but now that I'm here, it's hard not to. A few minutes later, the school gates slide open, and I watch as a big guy in motorcycle gear wheels his bike out. He straps his helmet under his chin, pushes the kickstand away with his foot, and within seconds he's roaring off down the street.

When my bus arrives a few minutes later, something stops me getting on and I let it go. It's a Tuesday morning and people are going to work. Sooner or later, more of those guardians will come out on to the street. Maybe I'll just sit here for a while longer and keep watch, see if I can work out which silly cunt might be Boho Birdie.

Five minutes pass. Then ten. I let another bus go by. The gates open again, and this time a woman emerges and starts crossing the street towards me. She's heading for the bus stop. I glance at her as she sits down on the other end of the bench, and my heart begins to thump. It's the one I thought looked like Marilyn; this time, she's only a couple of feet away from me.

I take another glance, hardly able to believe my own eyes. It is her. It has to be. Her hair's different. Shorter, messier, with a silly purple fringe. But apart from that . . .

Holy fuck! She must have fallen on hard times if she's reduced to living in an empty school.

I look away quickly. I don't want her to recognize me. Although I doubt she will – I've lost so much weight since my school days. I look nothing like I used to.

Oh. My. God. Does this mean what I think it does? Has she moved on from painting over her stupid photos to posting them on Instagram? Is Marilyn DeVere-Cairns actually Boho Birdie?

I clamp my hand over my mouth to stop a smug laugh from escaping. This could be payback time all over again.

17

Marlow

That night, when I get back from work, I'm too tired to do much more than heat up a ready meal in my microwave and climb into bed. All the exertion involved in moving, and the stress of coming back here again and meeting new people, has taken its toll. Not to mention the mystery of Hayley's disappearance and the shock of that message on the playground. No wonder I feel drained.

I send a quick WhatsApp to Dev. *You'll never guess what happened this morning!* The two grey ticks turn blue, and I wait for his response, but it doesn't come. Then I remember. He said he had to go to Birmingham today. He's probably still driving back.

I set my alarm for 3.30 a.m. If I'm going to get into

Hayley's room, I need to do it while everyone else is asleep. Which means I'd better get some rest while I can.

When the alarm goes off six hours later, I realize I must have dropped off straight away because I didn't even clean my teeth. I pull a thick jumper over my pyjamas, stuff my socked feet into my trainers, and grab my coat from the hook on the back of the door.

The corridor is dark and cold. I hesitate. It would be so much easier – and more sensible – to give up on this crazy idea and go straight back to bed, snuggle down under my duvet, and forget all about this girl I've never even met. But I'm up and dressed now, and since when have I ever been sensible? A sensible person would never have agreed to move into a classroom in their old school in the first place; a school associated with tragedy and sorrow and lost dreams. A sensible person wouldn't still be living this peripatetic life in their thirties.

But here I am, and now that I've made the decision to investigate, my body takes over and I find myself tapping the torch button on my phone, locking my door, and walking towards the fire doors at the end of the corridor. As I push the one on the left open and let it close slowly behind me, the sighing and sucking noise sounds unnaturally loud in the extraordinary stillness of the building.

The stair rail is cold under the palm of my hand as I make my way down, and I have the creepiest sensation that someone is right behind me. Some ghostly presence. I suppress a shudder and refuse to look over my shoulder. It's only my imagination, but even so, goosebumps stipple the tops of my arms. Elle's comment about the two little girls from *The Shining* comes back to me and I quicken my pace, keen to reach the ground floor as fast as I can.

Outside, there's a fat crescent of moon visible above the bell-tower. It's been raining, and a breeze drifts through the hedges bordering the playground, making the leaves tremble and rustle. It sounds almost like whispering, and I'm aware that my heart is beating a little faster. This is the witching hour, when the boundary between the living and the dead is said to be at its very weakest. Not that I truly believe in any of that, but still, there's definitely some-thing about this time that plays into our superstitions.

I flinch, then freeze. I'm not alone out here. Something just moved, at the very edge of my vision. A large, dark shape, I'm sure of it. I slide my eyes as far to the right as they'll go, then slowly, slowly, slowly, no more than a millimetre at a time, move my head in that direction, hardly daring to breathe.

I blink in the darkness. The shape has gone, melting into the night air like a phantom, but I still feel its presence. A vibration down the side of my body. A silent thrumming.

The sound of someone clearing their throat to my left startles me. I spin round and see the tall, bulky figure of Big Dave materializing out of the shadows, a sheepish expression on his face. 'Sorry, didn't mean to make you jump. Everything OK?'

My mouth hangs open and, try as I might to respond, the words don't come. Didn't Craig say much the same thing when he came up behind me at the swimming pool?

'Shit.' He scratches his head. 'I've scared the life out of you, haven't I? I'm so sorry, Marlow. I was just getting some fresh air. I couldn't sleep.'

'Me neither,' I say, finally recovering from the shock and finding the power of speech. 'Was that you, over there?' I point to where I first saw the movement.

'Yes, I was watching a fox.'

A fox. Right. Perhaps he didn't notice me. Is that why he didn't announce his presence sooner? Is that why he walked around and behind me first? So quietly I didn't even hear him.

'Anyway,' he says, 'I'd better head back to my room now. Get some shut-eye before work tomorrow.' He starts to walk away from me, then stops and turns around. 'Are you *sure* you're OK?'

'I'm fine, thanks. Just fancied some hot chocolate.'

Dave nods. 'Good idea.' His eyes crinkle as he smiles, and the tension I've been holding in my neck and shoulders starts to seep away. But not entirely.

I stand there for a moment as Dave trudges towards his room in the drama block, watch him push open the door and close it behind him. Silence settles around me once more and I start walking again, still spooked by what's just happened and cross with myself for being such a scaredy-cat. Cross with Dave too. What is it with him and Craig acting like ninjas?

I'm drawing level with the memorial garden now. The back of my neck starts to prickle as I remember the shadow I saw after the meeting on Sunday night, and how for one absurd second, I found myself wondering if it was Lottie's ghost. Once again, I think I see something move in there, behind the padlocked gate. An unfocused blur. My heart hammers in fright.

A fox darts out between the railings. I exhale in relief. Of course it's a fox. Maybe the same one Dave just saw. Or one of its pals. The city is crawling with them. Both of us stop dead in our tracks and stare at each other. Why on earth am I doing this? Why can't I just accept what Rob has told me? If he says there's a leak in the room, then maybe there *is* a leak. And he could be right about health and safety. I mean, if the ceiling came down on my head, I probably *would* sue the owner. Or the agency. I'm not even sure who'd be responsible, but one of them certainly would.

The fox continues to stare me out, its lambent yellow eyes unsettlingly intense. Maybe I should turn around and go back to bed. Stop obsessing over that classroom. Stop obsessing over Hayley.

But I can't. Not now. Because some deep, instinctive part of my mind *knows* that something isn't right. Admittedly, it's the part Dev would probably describe as 'woo woo', but just because something can't be explained by science, doesn't mean it's wrong. Why would she have left without saying goodbye to at least one of the guardians? Why would she have taken Nikhil's screenplay with her? And why isn't she answering any of Bryony's messages?

All these questions are rattling around in my head. If only I didn't need to know the answers. If only I didn't care about this girl I don't even know. This stranger. But I *do* care. It's not just curiosity that's pushing me to do this, it's concern. Concern for another human being who might be in trouble, and in the very place Lottie died. After all, if it weren't for me putting ideas into Lottie's head about hiding out in the art pods, she wouldn't have lost her life that day. So if someone else is in danger here, don't I owe it to the universe to try my hardest to help them?

I think of the beam of light that shone from Angie's eye, how I stupidly interpreted it as some kind of sign that I should come back here when my gut was telling me not to. Well, maybe it really *was* a sign and I'm here for a reason. To find out what's happened to Hayley.

The wind picks up and rain starts to fall, gently at first, then harder and faster. The fox tires of watching me and slopes off in the opposite direction. I've come this far; I might as well continue.

I open the door to the hall as quietly as I can, but still it creaks. I stand frozen for what seems like minutes on end, but everything is silent. Apart from my heart, that is. It's beating like the clappers.

I creep across the hall to examine the lock on the door of the classroom. It's as I thought. The original, old-fashioned mechanism has been removed by the agency and replaced with one that looks annoyingly robust. I've brought some Allen keys with me in my coat pocket, and a few other bits and pieces I've collected over the years. Not because I'm in the habit of breaking and entering, but because it pays to be prepared. There's nothing worse than forgetting your keys, being locked out and having to pay for replacements.

First though, I'll see if I can get into Rob's top drawer. The lock on that will be a lot easier to pick, and if the classroom keys are in there, it'll make this whole thing so much simpler.

I'm about to turn around and cross the hall to the office, when a low voice right behind me makes me shrink with fear. A woman's voice this time.

'Marlow, is that you? What on earth are you doing?'

It takes me a few seconds to realize who it is. It's Mags. Her hair is hanging loose round her shoulders, and she's wearing a long white T-shirt that just covers the tops of her thighs, an old cardigan and a pair of flowery DMs, the laces still undone.

My mind goes blank. What possible reason can I give her for creeping around in the middle of the night? If only she'd caught me walking towards the kitchen; I could have told her what I told Dave, that I wanted some hot chocolate.

I blink at her in confusion, willing myself to think of something coherent to say, something that will explain my actions. But nothing will. Nothing except the truth.

Whether it's the paralysed expression on my face, or the fact that I can't seem to string two words together, Mags's face suddenly changes. Her suspicion turns to concern.

'Are you OK, Marlow? You're not . . . you're not *sleep-walking*, are you?'

Without realizing it, Mags has offered me the perfect solution. I stare at her blankly, as if I've no idea who she is or what's going on. I take a few steps towards the office as if I haven't even heard her. As if I'm in some kind of trance.

I've never actually witnessed a sleepwalker before, but my performance seems to be doing the trick because Mags is already linking her arm in mine. She has gone into full caring mode now, as if she's still at work and I'm a confused old lady she's shepherding into an ambulance.

'Come on, sweetie. Let's take you back to your room.'

I allow her to steer me across the hall towards the door to the playground. She opens it and a blast of cold, wet air hits us full in the face. I guess I really ought to wake up now.

'What's going on?' I say, my voice shrill and panicky. I shrug her arm away from mine and stare at her, as if she's just accosted me. I hope I'm not overdoing this.

'It's OK, Marlow. It's OK. You've been walking in your sleep. You're safe now. I'm Mags, remember?'

I stare at her for a few seconds, as if I'm still in the process of waking. Then I switch back to my normal self and am full of apologies.

'I can't believe this has happened again. It's so embarrassing.'

'Don't worry about it. I'm just glad I was awake and heard something, or God knows where you'd have ended up!'

I smile, weakly.

Mags looks into my face, and I sense that she hasn't quite switched out of her paramedic role yet. 'Will you be OK getting back to your room?' she says. 'Do you want me to come with you?'

I shake my head. 'I'll be fine. I don't want to put you to any more trouble.'

Mags eyes the weather and then me. She shuts the door and points to a chair.

'It's no trouble,' she says. 'Wait there while I get my coat.'

A few minutes later, the two of us are hurrying across the wet playground, heads down against the wind. At the far edge of my vision, over by the caretaker's huts, I think I see something. A towering, dark shape that for one absurd and terrifying second I think is some mythical creature, standing watch from the shadows. A hulking great golem.

But when I force myself to turn my head and look straight at it, there's nothing there. Nothing except a tree. I must be going mad.

18

Elle

Elle is coming back from the toilets. She is almost at her room when she hears footsteps on the stairs. *Marlow.* She's the only other person in this block.

Elle pushes open the fire door as quietly as she can and peers down the stairwell to see the top of Marlow's head disappearing. She shrinks back. What the hell is she doing, creeping around at this ungodly hour?

Elle goes back to her room to grab her coat and slip her feet into a pair of Crocs. Then she sets off after her. Outside, she is careful to keep her distance by sticking to the perimeter, tucking herself so closely in to the line of hedges that drops of water from the wet leaves soak into her shoulders. She pulls the collar of her coat up around her neck, wishing she'd worn another layer. Wishing she wasn't here at all. But she *must* find out what Marlow is doing. She still feels guilty about not keeping a closer eye on Hayley.

Perhaps Marlow doesn't have her own kettle and is making her way to the kitchen for a late-night cuppa. But something about the furtive nature of her movements, the way she keeps stopping and looking about, makes Elle suspicious. Someone who is so desperate for a hot drink that they are prepared to venture out across a dark, cold playground in the middle of a rainy night would be walking a little quicker and more purposefully than that. Surely they would.

And what about last night, when Elle caught her in Rob's office? She's definitely up to something. Just like Hayley was up to something. And now Hayley is gone, and Elle has a horrible, sinking feeling about what might have happened to her.

She doesn't want the same thing to happen to Marlow. Or herself, come to that.

Elle freezes. Marlow has stopped again and is staring directly at the memorial garden. Flanked by darkness, the profile of her face is starkly illuminated by the white moon. She looks terrified, almost as if she's seen a ghost.

Elle follows her gaze, her heart thudding in anticipation as her eyes roam the length of the padlocked garden. She takes in the dark shapes of the trees, the silvery moonlight filtering through their branches, their trunks gleaming like white bones behind the railings.

She too has seen things in this place. But it's not the dead she's afraid of.

A fox tears across the playground and Marlow is on the move again. Elle watches her enter the hall and sets off after her. She is almost at the door when she hears voices from inside and darts to one side, flattening herself against the wall.

A few minutes later, Mags and Marlow emerge, arms linked, and hurry across the wet tarmac. Elle edges along the wall of the old building, the brickwork cold on her back, waiting until they've disappeared from sight. First Lou and Hayley, now Marlow and Mags. What the fuck is going on?

Now that Elle is here, wide awake, she might as well make use of the time and see if Rob is still up. She slips into the hall and turns right, moves swiftly and silently past the office and along the corridor towards the science block. He's there – he's always there – sitting on a lab stool, staring into space and doing that weird thing with his jaw.

Her stomach clenches at the thought of spending more time with him, but Craig is right. It won't be long now. All their hard work is about to pay off.

This will be the last time she does anything like this, the last time she mixes with this kind of company. Elle knows that now. All she wants is for it to be over, once and for all. The whole sordid business. She feels soiled by it. Tainted.

She wants to go home to Suffolk and see her family.

She wants to be normal again.

19

Marlow

When I wake up, I'm disorientated and groggy. It took me ages to drop off after the 'sleepwalking' fiasco with Mags. Thank God I've asked for the next couple of days off. I'm not sure I could have dragged myself into work today.

I check to see if Dev's responded to my last message yet, but he hasn't. I know he's got loads of work on this week, but I thought he might have got back to me by now. I've got a horrible feeling he's distancing himself deliberately – something he accuses *me* of from time to time. It's not so nice when the boot's on the other foot. I'll try calling him a bit later, see if I can find out what's going on.

Right now, I need coffee – badly – and not the instant shit I've been drinking lately, but the real stuff. I also need to get out of this place for a couple of hours, to clear the fog in my head and take stock. In the cold light of day, my decision to break into Hayley's room seems rather foolish. Wouldn't I be better off just speaking to Harry directly and telling him my concerns?

Half an hour later, after I've been over to the drama block and had a disappointingly tepid shower, I'm dressed and on my way out. It's a grim sort of day, but when I open the gates, I see a small crowd milling about on the pavement outside the railings a little further up, spilling on to the road. Some of them are holding placards that say, 'Save Lottie's Garden', and all of a sudden, one of them spots me and shouts out the words in my direction. Before long, they're all chanting the same thing, over and over again, and I don't know what to do. I'm like that fox last night, pinned to the spot.

There must be about thirty of them, but one face in particular stands out. There's no mistaking that high forehead and prominent nose, that steel-grey hair in a tight bun. My chest constricts. Even after all this time, she still has the power to make me feel like I've done something wrong. Miss Latham, my old headmistress. The very last person I want to see right now. Thankfully, she's deep in conversation with someone, but when I realize who she's talking to, my heart skips a beat. It's Lottie's dad.

I pull my hoodie up and hurry away in the opposite direction. I really, *really* don't want them to recognize me. I'm not sure I could bear the pitying look in Miss Latham's eyes at seeing one of her 'old girls' reduced to living like this. As for getting into a conversation with Lottie's dad, it would be unbearable. I should have kept in touch with her parents. It's one of the things people who've been bereaved always complain about, isn't it? That friends avoid speaking to them because it's too awkward. Too uncomfortable. I was a coward not to go and see them again after the funeral. To bump into him now, in these circumstances, would be awful. For all I know, her mother's here too, somewhere in that crowd.

But just when I think I've got away with it, one of the demonstrators runs after me and shoves a wodge of flyers in my hand. There's something about her that looks vaguely familiar. But no, I must be mistaken. She's a scrawny-looking woman with a pallid, unhealthy-looking complexion and an ill-fitting tracksuit. I've never set eyes on her before.

'Nice, comfortable place you've got here,' she says. 'Living your best life, eh?' There's something spiteful about the way she says this, something threatening about her face, almost as if James Brampton's decision to pave over Lottie's garden is somehow *my* fault. I can't get away from her – from all of them – fast enough.

When I reach the top of the street and turn the corner, I'm out of breath. Bloody hell, that was a close call. If they'd been standing right by the gate when I came out, I might have been spotted by Miss Latham or Lottie's dad. I'd have had no choice but to talk to them, and my precious anonymity – the only thing that's keeping me sane – would have been blown.

And what on earth did that crazy woman in the tracksuit mean about me *living my best life*? In an empty classroom in a draughty old school full of mice? She's unhinged, she must be. I stuff the flyers in my pocket. God only knows why she's given me quite so many. If she wants me to hand them out and spread the word, then why was she so aggressive?

By the time I find a coffee shop, my anxiety has subsided. But seeing Lottie's dad so unexpectedly has brought with it a fresh wave of grief. Poor, poor Lottie. She had her future all mapped out. First, a Fine Art degree at Central Saint Martins, followed by gallery assistant work if she could get it. But her main ambition was to create her own art and make a name for herself. She would have done, too. I have no doubt in my mind about that.

I can't bear to think of the pain all this must be causing her mum and dad. It's like a slap in the face from James Brampton. He can't possibly have any children of his own, to do something like this. To ride roughshod over a bereaved family's feelings.

Once again, I'm consumed with guilt. Not that it ever goes away for long. Why did Lottie choose that day of all the other possible days she could have chosen to follow my stupid example and hide out in one of the art pods? And why didn't I have the guts to reach out to her parents before now?

The familiar knot of distress twists and tightens in my stomach, as it always does when I open the door to my feelings. What kind of friend was I to turn my back on them the second the funeral was over?

A bad friend. The very worst.

And what kind of person am I *now* to run away from her father, and all the other people who care enough about her memory to make a stand against James Brampton?

I'm a despicable coward, that's what I am. Despicable.

Forcing myself to push away the thoughts before they spiral out of control, I buy myself a large Americano, then take it over to a table at the back of the cafe. Nothing good ever comes of reliving the events of that day, nor the self-recrimination that inevitably follows.

When I've drunk half of my coffee, I steel myself to take the flyers out of my pocket. The very least I can do is read what they say.

I put them on the table in front of me. That strange woman seems to have given me her own copies by mistake because there are some notes written in black felt-tip down the side of the one on top – someone's Twitter or Instagram handle, by the looks of it, and underneath that . . .

The little hairs on the back of my neck stand up as I read the words printed underneath. *I know who you are.* The words swim before my eyes, and an icy feeling trickles down my spine. I stare at them, my mouth gaping. What *is* this? She can't possibly know who I am. She must have mistaken me for someone else.

I tap the username scrawled above the message – @bohobirdie3 – into Twitter (I refuse to call it X), but the account is an inactive egghead. I try Instagram instead and bingo, there she is. Boho Birdie. It's one of those lifestyle accounts with loads of pictures of some kind of renovation project in a period property. There's something about these pictures. I can't quite put my finger on it, but they look . . . familiar.

I scroll through the grid until I come to one that makes me pause. The photo that fills the screen is of an open notebook next to a cactus in a beautiful, Moroccan-style ceramic pot. The two items are arranged on a wide windowsill and—

My breath catches in my throat. This is Mrs Barrie's classroom. It's the window of the room I'm currently living in – there's the tulip sun-catcher sticker, and beyond that, the fabulous view of the London skyline. Whoever took this picture must have done the exact same thing I did the day I moved in, and hooked the ugly old blinds out of the way first.

The caption beneath the photo reads: *This place was worth every penny. I feel utterly blessed to be able to look out on this view every day.*

I blink in confusion. It's as if this person, this Boho Birdie, is pretending it's her house. That she actually *bought* it.

I look at the message on the flyer again. *I know who you are.* Does that horrible woman think this is me?

Something is niggling away at the back of my mind, a half-formed theory I can't quite pin down. My brain is so scrambled from being ambushed on the street that I can't think straight.

I feel a headache coming on – a tight band of pressure low on my forehead. I finish my coffee and look at my watch. There's no way I'm going back to the school while the demonstrators are still there, and who knows how long they'll be hanging around. I get up and order another coffee, and a bacon roll to go with it. I'm not that hungry, to be honest, but this place is filling up now, and if I want to keep my table, I need to spend more money.

I continue looking at the Instagram account, trying to see which parts of the school I recognize. Boho Birdie is a liar. Or rather, she's not telling the whole truth. The way she's set up each shot gives the impression she's living in a stunning conversion. They are stage-managed pictures, carefully curated corners and sections of the school with specific focal points in each one – a vase, a candle, a chair, a book – and the background is always tantalizingly out of focus.

A couple of pictures have been taken of, and from, the little metal bench that's set into the circular paving area in the memorial garden. I think of how upset Mags was at being told the garden was going to be padlocked. Gilly was annoyed, too. I suppose it's possible that one of *them* might be Boho Birdie.

I continue scrolling and immediately identify one of the windows in the main hall, sunlight streaming through it and forming a yellow square on the parquet flooring. Three candles have been arranged on a small table below the window, and to the left of this table is a pair of green wellies, one standing upright, the other having fallen on to its side. It looks as if someone has just that moment come indoors to take them off, spotted the way the sunlight is hitting the floor, and been inspired to capture the image. It's exactly what I did before my first early-morning perimeter walk – minus the accessories, of course. It's an excellent picture. Really well composed. In fact, all of them are. This person certainly knows how to take a good photo.

The caption beneath reads: *My favourite spot in the entire house. Think I need a reading chair here. Watch this space.*

Sure enough, a few days later, there's a picture of a chair in the exact same spot with an open book lying on the sheepskin that's been draped over the seat. A well-thumbed book, by the looks of it. I zoom in. The title is blurred and unreadable, but I can tell from the shape of the single word and the three-part author name underneath what it is. *Rebecca* by Daphne du Maurier. I feel a squirm of discomfort in my belly. It's the same book I found in the bin and took up to my room.

The half-formed theory that's been lurking at the back of my mind assembles itself into a more solid shape. There's no caption with this picture but a whole paragraph of book-related hashtags, including #myfavouriteeverbook and #bookstotreasure. The unease that's been building in my gut intensifies.

My gaze returns to the most recent photo, taken from inside another room. For some reason I missed it the first time, but now I recognize the tree outside the window. It's one of a pair of silver birches that flank the East Gate entrance, on the landscaped belt of ground that separates the front of the school from the pavement beyond the railings.

It's Mr Barker's old room, the room Hayley has just vacated.

20

Rob

It's Wednesday morning, and Rob is sitting at his other desk. His work desk in the large college where he is employed as an ICT and AV Support Technician, a role which suits him very well. The only aspect of the job he doesn't enjoy is visiting one of the end users at *their* desk in order to give them support. He prefers fixing problems remotely if he can. If Rob could have his way, he would fix *all* problems in life remotely, without having to see or speak to anyone.

If only people were more like computers. *But alas*, he thinks, *they are not*. People are messy and unpredictable. People have unreasonable expectations and demands. People do not follow the simplest of rules. Hayley's stricken face flashes into his mind, as it so often does these days.

Rob shifts in his chair and blinks at his screen. It is unusual for him to feel sick, but lately he has been fighting back unexpected waves of nausea. Once or twice, he has had to rush into the toilets and retch into one of the lavatory bowls.

He would prefer to fish out the liner from the stainless-steel bin in his office and heave into that than put his face anywhere near a toilet bowl, especially one in the men's toilets, but he knows that this kind of behaviour would not be acceptable in a shared office, along with passing wind, even if silent. These are the things Rob has picked up over the years and which he adheres to, albeit reluctantly.

Once again, he tries to distract himself with thoughts of how an intruder might have found their way into the school grounds to chalk that message yesterday morning. Rob has a degree of sympathy for the campaigners and sincerely hopes that they are successful in their quest to preserve the garden for posterity.

He has even, on one occasion, attempted to talk to James Brampton about the matter himself, informing him that, according to his own very detailed calculations, the playground is more than large enough as it is to accommodate one vehicle for each new residential dwelling planned, plus ten extra places for guest parking – once the caretaker's huts have been removed – but he received disappointingly short shrift for his efforts and has not approached him since.

However, the idea that the campaigners have had the temerity to breach the school's security does not sit well with him. He is the Head Guardian, after all, and although it isn't strictly within his job description to prevent unauthorized site access – that task falls specifically to Guardian Angels Inc. – he nevertheless feels the full weight of responsibility.

Much as Rob supports the laudable aims of the campaigners, he cannot and *will not* condone this wholly inappropriate way of getting their message across. Such behaviour is, in fact, far more likely to make that dreadful bully of a man, James Brampton, dig his heels in and go ahead with his car-park plans, rather than rethinking them in line with common sense and decency. Qualities, Rob thinks, which are sadly lacking in today's society, and sadly lacking in James Brampton in particular.

But this morning, try as he might to take his mind off things by mapping the perimeter of the school in his mind and identifying any possible weak points, this latest bout of queasiness is growing steadily worse. He heads for the toilets yet again.

Afterwards, when he is washing his hands thoroughly at the basin, he realizes something that almost makes him start heaving again. He grips the edge of the basin so hard, it's a wonder he doesn't loosen the mounting brackets and bring the whole thing crashing down on to the floor.

His fingerprints will be all over her things. His DNA, too.

Last night, he thought about confiding in Elle, but every time he opened his mouth, different words came out. Safer words. He thinks she's on his side. He thinks she's a friend. Is it possible she could become more than a friend? He can't always read the signs.

He screws up his eyes to stop tears of frustration, tears of fear, spilling out.

He *never* reads the signs. That's why he's in this almighty mess.

How could he have been so unbelievably stupid?

21

Marlow

Outside on the street, I head off in the direction of a small park where Lottie and I used to go sometimes after school. I need to give the campaigners time to disperse before going back. They'd better not be hanging around all day.

Apart from a woman with a couple of toddlers in the playground area, a solitary jogger with earbuds in, and a man walking a cockapoo, the park is more or less empty, and I soon find a bench to sit on. It isn't long before memories of Lottie and me sitting in the very same place come flooding back. All those schoolgirl dramas we used to share. All the giggling and talking about boys, and who we fancied out of our friends' brothers, and why it was never the ones you wanted to send you a Valentine's card who actually did. In Lottie's case, it was the pimply son of one of her mother's acquaintances; in mine, the geeky friend of a cousin.

A solitary tear rolls from the corner of my eye down the side of my nose, and despite my sadness, I can't help smiling.

I pull out my phone, suddenly anxious to study the Boho Birdie Instagram account in more detail; in particular, the photograph of Hayley's room.

I zoom in. It's been completely transformed, and every little bit of it is beautiful. Three white voile panels hang at the windows, each one gathered at the middle so that they look like three huge Ys. Part of a double bed can be seen. It's covered in a variety of patterned blankets, layered on top of each other, with cushions scattered over. Hanging plants in baskets adorn the bare white walls, and there are several rugs on the parquet floor, which, unlike the floors in the rest of the school, has been polished until it gleams. The old cast-iron radiator, where once my classmates and I gathered to warm our cold hands in the winter months before class, is painted brilliant white. It's exactly the style of decor I love. It's how I would have decorated the room if it were mine.

I check the date this photo was posted. It was last Thursday, the day before I got the call from Harry telling me about the vacancy. I study the picture again. There is no sign of any leak, not as far as I can see.

The caption reads: *My bedroom is my sanctuary.*

I look up at the sky and the chink of light trying to escape from behind the clouds, and try to process this new information. As a property guardian, when you find some-where nice to live, somewhere you've spent time and energy – and in some cases, a fair amount of money – to make your own, the only thing that would prompt you to move out would be a notification from the agency that the owner was ready to develop the property.

Either that or finding a better place to live, moving back into the mainstream property market. But if that were the case, you wouldn't have to move out so fast that you didn't have time to say goodbye to your friends.

I try to think of all the possible family emergencies that might warrant such a hasty departure, but even a sudden and unexpected death or the serious illness of a close relative wouldn't necessitate clearing out of a place you considered your 'sanctuary' in such a peculiar hurry.

I scroll through the grid again, my conviction that some-thing bad has happened to Hayley growing stronger with each passing second. Surely someone with such an obvious passion for photography and a thriving lifestyle account with a large and engaged following would be unlikely to stop cold like this, without posting a little holding message first. She must have taken hundreds, if not thousands of photos while she was living here. There would be nothing to stop her posting some of those, until she'd settled in some-where else and could amend her narrative and start again.

I've never even met this Hayley, but already I feel a con-nection with her. Anyone capable of making Mr Barker's old geography classroom look like something out of a glossy magazine is to be admired.

I try to imagine her flitting around the school at different times of the day and night, setting up her Instagrammable pictures and snapping away. Capturing little scenes from an imaginary life and sending them out into cyberspace. Waiting for the likes and comments to come in. Waiting for validation. It doesn't matter to me that she hasn't been entirely truthful with her followers. She's a creative, like me. She lives by her own rules.

I feel a small ripple of unease at the memory of that woman's face. What did she accuse me of doing? Something sarcastic about living my best life.

I go into my own Instagram account and read through my profile, the one I drafted over and over again before I was happy with it:

Marlow she/her
Property Guardian

I live in the places you don't want to. Some of them are beautiful. Others aren't. I take pictures of them all and stick them on here.

How strange to think that both Hayley and I were inspired to take the very same picture of the view from Mrs Barrie's old classroom, and one of the light falling on the floor of the old hall. Could those binoculars have belonged to her? And the flask of coffee? Did she write that thing about Dave and Bryony on the flipchart? But why would she be spying on them?

Something else occurs to me. Something I'd almost forgotten. The graffiti on the back of the toilet door. Did she write that too? And if so, for whose benefit?

I pull out the flyer and re-read the words in black felt-tip. *I know who you are.*

The relief I feel that the crazy woman who waylaid me in the street doesn't know me after all is only fleeting, because she's obviously got it into her head that *I'm* Boho Birdie. But why would she think that unless she's actually seen me at my window, and put two and two together to make five?

I get up and start walking round the park. The only way she could have done that is if she's been on site. My heart begins to thud, and I remember what she said to me when she shoved the flyers into my hands. *Nice, comfortable place you've got here. Living your best life, eh?*

The image of that chalked message on the playground comes into my mind. *DON'T GET TOO COMFORTABLE.* Could that have been her? And if so, how the hell did she get in?

22

Marlow

When I return to the school a couple of hours later, sick of walking round in circles and killing time, there's no sign of any of the protestors. And, more importantly, no sign of the woman in the tracksuit.

As I wait for the gates to slide open, I can't help looking over my shoulder. Is this what it's going to be like from now on, feeling like I'm being watched all the time? And not only inside the school, but out on the street too.

For the rest of the day, I force myself to sort out my room. If Hayley *was* using it as some kind of lookout, then there must have been something worth looking *at*.

A couple of times, I call the agency, but it keeps switching to voicemail, and try as I might to come up with something to say that doesn't sound completely mad, in the end I give up. Besides, I'd like to talk to Dev about it first.

I reach in my pocket for my phone and see that he *still* hasn't responded to my message. I don't care how busy he is, he could at least have sent me a couple of words to acknowledge it. I'm about to call him, then change my mind. He obviously doesn't want to speak to me at the moment, and he already thinks I'm making a drama out of things.

I need to figure this one out myself.

I'm in the middle of assembling my canvas wardrobe, or trying to, when there's a knock at the door. It's Bryony.

'Just thought I'd check and see how you're settling in,' she says. 'I'm working Saturday this week, so I've got the day off.' She spots the half-finished wardrobe over my shoulder. 'Do you want a hand with that?'

I hesitate, but only for a second. She seems nice enough, and it would be rude to refuse her offer of help. Besides, it's been taking me far longer than usual to put the frame together, and I'm getting frustrated with it. I stand aside so she can come in.

'That'd be great. Thanks. I keep forgetting which pole goes where.'

Bryony laughs. 'I'm not sure I'll be much better, but maybe we can figure it out together.'

I feel a stirring of gratitude towards her, and for the first time in ages, I wonder what it would be like to have a really close female friend. The sort of friend I had in Lottie.

After much umming and aahing and several false starts, the wardrobe is finally up.

'Do you fancy a coffee? I've only got instant, I'm afraid.'

'Fine by me,' Bryony says. 'I don't even like the fresh stuff. Have you got enough milk?'

I go over to my little fridge and check the carton. 'Yeah, plenty. Kettle's empty though. I'll just go and refill it. Won't be a sec.'

When I return, she's standing at the window. 'Nice view you've got here.' There's something different about her voice. She doesn't sound quite as friendly as she did before.

My eyes land on the binoculars I've left out on the sill. Shit. She must have seen them and jumped to the conclusion that they're mine.

'Yeah,' I say. 'Someone here obviously thought so.' I nod in the direction of the binoculars, cursing myself for not putting them away. 'They were here when I moved in.'

A slight frown flickers across her forehead. She picks them up and puts them to her eyes. 'Jesus, you can see right into our rooms. I had no idea.'

'I figured whoever was using them might not have realized this room was going to be occupied, and that when they did, they were too ashamed to ask for them back. Not that I want them,' I add. 'But, well, money's a bit tight at the moment. I thought I might be able to sell them on eBay or something.'

I feel my cheeks reddening. Still, it's better for her to think of me as an opportunist thief than a Peeping Tom.

'I think I've seen these before,' she says. 'Somewhere else.'

'Really? Where?'

'On top of the little staircase that leads up to the bell-tower. Me and—' Now it's her turn to blush, but I pretend not to notice. I think she was going to say Dave. 'Me and one of the others were exploring the site once.' She giggles. 'Rob's tour leaves out all the best bits, so we decided to do our own. We found the old access door, and went and had a look. Some-one must have beaten us to it and left these up there.'

'I thought they might be Hayley's,' I say, 'seeing as no one else seems to be missing them.'

Bryony lowers her eyebrows. 'Well, if they are, she must have forgotten they were here. Just like she forgot to say goodbye, or give me my seventy quid back. If I'd known she was going to do that, I'd have swiped these for myself.' She replaces the binoculars on the windowsill with what looks like reluctance.

'So she still hasn't replied to any of your messages?'

'Nope.'

I plug the kettle in. 'How well did you know her?'

'Fairly well, or so I thought. Well enough to get drunk with her a couple of times. Well enough to lend her some money.'

I gesture to a chair, and she comes over and sits down, taking one of the biscuits I offer her.

'Are you worried about her?'

Bryony wrinkles her nose. 'More worried about my dosh, to be honest. I mean, it's not like we were close friends or anything. We just . . . had a laugh together sometimes. It is odd, though. She really seemed to love it here. Said she was dreading the day we all got chucked out.'

141

She takes the mug of coffee I hand her and rests it on the floor by her chair.

'She never really opened up much. But then, you meet so many different people when you live like this. I guess we're all a bit guarded sometimes, aren't we?' She giggles. 'The guarded guardians. I don't know, maybe she found somewhere nicer to live.'

I study Bryony's face. I can't think of many places that would be much nicer than the room pictured on that Instagram account. Which makes me pretty certain that Bryony has never been inside it.

'The thing about telling people you've had a family emergency,' she says, 'is that it's one of those catch-all phrases. An excuse people give when they want time off work and don't want to give you any details. Or when there aren't any details to give in the first place because they just fancy fucking off somewhere for a couple of days.'

She smirks. 'She probably turned the waterworks on and gave Harry some sob story. He's a sucker for a damsel in distress, especially if she's pretty.'

'Is he? I've never seen that side of him. Mind you, I'm not pretty and I've never really got the hang of flirting.'

Bryony gives me a pointed look. 'Really? You seemed to be doing OK the other night with Dave.'

I blow across the top of my coffee. Well, *that* was unexpected. There's definitely another side to ever-so-friendly Bryony. I deliberately keep it light, as if I haven't heard the accusation in her voice or seen the flint in her eyes.

'You're joking. I think I'm probably Marmite where men are concerned.'

'Anyway, take it from me,' she says, back to her chatty self. 'Hayley was a *stunner*. I'm not surprised Nikhil gave her his screenplay to look at. Living with Gilly must be taking its toll on the poor man. She'd test the patience of a saint, that one. All sweetness and light one minute, then seething with suppressed rage the next. He's only got to look at another woman and she's all—' Bryony purses her lips and flares her nostrils to demonstrate what she means. 'I don't know why he puts up with her, to be honest.'

By the time we've finished our coffee, Bryony has given me the lowdown on the other guardians. I know all about Nikhil and Gilly trying for a baby. ('If you ask me,' she says, 'Nikhil should run a fucking mile.') I know that Elle and Craig are having difficulties in their relationship, that Elle is sick and tired of being a property guardian, and wishes Craig had the gumption to get out of retail and find himself a better job. ('I mean, she can talk,' Bryony says. 'Why's it always got to be the fella who makes things happen? If she wants more money, why doesn't *she* look for a better job?')

I also know that Mags is a sweetheart and would give you her last drop of milk if you needed it, but that Lou is best avoided at all costs. ('What Mags sees in her is beyond me,' Bryony says. 'Face like a slapped arse and a temper to go with it. Mags reckoned she had a crush on Hayley. Maybe *that's* why she's scarpered.')

And finally, I know that Rob's diet consists entirely of Pot Noodles and salad-cream sandwiches, and that he 'resents every single one of us for being here, because he managed the place perfectly well on his own before we all pitched up to shit on his parade'.

I'm tempted to ask her about Big Dave, seeing as he's the only one she hasn't yet mentioned, but after her comment about me flirting with him earlier, it's probably not a good idea. Besides, I'm growing tired of this one-sided conversation. There's only so much gossip I can take in one day, and chances are, it'll be *my* character she's assassinating next. I'll be 'the plain girl with purple hair who likes spying on people', or worse, 'the sort to steal anything you leave lying around and stick it on eBay soon as look at you'.

'How come Rob was here on his own?' I ask instead.

She shrugs. 'I dunno. Someone's always got to be the first to move in, haven't they?'

When at last she leaves, I close the door behind her and exhale in relief. Bryony might have had a few drinks with Hayley, but she clearly wasn't trusted enough to be invited into her room, and now that I've got to know her a little better, I can understand why. So much for thinking she and I might become friends. It makes me appreciate Dev all the more. Quiet, gentle, kind Dev. I should be making more of an effort with the friend I *already* have rather than contemplating making new ones. And I would, if only he'd respond to my message.

I wander over to the window, my eyes sliding from the

144

binoculars to the playground. It might have been the view that first brought Hayley up here, but something else kept her coming back. Did she write that strangely precise sentence about how long Dave and Bryony had been seeing each other, then tear up the paper, leaving only the imprint?

But why was she spying on them in the first place? And what else might she have seen?

I think of the cardboard sign covering the window in the door of her room – her *locked* room. I think of her book – her favourite ever book, if her hashtags are to be believed, discarded in the bin like a worthless piece of trash. The book that used to belong to her grandmother. And I think of that message, written on the back of the toilet door at the end of my corridor and ringed in red. *HG DEFINITELY INVOLVED*. This is a puzzle I just *have* to solve.

I check Boho Birdie's Instagram, but nothing new has appeared since I last looked. A small part of me still clings to the hope that another post will pop up soon and I can stop worrying, but something tells me it won't. Something tells me that this account will remain inactive. Because while I have no real proof that Hayley is in danger – certainly not the sort of proof that I can take to the local police station and expect to be taken seriously – the instinctive part of me that senses things, that knows things I can't possibly know and yet invariably gets it right, is fully switched on.

And right now, it's screaming.

23

Hayley

I jolt awake. Again. More tape on my mouth. I'm not in the dirty bathroom any more. Where am I? What's happening?

Something is wrong. Something is terribly wrong. My head feels like it's splitting open, and I can't move. But I *am* moving. I'm in a vehicle of some kind, curled on my side with my hands tied behind my back. It's cramped in here, and it's dark. So dark.

Panic hits me at the same time as the pain. Intense pain in my shins.

A memory: my legs kicking out. A hard edge ramming down on them.

I blink in the darkness. There is a tang of petrol in my nostrils and something else. A damp and mildewy smell. My left cheek is pressed up against something rough and scratchy, like old carpet. I'm in the boot of a car. Someone has put me in the boot of a car. *He* did.

How did he get me in here? Why don't I remember?

This is a nightmare, it must be. Any second now, I'll wake up sweating and scared, but I'll be in bed. I'll be safe.

No, I will not be safe. The realization rips through my body like an electric shock. This is real. This is actually happening. To me. Right now.

The vehicle starts to rattle. We're on bumpier ground now. Cold dread creeps into my body, sending my thoughts in ever more gruesome directions. Bumpy ground is not good. It means we're not on a road any more. It means we're going somewhere remote. Somewhere deserted.

Oh God. Please God, no!

Wherever he's taking me, I'm not getting out of this alive. Not now he knows what I've seen.

Hot, salty tears sting my eyes. This is my fault. What was I thinking going in there? What was I fucking *thinking*?

The car stops. Terror seizes me in its vice-like grip, every fibre of my body straining with tension as I wait for the boot to open. As I wait to discover my fate.

24

Marlow

I hang the last of my clothes in my newly erected canvas
wardrobe and make a plan. I *was* going to try to get into
that classroom again this afternoon, while everyone else is
at work. But now I know Bryony's on site, I think I'd better
wait till tomorrow. That's assuming no one else decides to
have a day off in the meantime. Craig will be here, of course,
but he should be sleeping.

Still, there's nothing to stop me from wandering about
and investigating some of the places I recognize from the
photos on Boho Birdie's account. It will be like following
in Hayley's footsteps. Going where she went. Seeing what
she saw.

I put on my coat because it has nice deep pockets to
hide the binoculars in. What Bryony said just now about

spotting them in the bell-tower once has got me wondering how much of the campus you can see from up there. Pretty much all of it, I should imagine.

I grab my keys, lock up, and take the stairs down to the ground floor.

Crossing the playground towards the hall, I remember how scared I was when I did this before, in the dead of night. Scared of shadows. Scared of ghosts. As I think this, I can't resist looking in the direction of Lottie's garden. Padlocking the gate seems way over the top to me, especially now the statues have been removed. Mags and Gilly are right to be upset, considering they've been watering the plants all summer.

Once I'm inside the old building, I'm suddenly overcome by a terrible sense of melancholy. There's something really sad about an empty school. Especially this one. A building designed to be full of young people now stands like a museum piece. It was dated enough when I was here, but now it looks positively archaic. Each classroom I pass looks as if the inhabitants were forced to leave in a hurry, taking only what they could grab on the way out. Pictures and charts have been ripped from the walls, in some cases leaving the paper corners still attached with sticking tape. Chairs have been overturned, tables too in places; scrunched-up paper and discarded pens and pencils lie scattered on the floor.

I wouldn't be at all surprised if, between the school closing down and James Brampton buying it, local teenagers found their way in and did a bit of ransacking. Or urban explorers, keen to take pictures of decaying structures – old hospitals and care homes, abandoned warehouses, that kind of thing. It's one of the reasons I was attracted to property guardianship in the first place, because it's a legitimate way of doing just that, although I can't pretend that cheap rent wasn't also a factor.

The urge to take some close-ups of what's left of the wall art distracts me for a few minutes, and I find myself focusing on the colours and textures, the marks left by the tape. Then I remember why I'm exploring in the first place and shove my phone back in my jeans pocket.

I'm now approaching the end of the corridor where the barrier is. It's easy enough to shift it to one side and squeeze past, but I make sure to put it carefully back into position before going any further, just in case Rob or one of the others comes back early and notices it's out of place.

The old chemistry lab is almost exactly as I remember it, only gloomier and emptier and with most of the lab stools missing. The cabinets at the side still have a few dusty funnels and flasks on the shelves, and stacks of old packets of litmus and filter papers. Before I know what I'm doing, I'm taking more pictures. I can't help myself. This place is one big photo opportunity, and though scenes like this would never have made it on to Hayley's Instagram account, they're perfect for mine.

In one of the sinks at the end of the bench at the back is an empty Pot Noodle container. So I was *right*. Rob was lying when he said he'd never been in here. Just like he was lying about the leak in Hayley's room. What else is he lying about?

I wonder why he comes in here. It's not exactly comfortable, and there's an underlying chemical smell – hardly a place to sit and enjoy a meal. Not that you can call a Pot Noodle a meal.

I have a quick wander through the physics lab, but there's even less to see in there. If I was hoping to find something that might give me more clues as to what's happened to Hayley, it won't be in this part of the school.

The bell-tower though. She must have been up there if Bryony noticed the binoculars on the stairs once. And there are several arty shots of brickwork and sky that can't possibly have been taken from anywhere else. I make my way back past the barrier until I reach the recess next to the staffroom, now Rob's room. From there, a set of roped-off stairs takes me to a small platform and a door, behind which a second staircase leads up to the bell-tower.

The fact that this door isn't secured when these stairs are meant to be a safety hazard makes it even more suspicious that Rob insists on keeping Hayley's room locked. Surely a rickety set of stairs leading all the way up to the roof of the school is far more dangerous than a leaky ceiling?

I start climbing, testing each step as I go. When I finally reach the top and poke my head out of the little parapet where the bell hangs, I have a bird's-eye view of the school. Careful to keep my balance, I take the binoculars out of my pocket and look through them, slowly rotating my head as I do. I can even see the playing field beyond Block C from up here, and there's a perfect view of the PE block and the entrance to the swimming pool. The whole place is deserted. Which makes it an ideal time to go and see if I can still access the pool via the gym store cupboard.

But when I climb down and reach the doorway leading on to the platform, I hear footsteps in the recess below and freeze. Whoever it is begins to climb the first flight of stairs, and I'm torn between making my presence known by bursting out of the bell-tower and waiting here for them to discover me. Either way, I've been caught snooping around in a place that's supposed to be out of bounds. But then, aren't they doing exactly the same thing?

Just as I'm on the verge of springing out and getting the confrontation over and done with, I hear a woman crying. I peer through the crack in the door and see Gilly lowering herself down on to the top step, cradling her face in her hands. I breathe a sigh of relief that it isn't Rob and clear my throat.

Gilly looks up, startled, as I open the door and come out. 'Sorry, I thought you might be Rob, about to lecture me on staying away from the no-go areas. Are you OK?'

Gilly wipes her eyes with her fingers and shakes her head. 'Not really, no. I thought I'd be alone up here.'

I sit down on the step next to her. 'You can be, if you like. Just say the word and I'll go. But if you want to talk, I'm right here.'

She takes a tissue out of her pocket and blows her nose. 'We're practically strangers. You don't want to hear all my woes.'

'Sometimes it's easier talking to a stranger. And I'm a good listener.'

Gilly sniffs and tucks the tissue up the sleeve of her jumper. She's wearing the same kind of bandana on her head that she was wearing the other night at the meeting. Only this time, it's bright orange.

'Thanks, but I don't think so. I hardly know you.'

'Well, if you change your mind, you know where I am.'

I'm halfway down the stairs when she blurts out, 'I'm pregnant,' and starts crying all over again.

I go back up and sit down next to her, confused by her tears. According to Bryony, Gilly desperately wants a baby. But of course, I'm not meant to know that.

I find myself adopting the gentle tone of a therapist. 'And how do you feel about it?'

Gilly lets out a strange little laugh. 'On the one hand, I'm elated. Over the moon. It's what I've wanted for so long.'

'And on the other?'

'On the other, I'm terrified. And frankly, appalled. Because . . .' She exhales noisily. 'Because I don't know whose it is.'

'Ah.' Now I see her problem. 'Can't you work it out from the dates?'

'Not really. It could be either of them.' She clasps her head in her hands and rocks over her knees. 'Oh God, I can't believe I'm telling you all this.'

To be honest, nor can I. But then, I did ask.

I let the silence sit between us, because I don't think it's my business to probe her on the details. After a moment, she turns to face me. 'It's either Nikhil's or . . .' Her voice has started to break. 'Or Dave's.'

'Dave's? You mean, Big Dave's?'

She nods, and it's as much as I can do not to stare at her open-mouthed. I wonder if Bryony knows about this. She can't do, or she'd have said something earlier in my room when she basically unspooled the contents of her entire head. I wonder if Gilly knows about Bryony and Dave.

'What are you going to do?'

'I don't know. I'm going to have to tell him, aren't I?'

'Who? Nikhil or Dave?'

'Nikhil, of course. He's my boyfriend. We've been trying for a baby for ages. Which makes me think it must be Dave's.'

'Are you definitely pregnant? Have you done a test?'

'Yes. I've done six. It's cost me a fortune. All positive. Oh God, Marlow. What have I done? I should never have slept with Dave. I can't believe I did. I love Nik *so* much. But, well, me not getting pregnant has put a lot of strain on our relationship. I've been so worried that he'll get tired of me, that he'll start looking elsewhere. We've been snappy with each other, and it's made me so low. Dave took advantage of my vulnerability, but I let him. I *let* him. Oh Marlow, what the hell am I going to do?'

25

Elle

Elle arrives back at the school at around half past four in the afternoon. She has spent most of the day in a team meeting, and now she has a migraine. It feels like a vice tightening around her temples, and her left eye is throbbing.

One of her colleagues, a cocky little Welsh git called Gavin, called her a part-timer when she left early. 'Only a bit of banter,' he'd said, when she told him to fuck off and get a life. She should have kept her mouth shut. He'll be even worse from now on. Pricks like him always are.

The cool, dark interior of the school is almost soothing after the fluorescent lights she's been sitting under for most of the day. As she passes the little recess near Rob's room, she sees Gilly and Marlow ducking under the rope that cordons off the stairs. Gilly's face is blotchy with tears.

Elle waits for one of them to say something by way of explanation, but neither of them does. Gilly hurries off and Marlow just smiles, as if she has every right to be coming down a staircase that is supposed to be out of bounds. Something about Marlow is a little off, Elle thinks. First she catches her in the office, going through Rob's drawers; then she sees her creeping across the playground in the dead of night and returning to her room with Mags; and now this, today, with Gilly.

Elle doesn't trust her – but then, she doesn't trust anyone in this place.

26

Marlow

It's the middle of the night. I wake, hot and sweaty, a scream still echoing in my ears. It takes me several seconds to work out where I am. When I do, I try to get out of bed, but my legs are all tangled up in the duvet and I end up half falling on to the floor, where I stay on my hands and knees until my heart stops pounding and the sweat cools on my back.

The nightmare is still so vivid and frightening. I was trapped in a burning building and hammering on a window, trying to break the glass with my fists. I was me and yet I was Lottie too. We were one and the same person. Down below, I saw all my classmates screaming and pointing up at me in panic. The other guardians were there too, including Gilly, with her orange bandana on her head and a massively pregnant belly.

Then I saw a dark, ominous figure standing at the very back of the crowd, a horrible smile playing at the corners of her mouth as she watched me burn. Except then she morphed into that dreadful woman who thrust the flyers at me in the street, her face suddenly inches above mine, sneering down at me like an evil gargoyle.

The encounter has obviously unsettled me if it's infiltrating my dreams. It was the way she looked at me yesterday. As if she knows who I am. Who I *really* am. As if she hates me.

I clamber to my feet and make my bed. For some reason, she's got it into her head that I'm responsible for that Instagram account. But why me? She must realize I'm not the only one who lives here.

I sit on the side of my bed and massage my temples, trying to persuade myself that I don't need the toilet and should climb straight back into bed and go to sleep. But sooner or later, I know I'm going to have to force myself out of this room and along that cold corridor into the even colder toilet block.

Reluctantly, I slip on my trainers and dressing gown. I'm tempted not to bother locking the door behind me. Craig's on his night shift so it's only Elle downstairs, but how well do I really know her? How well do I know any of them? And after Elle's warning to 'keep my head down' the other night – not to mention that look she gave me when she caught Gilly and me coming down the roped-off staircase – maybe I shouldn't take any risks.

The lights in the corridor are on a timer, so I take my phone with me for back-up and walk as briskly as I can down the windowless corridor. I'm plunged into darkness about three-quarters of the way along, and even though I know I'm alone up here, I'm scared. I can't stop thinking about that woman in the street.

I open the door to the toilet block. If she recognized the view from my window, that must mean she knows this school as well as I do. She *must* do.

I close the cubicle door and brace myself for the icy toilet seat. I won't look at the graffiti again. I won't. But I do. Of course I do. I look at it every time I come in here. It's impossible not to.

HG DEFINITELY INVOLVED.
New SPG (HG?) – 2.13 a.m. in, 2.40 a.m. out.

I look at the time on my phone and make a decision. It's 2.25 a.m. If Hayley was in the habit of coming up to my room in the middle of the night and keeping tabs on the other guardians, then maybe I should keep tabs on them too. If this 'New SPG' (whatever that means), who might possibly be the Head Guardian, entered somewhere at 2.13 a.m. and left at 2.40 a.m., then perhaps they might do it again tonight. It's unlikely, I know, but it's not as if I'm going to get much sleep anyway. Not now my brain is wide awake and intent on solving puzzles.

Back in my room, I make myself a small mug of tea and take it over to the window, along with the half-eaten packet of biscuits I shared with Bryony earlier. If I don't put any lights on, nobody can see me up here. Not that there's anyone about. The playground is deserted, and no lights are on in the other buildings.

I sit here for what seems like ages, absent-mindedly twisting and turning my Rubik's cube. I've more or less given up ever mastering it, but something about the feel of it between my fingers and the repetition of the movements is comforting. My mug is empty, and I've just eaten the last of the biscuits. I really should go back to bed now. If I'm going to get into Hayley's room tomorrow, I want to do it as soon as I can after everyone's gone to work.

I yawn and stretch, aware that I've just dropped off and woken up again. This was a silly idea anyway. I don't even know for sure that it *was* Hayley who wrote that message on the back of the toilet door. It could have been anyone, at any time. But just as I'm rising from my chair, I see something. My stomach tightens. It's a dark shadow in front of the gate to Lottie's garden.

I cup my hands either side of my eyes and lean against the glass of my window to get a better look. Someone is crouching in front of the gate, as if they are peering through the bars; a man by the looks of it. There's someone else with him too. A smaller, slighter figure, almost certainly a woman. If only there wasn't so much cloud cover, I might be able to see their faces.

Now they're moving away from the gate. What the fuck are they up to?

I follow their progress, assuming they're headed for the hall as that's the direction they're going in, but then they veer off to the left and disappear round the side of the building. I wait to see if they come back out, but they don't. Which means they're either lurking about in the shadows, or they've entered the building via the door that leads into the refuse room at the back of the kitchen.

For a few minutes, I consider going over there on the pretext of needing to make myself a hot chocolate, but fear holds me back. I have no idea who these people are or what they're up to, but it must be something dodgy if they're creeping around like that in the middle of the night. Are they part of the campaign? Have they left something in there for us to find? Another message?

I stand at the window for a little while longer, torn between thinking I should alert the others straight away – Elle is only a couple of floors below me, so I could go and knock on her door right now – and thinking I should just call Dev first thing in the morning and ask him to come and get me. Clear out of this place for good and never come back. Especially now that there's every chance I might run into Miss Latham or Lottie's dad next time I step out of the gates.

But then I think of Hayley, and I know I can't leave yet. I *have* to find out what's happened to her.

When I get home, there is loud music blaring out from the living room and shrieks of laughter. Strangers are milling about in the kitchen, helping themselves to sausage rolls, cheese and crackers, and an assortment of crisps and pretzels. Bottles of wine and gin, vodka and tonic water have also been put out. And a cake with the words 'Happy Birthday Jemma' iced on it. Jemma is the girl who lives in the other room next door to mine. The girl who makes noises like a wounded animal when her boyfriend stays over. I had to bang on the wall once and tell her to shut the fuck up.

As I walk in, there is a brief but noticeable lull in the conversation. Helena, the girl who's still waiting for her bank card, gives me a tight smile.

'Nice of you to invite me to the party,' I say, helping myself to a paper plate and piling it with food. I'm not particularly

162

hungry, but it seems a shame to pass up a free meal, and if I don't eat it all tonight, I can always finish it in the morning.

Helena exchanges a look with a bearded man standing next to her, and he grimaces. I pour myself a large vodka and add a splash of tonic.

'Oh, I think that's Jemma's vodka,' someone behind me says.

I pour some more out and say, 'Oh good. That's my favourite brand.'

Someone behind me sniggers, and Helena rolls her eyes. 'And she wonders why we didn't invite her.'

I take a large swig of my vodka and head for the stairs, glass in one hand, plate in the other. 'And you wonder why you don't get any post.' Oops, I didn't mean to say that – it just slipped out. What am I like?

'What did she say? Did she say something about post? Have you been taking my post? OMG, you bitch! Have you got my fucking bank card?' She's right in my face now, her stupid eyebrows like fat brown slugs. She's got red lipstick on her teeth.

It's a hugely misleading description, 'housemates'. These people are not my mates. They never have been and they never will be, so what's the point in pretending?

'Not any more,' I tell her, and with that, I go upstairs to my room and lock the door. I rest my plate of food and my glass of vodka on my bedside table, put my noise-cancelling earphones on, and fire up the old laptop. Then I change into my lounge pants and baggy T-shirt, climb under the duvet, and get ready for a spot of trolling.

When I wake up the next morning, an envelope has been

pushed under my door. It's got my name on the front, and when I open it up, it's a handwritten letter signed by Helena, Jemma and Cari. It says they'll be contacting the landlord with another complaint about me, and if I've got a shred of decency, I'll start looking for somewhere else to live.

I screw it up and lob it into the bin. My last shred of decency vanished years ago.

27

Rob

It's Thursday morning, and Rob has just opened an email from Harry Kiernan informing him that James Brampton has decided to do an impromptu site visit this morning.

Rob is furious, because this isn't the first time this has happened. Why can't the wretched man schedule his visits ahead of time, so that they are in the diary where they should be? He reads on. Harry says he will try to rearrange his schedule in order to accompany Brampton, unless there's a chance that Rob can leave work and return to the site straight away?

No, Rob replies, stabbing at his keyboard in frustration. It's not Harry's fault, he knows that, but he's furious with him too, for thinking he can just leave his desk whenever he pleases. If Rob had known about this visit, he would, of course, have arranged to work a half-day so he could be there. As Head Guardian, he *should* be there. How can Rob do his job properly if he isn't informed of things in good time?

Rob swallows hard. If Brampton isn't satisfied with security, then the agency's contract will be on the line and so too will Rob's position as Head Guardian. Even though he's done everything he can to fulfil the demands of his licence and make himself indispensable. Even though he's gone above and beyond the call of duty.

Not for the first time, Rob wishes he were the sort of person who could get up from his desk and leave the office, walk out of the college without a backwards glance, and go straight home to the school. That type of person would send an explanatory text to their manager and deal with any consequences the next day.

But Rob is *not* that kind of person. He follows protocol when it comes to requesting leave. He does not make excuses or lie. At least, not unless he is told to by one of his superiors. Not unless it is part and parcel of his job, and even then, he finds it hard. Like that time he was expected to tell a half-truth to an Ofsted inspector. 'Except it isn't a half-truth, Rob,' his manager had explained. 'It's simply putting a positive spin on something for the greater good of the college.'

Rob felt powerless then and he feels powerless now. What little control he's clinging on to is fast slipping away.

But who is he fooling? He has no power. He has no

control. Recent circumstances have brought that message home with a vengeance.

A distant memory flickers: another bad-tempered man – an over-protective father – threatening him on the street. Telling him to go away, when all he was doing was looking. He had every right to be standing there on a public street. And then the atmosphere when he went home to his parents. Walking in on their argument. Realizing they'd had a phone call and that the argument was about him.

The shame of it. The confusion.

Something is nagging away at the back of his mind again. Some vital piece of information that refuses to be dragged into the light for inspection. He puts his elbows on his desk and massages his temples with his fingers. Perhaps if he pushes all the other thoughts away so that they cannot distract him, it will reveal itself and he will know what to do.

But now his work phone has started to ring, and Rob has no choice but to answer it.

28

Marlow

I'm standing outside the office, pretending to scan the noticeboard. I'm as sure as I can be that, apart from Craig, whose snoring I heard from two floors up, I'm the only one left on site this morning. As soon as I've plucked up the courage, I'm going to nip into the office, unpick the lock on Rob's top drawer, and hopefully get my hands on the key to that classroom.'

But just as I've psyched myself up to do it, a door further along the corridor swings opens and Lou comes out. Fuck! I'm beginning to think I'll never get into that bloody room.

'I don't believe any of that sleepwalking shit,' she says, as she walks towards me.

So that's her opening salvo, is it?

Let's try this then. 'Hello, Lou. Isn't it a lovely morning?

I replaced your fruit and veg, by the way. Did you see? I really am sorry. I should never have taken your stuff in the first place.' I give her a winsome smile, which obviously throws her.

She narrows her eyes, which are minus the heavy make-up today. She looks much nicer without it. 'No, you shouldn't have,' she says. 'But . . . but thanks, anyway. And you didn't need to buy me a whole bag of apples.'

Now I'm the one taken aback. She was almost nice then. 'What were you saying just now, about my sleepwalking?'

She sniffs. 'Just that I don't believe it. You're up to something, I know you are.'

'What makes you say that?'

She gives me a strange look. 'You were trying to get into Hayley's room, weren't you? I heard you ask Rob about it on Monday evening. I saw you go into the office.'

Bloody hell. What kind of place *is* this, everybody spying on everyone else? Where was she hiding then? Did she hear that peculiar conversation I had with Elle?

'I *was* sleepwalking.'

'In your coat?'

'How do you know I was in my coat?'

'Because I heard the commotion and came out and saw you with Mags, saw your *Oscar-winning* performance.'

I look her in the eye. 'For your information, I do all sorts of things when I'm asleep. I even climbed into a friend's van once and tried to drive it. Luckily, he caught me just in time.'

Lou raises her eyebrows. She doesn't believe me, but if

she googles it later, she'll see that this sort of thing can, and does, happen. I did some research yesterday, in case Mags asks me any questions about it the next time she sees me.

'You know when you asked me what the agency said when they offered me a room here? Why did you want to know?'

Lou looks conflicted, as if the conversation has taken a direction she both wants, and doesn't want, to pursue.

She shrugs. 'I was interested, that's all.' She lowers her voice. 'The Hayley I know wouldn't have left without saying goodbye.'

'How can you be sure about that? How well did you know her?'

Lou takes a long while to respond, and I think I see the exact moment she makes the decision to drop the attitude and actually talk to me. She gestures with her head towards the kitchen. I follow her inside and she closes the door behind us, moving over to the far side of the room, the side that looks out to the front of the school. Not that we can see anything – the windows are too high up.

When she speaks, her voice is barely above a whisper, even though we're the only ones in here. She seems scared.

'I was with her the day before she's supposed to have left. She never said anything about going. Nothing at all.'

I think of what Bryony said about Lou having a crush on Hayley. 'When you say *with* her, what do you mean? In her room?'

A slight flush creeps into Lou's cheeks. 'No,' she says. 'In *your* room.'

'Oh.' My brain scrambles to make sense of this information. 'So . . . is that where the two of you . . .?'

Lou shakes her head. 'No. And for God's sake, don't mention any of this to Mags or I'll never hear the end of it. We were just friends, that's all. I was helping her with something.' Lou's face is pinched and drawn. All her previous aggression is gone.

'Have you tried calling her?'

'Yes, from work I have. I don't want Mags ever checking my phone and seeing. But it just keeps going to voice-mail.'

I rub the tops of my arms. It might only be September, but it's as cold as a fridge in here. 'Shall I make us some tea or something?'

Lou nods. 'There's some in a blue caddy in the second drawer down of that thing.' She points to a tall metal cabinet.

'Where are the mugs and spoons?'

'Here, let me do it. It'll be quicker.'

Five minutes later, we're sitting down, sipping tea, and I can't help thinking how weird it is to be doing this with Lou of all people. Especially given how sullen and rude she's been with me up until now.

'What were you helping her with?'

Lou presses her lips together. 'I'd rather not say, if you don't mind. It was . . . it was private.'

I nod. It's clear Lou needs to get something off her chest, but I'm going to have to give her time to say it.

'I feel so guilty that I didn't go up there with her that

171

night,' she says, almost as if she's forgotten I'm here and is thinking out loud.

'What do you mean? What night?'

Lou is silent for a moment before answering.

'The night before she left. She wanted me to . . . Oh fuck, I'm going to have to tell you or none of it will make any sense.'

She looks me in the eye. 'She and Big Dave had been seeing each other. In secret.'

I'm aware of my jaw dropping and clamp it shut. I think of how he sidled up beside me and offered me a smoke the first night I was here, how he surprised me in the playground the other night, kept asking if I was OK. I think of his crinkly eyes and warm smile, and feel the muscles in my face tighten. He comes across as this nice, kind man, but in reality he's an absolute bastard who was playing around with all *three* of them: Bryony, Gilly *and* Hayley. It just goes to show how wrong first impressions can be.

'Hayley really liked him,' Lou says. 'They'd started sleeping together. Or rather, *not* sleeping together, if you know what I mean.'

'Go on.'

'The thing is, she got the sense she couldn't entirely trust him, that he wasn't the person he made himself out to be.'

Too bloody right, he wasn't, but I don't say anything. Not yet anyway. I let her continue.

'She was conflicted about it and needed to talk.' Lou blushes and looks down at her lap. 'I *liked* her. I knew nothing would come of it. Hayley wasn't into girls and

172

I'm happy with Mags – I *am* – but it gave me the perfect excuse to spend more time with her.'

She chews the inside of her lip. 'We actually had a lot in common.'

'Yeah?'

'Yeah. Family issues, stuff like that.' Lou frowns. 'My parents reacted badly when I told them I was gay. Tried to persuade me it was just a *phase* I was going through.' She rolls her eyes. 'I don't have much to do with them now. They've never really accepted me for who I am.'

'I'm so sorry to hear that.'

'And Hayley *hated* her family. Her dad abused her when she was younger.' Lou looks directly into my eyes. 'Sexually abused her.'

'Oh God no, that's awful. Poor Hayley.'

Lou nods. 'She finally plucked up the courage to tell a teacher, and the whole thing blew up into a full-scale investigation. But she wasn't believed. The case was dropped. Can you believe it?'

Anger rises inside me. Whenever I hear something like this, it brings to mind all the other times I've heard a news story about someone getting away with abuse, sometimes for years and years. For ever, in some cases. It makes me livid.

'What do you mean, she wasn't believed? Why?'

Lou sighs. 'She used to take drugs, you see, as a teenager. She was a bit of a wild child, from what I can gather. Her family accused her of being an attention-seeker, out to punish them for giving her a hard time over the drugs. But that was the reason she took them in the first place! Because of her dad. It was her form of escape.'

Lou sniffs loudly and shakes her head. 'We were up there talking about all this one afternoon while Mags was at work – I was on a half-day and Hayley had thrown a sickie. Suddenly, we spotted Dave and Bryony standing at her window and they were kissing. They obviously had no idea anyone could see them, because the only building that overlooks the drama block is that one side of Block C. There's only Craig and Elle in that building – well, until you arrived – and their room looks out over the play-ing field at the back. There was no way Dave or Bryony would've known me and Hayley would be up there, so there they were, snogging away for bloody ages.'

Lou sighs and shakes her head. 'Hayley was furious. She knew she'd been played. Big Dave had made out he was falling in love with her, gave her the impression that he hadn't had a proper girlfriend before because he was self-conscious about his weight. She wanted to broadcast what a two-timing bastard he was, so she wrote some daft shit on the flipchart and was going to pin it up on the notice-board outside the office so everyone could see.'

A *three*-timing bastard, I think, but again, I let her go on. If she doesn't know about Dave and Gilly, she's not going to hear it from me.

'I told her she'd regret it if she did that, and she should just let it go. Tell Dave she and him were over. Not even give him an explanation. I told her that he was beneath her contempt, and that if she did something like that it would just send him the message that she was jealous and upset, and he needed to see that she didn't give a shit. But she was adamant she wanted to do it. In the end, I ripped the sheet off and tore it up. Told her to sleep on it at least. And I was right. She'd changed her mind the next morning and thanked me for stopping her.

'After that, though, she had this thing about spying on them. Talk about rubbing salt into a wound. She even took a pair of binoculars up there.'

'I know. They're still on my windowsill.'

Lou's eyes widen. 'She wouldn't have done that, left an expensive pair of binoculars behind. She just wouldn't. She looked after her stuff. Shit! Maybe they saw her watching them. Maybe they—'

'Come off it. Big Dave and Bryony might be pissed off that she was spying on them, but I doubt they'd do anything to—'

'No! Not Dave and Bryony! The men who've been going into the swimming pool.'

29

Marlow

Now it's my turn to look surprised. 'Men going into the swimming pool?'

Lou leans closer. 'I haven't told you that bit yet.' Her voice is low and urgent. 'It started with her monitoring Dave and Bryony, but then she saw something else.'

She glances towards the door before continuing. When she does, she's whispering. 'I wasn't with her the first time she saw it. To be honest, I was starting to get a bit fed up of seeing a couple I had zilch interest in making out, and listening to Hayley get more and more worked up about it. I was also feeling a bit guilty about seeing her behind Mags's back. But when she told me what else she'd seen, I couldn't resist going back up there with her to see for myself, and . . .'

Lou looks down at her lap again. 'The truth is, I missed being with her.' She looks up, sharply. 'Don't judge me.'

'I'm not.' I lean forward. 'So what's this about men going into the swimming pool?'

'First off, she saw this guy in a high-vis jacket and hard hat going into the swimming pool one day. He was in there for about fifteen minutes – then he came out and left via one of the padlocked access points at the side. Looked like a builder maybe, or a tradesman of some kind.'

Lou chews the inside of her bottom lip before continuing. 'The thing is, when he went in he was carrying a large toolbox, but when he came out, he just had a clipboard.' She frowns. 'Normally, we're given a heads up if there's going to be a site visit, and we hadn't been told to expect anyone. In any case, the building works aren't supposed to start until next autumn. We've been given assurances by the agency that our licences will extend till then. Hayley asked Rob about it, and he said it was one of Brampton's men and he knew all about it, that it was a planned visit.'

'But you don't think it was.'

Lou shakes her head. 'No, because the next time we were up there, it happened again. Only that time there were three of them. All in high-vis jackets, all wearing hard hats, all carrying toolboxes. They were in there for about forty-five minutes, before coming out minus the toolboxes and carrying clipboards.'

'That does sound a bit odd.'

Lou nods. 'We assumed Rob was lying. I mean, why would Brampton have builders going in and leaving tools on site if work wasn't scheduled to start for another year? It doesn't make sense. Hayley was convinced he'd changed his mind about the start date, and that we were all about to be given our marching orders. She was furious. She said she'd only agreed to this licence because Harry had assured her it was long-term.

'So from then on, the focus switched from Dave and Bryony to the swimming-pool guys. We either went up there together when we could, or we took it in turns. Obviously we couldn't keep watch every day, but I work remotely a lot of the time now – have done ever since the pandemic – and Hayley did too.'

'What did she do for a living?'

'She had a few different jobs, one of which involved listening to audio tapes of meetings and typing up minutes and reports, so she often did that from your room.'

Hence the flask of coffee, I think.

'We even went up there at night sometimes.' Lou gives me a sheepish look. 'This might sound stupid, and it probably goes to show how boring my life is, but it was kind of exciting. Like being a couple of private eyes on surveillance. I could only do it when Mags was on night duty, but I have a feeling Hayley did it more than she let on. I think at least a part of that was wanting to see what was happening with Dave and Bryony too. She couldn't quite let that go.

'But then one night, when she was up there alone, she saw a man in black wearing a balaclava unlock the padlock to the swimming pool and go inside. He was in there for about twenty minutes. She assumed it was Rob as he keeps the key to the padlock, but I guess someone else could have got hold of it.'

I think of that time Craig came up behind me while I was peering through one of the windows of the pool. Could it have been him?

'The only person it definitely *wasn't*,' Lou says, 'was Big Dave. His size would have given him away, and anyway, he was too busy banging Bryony.'

'Nice bit of alliteration there.'

Lou smirks.

'And was he carrying anything?' I ask.

'No. But it's weird behaviour, right? I mean, you don't prowl around at night dressed up like a cat burglar unless you're up to something.'

'And where did he go afterwards?'

'Back across the playground and into the hall, which made her even more convinced it was Rob.'

Something in my mind suddenly slots into place. 'How did you and Hayley communicate with each other if you didn't want Mags ever seeing her name on your phone?'

'We left each other little messages.'

I think of that strange piece of graffiti that didn't make any sense: *New SPG (HG?) – 2.13 a.m. in, 2.40 a.m. out.* SPG. Swimming-pool guy. HG. Head Guardian, Rob Hornby.

'You didn't, by any chance, disguise them as graffiti on the back of a toilet door?'

Lou's mouth falls open. 'How do you know that? Oh, of course – it's *your* toilet now. Anyway,' she continues, 'one time, when we were up there together, we saw the same guy – at least we think it was the same guy, bearing in mind I didn't even see him the first time – go into one of the huts on the other side of the playground. He was in there ages. We got so cold and tired waiting for him to come out, and I had to go to the loo. When I came back, Hayley had fallen asleep in her chair at the window. We waited another half-hour, but by then we were both so shattered we called it a night. I have no idea whether he came out in the five minutes Hayley nodded off, or whether he was still in there.

'Hayley said it was getting more and more suspicious, and we should bypass Rob altogether and speak to the agency, or go straight to the police, but I thought we should carry on monitoring them for a while longer.'

Lou lowers her gaze, looks embarrassed. 'I knew that if we told anyone, that would probably be the end of us meeting up in private, and I . . . I wasn't ready for that.'

Lou presses her fingers into her eyes and shakes her head. 'We agreed we'd talk it through and make a decision the following night, but Mags's shift got changed out of the blue, so I couldn't meet her as planned.'

She takes a long breath in and out. 'The next day, she was gone. I think she must have done something stupid, like trying to get into the swimming pool. She'd talked about doing it before.'

Lou's shoulders slump. 'I should have been with her that night. I'd have stopped her.'

'I've seen something weird too,' I say, and Lou looks up. 'Last night when I couldn't sleep.'

'What was it?'

I tell her about the two people I saw peering into the garden. Lou's face darkens.

'Something is definitely going on here,' she says.

'Have you spoken to Harry or the receptionist at the agency?' I ask her. 'They must have contact details for Hayley's next-of-kin.'

'Yes, but . . .'

'But what?'

Lou exhales through her nose.

'When we were chatting about our families and all the shit we'd both been through, she told me she'd cut all contact with them. I mean, I'm not exactly best buddies with my parents, but we do occasionally speak, and they know where I am. But Hayley, she'd cut ties with them *completely*.

'It was a safety mechanism more than anything. Her dad came looking for her once, when she was living in a squat somewhere. He'd managed to wrangle her whereabouts from an old friend she was still in touch with. She said it made her extra careful after that. Told me she'd even started using some cousin in Australia as next-of-kin on official forms. Someone who died three years ago. The last thing she wanted was her dad turning up, if she was ever in an accident.'

'Oh, I see.'

'And the thing is, I don't know for sure that anything's

happened to her, do I? I don't have any actual evidence. And if she *has* just taken off, and the police get involved, she'll be furious with me. Hayley hated the police after how she was treated.'

Lou looks close to tears. 'And even if I did tell the police, I doubt they'd think it was worth pursuing, especially if they trace her family and find out about her history with addiction.'

'OK. I think the first thing we need to do is get into her room and see for ourselves if Rob is lying about there being a leak. Then we need to have a look in the garden. See if we can work out what our mystery couple might have been doing in there.' I clear my throat. 'You were right about the other night, by the way. I wasn't sleepwalking.'

'I *knew* you were lying,' Lou says, but this time she sounds pleased rather than angry.

I take our mugs over to the sink and give them a quick rinse. 'We're going to have to find out where Rob keeps the key first though. I've got a feeling they might be in his top drawer. A couple of paperclips should do the trick.'

Lou reaches into her back pocket. 'I'm one step ahead of you,' she says, unfurling her fingers to reveal a gold key in the palm of her hand. 'I unpicked it last night.'

30

Marlow

Lou and I stand in the middle of Hayley's room, absorbing the scene. We have been inside for a few minutes now and neither of us has said a single word.

There is no leak in this room. No wet patches on the ceiling or discoloration of any kind. No puddles on the polished parquet floor. The room is devoid of personal possessions, but the furniture is still here. An occasional table, a small writing desk, two chests of drawers, an armchair and the bed, which has been stripped and dismantled. The mattress, the wooden base and the frame have been propped against the wall. The mattress looks new and clean.

Lou opens each of the drawers in turn. They are all empty.

'But why would she leave all her beautiful furniture behind?' she says.

'Maybe she's intending to collect it later.' But even as I say these words, I know it can't be true. Because if it was, why wouldn't Rob have said so? Why is he pretending the room is a health-and-safety hazard when clearly it isn't? This room has been well looked after. *Loved*. But then, I already knew that from looking at the Instagram account.

Lou is now crouching down on the floor, picking up little bits of soil in her fingers and frowning.

'That must be where the hanging plants were taken down,' I say, half to myself.

Lou turns to me, sharply. 'How do you know she had hanging plants? You've never been in here before. You've never even *met* Hayley.' The old Lou has returned. There is suspicion in her voice. Distrust. Our newly formed rapport is still a fragile, tenuous thing. I've only got to look at her face to see that.

I take my phone out of my pocket and find the Boho Birdie account, show her the picture of this room. Lou stares at it in astonishment, then at me. Her face crumples in confusion.

'What *is* this? I don't understand. Who's Boho Birdie? What the fuck is going on?'

So I tell her about my encounter with that awful woman yesterday, about her accusation.

Lou scrolls through the photos, and I see the look of recognition and incredulity pass across her features.

'I can't believe she was doing this,' she says. 'Why would she?'

I shrug. 'Who knows? They're good though, aren't they? The photos?'

'But she's *lying*. She's calling it her *house*, as if she owns it. It's so . . . *dishonest*.' Lou shakes her head, as if she still can't quite believe what she's seeing. 'It explains a few things though.'

'What things?'

'Why she was so secretive, for a start. And why we'd sometimes see her lugging stuff around. Candles and cushions and things. She'd always have a ready excuse on her lips. "Just trying to find a sunny spot to do some yoga" was one of her favourites, as I recall.'

'But this doesn't change anything, does it?' I say. 'I mean, she might have been lying about why she was carrying things round the school, but she wasn't lying about the strange goings-on she saw from my window. Because *you* saw them too. The builders coming out of the pool without their toolboxes. The man in the balaclava at night, going into one of the huts.'

Lou nods. 'You're right. I suppose I'm just feeling a bit disappointed in her, that's all.'

I spot something then, something I didn't notice before. I walk over and pull at a tiny section of cream-coloured cloth peeping over the top of the radiator. As I draw it out, I realize that it's one of the curtain panels that were hanging at the window. A beautiful wide rectangle of delicate voile, imprinted with tiny gold daisies. It's beautiful.

185

My eyes travel up to the tops of the windows and there, hanging down at an angle where it has come loose from its fixings, is the plastic curtain rail.

Lou comes over and follows the direction of my gaze. Then she stares at the voile panel draped over my hands.

'Looks like someone got hold of the panels and yanked them off,' she says, voicing my exact thoughts. 'Someone in such a hurry they didn't care if they broke the rail, and they didn't even notice one of the curtains had slipped behind the radiator.'

The sudden whirring noise of the school gates opening makes us both panic.

Lou heads for the door. 'We'd better get out of here.'

But we can already hear the main door opening. I put my finger to my lips and shake my head. 'There's no time for that,' I whisper.

There are two male voices. One loud and deep, the other slightly higher, almost bored-sounding. I recognize the second voice straight away.

'It's Harry Kiernan,' I say.

'Shit!' Lou says. 'I think the other one must be James Brampton, the owner. But there's nothing on the notice-board about a site visit today.'

We wait in the classroom while James Brampton's loud, self-important voice drones on about timescales and quantity surveyors and financial considerations. Every so often, Harry pipes up with a 'Ya, ya, absolutely.'

Eventually, we hear them open the door to the play-ground and go outside. The second they've gone, we get out of the classroom, lock the door, and put the key back in Rob's top drawer.

'Wait,' Lou hisses at me as I turn to leave. 'I've got to relock the drawer in case Rob turns up. He's usually here for site visits.'

I stand guard anxiously at the office door, while Lou fiddles around with a couple of paperclips she pulls from her back pocket, the ones she must have used to pick the lock in the first place. She's taking too long.

'What's the problem?'

'I can't seem to do it.'

'Here, let me have a go.'

My hands have started to tremble, and my neck feels all sweaty. If Harry and James come back and catch us doing this, we might be evicted on the spot. It's hardly trustworthy behaviour, is it, breaking into the Head Guardian's top drawer? Even though, strictly speaking, we're trying to lock it now.

And then, almost as if I've made it happen simply by thinking it, the two men are back. I'm still crouched down in front of Rob's desk, but Lou is in full sight, standing in the doorway, her face frozen with indecision.

'Hi there, everything OK?' Harry says. His voice is light and affable. Lou appears to have lost the power to speak, and I realize that it's up to me. I have to make this right and I have to do it now.

I stand up and pretend to be examining the computer screen. 'I came in to borrow a pen and thought I saw someone lurking round the swimming pool on the CCTV.' After

Lou's revelation in the kitchen, it's the first thing that enters my head. 'I got scared and went to find Lou.'

'That's right,' Lou says, quickly recovering and throwing herself into the part. 'I was just going to call you, Harry. Thank God you're here.'

James Brampton's face darkens in anger. He strides over to the screen and peers at it, starts tapping various buttons on the keyboard and bringing up different viewpoints, different angles. He is a large, broad-shouldered man who looks as if he's accustomed to taking up more than his fair share of space. He doesn't even say 'excuse me', just assumes I'll step to one side. Frankly, I'm glad to. Whatever scent he's wearing has an astringent, herby tang to it that makes me feel slightly queasy.

Harry joins us. 'What did they look like?'

My heart starts to slow. It was the right thing to say. They're more concerned with the possibility of an intruder on site than finding Lou and me lurking in the office.

'I couldn't really tell. I think it was a man, but it could have been a kid. A teenager. Maybe they saw the cameras and scarpered.'

James Brampton is still staring at the screen, a deep furrow between his eyebrows. He is chewing the inside of his lower lip.

'Do you think it's the same person who managed to get in and chalk that message?' Lou says.

James's head whips round to look at her. 'What message? You mean someone's already broken in? Why is this the first I've heard of it?'

Harry glares at Lou. 'I, er, I'm sure I emailed your sec-
retary about it. Some joker chalked "don't get too
comfortable" on the tarmac.'

'When did this happen? Last night?'

'No, it was, er . . .' Harry blinks as he tries to remember.

'It was on Tuesday morning,' I say. 'Early. At least, that's
when I first saw it.'

I'm about to tell him what I saw last night – the two
people in the playground – but if I mention that now,
Harry's going to wonder why on earth I didn't alert Rob
first thing this morning, or contact the agency direct.
Besides, Brampton is already apoplectic. Next to his rugby-
prop physique, Harry looks puny. I'm no expert in body
language, but it's clear he feels threatened by this bully of
a man. I don't want to make it any worse for him.

'For fuck's sake, Kiernan, what am I paying you for?
Your agency's meant to be looking after this place. Did
you check for any security breaches?'

Lou nods, vigorously. 'We went round the whole site.
There weren't any.'

James Brampton exhales forcefully through his nostrils, his mouth closed. He looks at his watch. 'This is all
I need. I've got four more site visits to do today.' He glares
at Harry. 'So how the fuck did they get in? Did anyone
have any overnight guests? Could it have been someone
playing a practical joke, do you think? Someone already
on the premises?'

He's looking at me now. I shrug. 'I've no idea, sorry. I'm
quite new here, so . . .'

But James Brampton is already bored with my answer. He takes one last look at the security cameras, then marches out of the office.

'Come on, Kiernan,' he shouts over his shoulder. 'Let's see if the little fucker's still on site.'

3 1

Marlow

When James Brampton and Harry Kiernan return to the office, Lou and I are in the kitchen, pretending to make some coffee. We wait until we're sure they've left the school grounds before heading over to the garden.

'There could be rational explanations for everything that's been going on here,' I say. I'm trying to convince myself as much as I am Lou, to quell my nerves. The trouble is, it's not working.

Lou turns to look at me. 'Such as?'

Now that I've started this somewhat hopeful line of conversation, I feel compelled to see it through. Perhaps if I say the words out loud, I'll start to believe in them. 'Maybe Hayley realized that it's only a matter of time before the building work starts and she'd have to clear out anyway. And perhaps—'

No, I can't tell her the next thing that pops into my mind: that perhaps she guessed Lou had a crush on her, and what with Big Dave turning out to be a lying git, she'd had enough of both of them and wanted to leave before either of them came back from work.

'Perhaps what?'

I have to think on my feet. 'Perhaps Rob has earmarked the room for himself. He saw how nice it was after Hayley left and is working on a way to move himself in there, after a decent amount of time has passed and his mythical leak can be fixed. He's probably hoping I'll be well and truly settled in Block C by then and will stop going on about it.'

Lou frowns. 'And the man in the balaclava Hayley saw going into the swimming pool in the middle of the night?'

'Hmm. You said she assumed it was Rob because he has the key to the padlock. I'd say that's a fairly safe assumption, wouldn't you? Admittedly, I don't know Rob that well, but he does seem pretty obsessed with policing this place. He got quite shirty with me when I asked him if I could look at the pool.'

'Why did you want to look at the pool?'

'I'm a photographer. Abandoned buildings are incredibly atmospheric. Anyway, maybe he likes carrying out his own security checks. When he was giving me a tour of this place, he let slip something that made me think he's already had a good rummage around in the science block, and that's out of bounds too, isn't it?'

We've reached the garden now.

'What about the figures you saw crouching in front of the gate?' Lou says. 'That doesn't sound exactly normal, does it?'

'No, it doesn't.'

'Or the man Hayley and I saw going into the old care-taker's hut and not coming out for ages.'

'Also true.'

'Or the fact that Hayley left all her good furniture behind.'

'I don't know. Maybe she deliberately left it behind because she fancied a fresh start.'

Lou snorts. 'Come off it. You don't just abandon good quality furniture. She'd have at least wanted to sell it, or offer it to a friend. And what about the binoculars? There are just too many things here that don't add up.'

She's right. Of course she is. And I haven't even told her about the negative energies I've been picking up ever since I arrived. The visceral certainty that Hayley is in danger.

Lou grips the bars of the garden gate and peers inside. 'Are we sure about this?'

'Yes.'

We look around to make sure we're not being observed. Then Lou interlocks her fingers to form a step so that I can scale the gate.

'What about you? How are you going to get over?'

Lou grins. 'I used to date a girl who was into Parkour. Let's just say, she taught me a few tricks. Come on.'

'Hang on a minute.' I peer at the padlock. Something

about it doesn't look quite right. Then I realize what it is. It's been sheared through with bolt-cutters.

Lou follows my gaze and gasps. 'What the hell?'

We stand there, staring at it, unsure what to do next.

'Rob will go apeshit,' Lou says.

'I can't imagine James Brampton will be best pleased either. Or Harry, seeing as he's the one who's going to get it in the neck.'

'We should call Harry now. Let him know straight away. It's got to be something to do with the campaigners. Unless Mags and Gilly have gone rogue and decided to do some guerrilla gardening.'

We both giggle at that. 'Let's carry on with our search first,' I say. 'Plenty of time to fill him in later.'

With one last look over my shoulders, I push open the gate and step into the garden. Lou follows me in.

It feels very strange to be in here again after all these years. Lottie is buried in a cemetery several streets away, but it feels almost as if I'm standing on her grave, and for a minute, I think I'm going to break down and start crying.

Lou is already prowling round the garden, peering behind the bushes. I take a few deep breaths before making myself do the same thing in the opposite direction. The lack of any kind of breeze gives the garden an unnatural stillness. I try to ignore the wave of apprehension that comes over me. Neither of us knows what we're looking for, but I feel sure that we'll know what it is when we see it. There are muddy footprints on the circular piece of paving in the centre of the garden.

'Marlow, come here and look at this.' Lou's voice is hushed but solemn, and a ripple of disquiet washes through me. I walk over to where she's standing, steeling myself for whatever it is she's found.

At first, I'm not sure what she wants me to look at, because all I can see are clumps of lavender past their best and a few straggly weeds. Then I see what she's pointing at. A solitary cut rose, lying towards the back of the border where one of the statues used to stand.

'So that's all they've done? Left a rose in her memory?'

'Well, it isn't *all* they've done,' Lou says. 'They've also broken into the site and damaged a padlock. It makes you wonder what they might do next.'

I nod, but the campaigners' next move isn't what's worrying me here. In fact, I rather admire their determination to keep Lottie's memory first and foremost in James Brampton's mind. But seeing this rose lying on the freshly turned soil where the plinth used to be, and thinking about Brampton's stubborn refusal to agree to preserve the memorial garden, has my mind travelling down a very different route. One that has nothing to do with Lottie and everything to do with Hayley.

A horrible feeling of dread descends on me. If the campaign to save the memorial garden is successful, it will remain where it is and become a permanent feature of the planned new development. The three statues on their heavy stone plinths will be returned to their rightful place by Lottie's parents. There'll be an article about it in the local newspaper, probably even some kind of official reopening ceremony. New residents will move into the renovated and refurbished school buildings and pass the garden every day, maybe even sit for a while on one of its benches, enjoying the peace and stillness.

And if the campaign *isn't* successful, the plans will proceed and Brampton will turn the garden into a car park, covering the whole area in a thick layer of tarmac.

My stomach twists. Because either way, what better place to bury a body?

32

Hayley

I hear a door opening. Feel a slight movement as he gets out of the car. A bottomless pit of dread opens up inside me.

This is it, Hayley. This is how your life ends.

I start to cry. My whole body convulses with sobs. I don't want to die. *Please God, don't let me die!*

I hear the crunch of his footsteps. Sounds like gravel. Is this where I'll meet my end? On some deserted piece of wasteland in the middle of nowhere? No one to hear my cries? No one to find me when it's all over?

Let it be quick. Please God, let it be quick.

But where is he going? Why is he walking away? Surely he's not going to . . .

Sweat pours down my face and coats my back. Surely

he's not going to leave me here to die? On my own. In the dark. Unable to move. A long, slow, agonizing death.

I try to shuffle nearer the door of the boot. There must be a release button in here somewhere, but I can't see it. My ankles have been tied together but I can still move my legs, if I forget about the throbbing pain in my shins. I lever myself into a position where I can kick against the door with my feet, but it's useless. I know it is. A waste of time and energy. I can kick and kick all I want, and it won't make a blind bit of difference. I'll still be trapped in here. Trussed up like an animal. Left to die of thirst and hunger and lack of oxygen.

If only I could rip this tape from my mouth, I'd scream at the top of my lungs. No one would hear me, but maybe he would. He can't have got far. I can't hear any other engine noise, so I don't think he's got into another car. I want him to hear me calling him a coward. A fucking miserable coward who hasn't got the balls to finish me off.

But I can't even do that. Because my hands are tied securely behind my back, and there's no way I can remove this tape without them. I rub my cheek on the scratchy bit of carpet that lines the boot, try to loosen the edge of the tape, but it's stuck fast. All I'm doing is making my cheek even more sore than it already is.

I freeze. The footsteps are coming back. My heart pounds in my chest. He's getting closer now. The footsteps stop. He's standing right behind the boot. I can sense his presence. Rigid with fear, I watch as the boot opens, expecting to see light, but it's as dark outside as it is in here. Someone I've never seen before looks down at me. Oh my God. He's got someone else to do his dirty work for him. I should have known. For a second, I think this stranger is going to say something, but then he leans in and picks me up as if I'm no heavier than a child.

There's a dull, roaring sound in the distance, and now I see that it isn't a piece of gravelly old wasteland after all. It's a beach. A deserted pebble beach. I'm being taken to the line where the pebbles meet the sand dunes. He deposits me in a pile of litter as if I too am something to be discarded. Worthless trash. Except this isn't typical beach litter.

Hot, silent tears splash on to pieces of screwed-up tin foil, dirty old dessert spoons and used needles. I hope to God that Lou doesn't take it upon herself to go looking for me. I can't bear to think of the same thing happening to her. Because now I know why I've been brought to this particular spot.

Now I know how my life will end.

33

Marlow

I gesture at the garden gate. 'We need to get into the pool and see if we can find out what's going on, but we have to do it now, before all the others come back.'

Lou looks at me as if I'm mad. 'And how do you propose we do that? There's a massive great bolt and padlock on the entrance, and a CCTV camera pointed right at it. And I don't remember seeing any padlock keys in Rob's drawer. He must keep them somewhere else.'

'I wonder if there's another way in?'

Lou frowns. 'I'm pretty sure there isn't. All the windows except for a small one at the side are boarded up. Even if we managed to break it without setting off some kind of alarm, I doubt we'd be able to climb through.'

'I mean via the PE block. They're adjoining buildings, aren't they?'

It would be a lot quicker and easier if I just came clean and admitted to Lou that I used to go to this school. Then I could tell her about the store cupboard with doors on both sides. But every time I'm on the verge of explaining, something holds me back.

'At my old school, we had a similar set-up,' I say. 'There must be a door that leads through into the pool. Staff access maybe?'

Lou shakes her head. 'There *was*. You can see it when you're standing in the gym, but it's been boarded up. Honestly, Marlow, you're not going to be able to get through that way unless you've got some serious, heavy-duty tools.'

'Yeah, but that might not be the only access point. At my school, there used to be a couple of store cupboards that were accessible from both buildings. It's worth a try, isn't it?'

Lou looks dubious. 'I guess so.'

'And we won't exactly be doing anything wrong by being in the gym. If anyone comes in, we can say we were looking to see if there were any old netballs or other bits and pieces we could use.'

'I don't think anyone's likely to come in. Everyone should be at work, except Craig, and he'll most likely be asleep.'

'He is. I heard him snoring when I was on the stairwell.'

'Let's go round and knock on everyone's doors first, just to be on the safe side,' Lou says.

'Good idea.'

We leave the garden, making sure to close the gate behind us and position the padlock so that it's exactly how we found it, the shorn edges lined up so that from a distance, it still appears locked. Then we go back across the playground and into the main hall.

Lou raps on Rob's door first. She waits for a minute, knocks again, then waits some more. She puts her ear against the door.

'Right, let's go and check on the others,' she says, and the two of us set off across the playground once again. It all feels a bit surreal. Scary too. But I have to admit, it's exciting. I feel more alive than I have in years. I feel like I'm here for a reason.

We pass the drama studio, where less than a week ago I thought Lou was one of the rudest people I'd ever met. Now look at us, united in a common purpose. Lou goes up to check on Big Dave and Bryony, while I stay downstairs and knock on Gilly and Nikhil's door. There is no response and no sound from within, but as I'm turning away, I register the two pairs of muddy shoes lined up outside their door and immediately think of the footprints on the paving stones in Lottie's garden. The mud on these shoes could have come from anywhere though. From the playing field when it's their turn to do the early-morning perimeter walk, or from a stroll on Hampstead Heath or along the canal. Right now, I have more pressing things to think about.

'I suppose we'd better check to see whether Craig is up and about,' I say to Lou when she reappears, remembering that time he came up behind me when I was trying to peer into the pool corridor.

We cross over to Block C and take the stairs up to Elle and Craig's room, but by the time we reach their floor and turn into the corridor, we can already hear the regular rumble of snoring. We exchange a satisfied glance and turn back.

Once we're in the PE block, it's as much as I can do not to steer Lou straight to the cupboard so we can press on while we know for sure we're not going to be disturbed, but I can't make it too obvious that I already know it's there. So I go through the motions of searching the changing area with her and opening various doors. We step out into the corridor. It might even be better if Lou finds the right door herself. She's already heading towards the large store cupboard. I hang back and let her go in and fumble around for a light switch, waiting for her to come out again, eyes wide with excitement.

She beckons me in. 'You were right! Come and look.'

I follow her in, closing the door behind us so that we are both standing in the store cupboard. Where once the shelves were piled high with equipment, now they are empty apart from a couple of faded relay batons, a few grotty-looking gym mats and an old, deflated netball. Lou has pushed a tall trolley to one side, old items of sportswear and lost or discarded trainers heaped in its wire baskets, and there is the door.

'You're a genius, Marlow. I'd never have thought to move the trolley if I hadn't been looking for a door.'

I accept the compliment, but can't help feeling a twinge of regret that I didn't tell her the truth from the start. It doesn't seem right, stringing her along like this, but it's for a good reason, I tell myself.

On the day of the fire, it was my fault that Lottie was in the art studio, my fault she died in that terrible, frightening way, and though there's nothing I can do to change that one immutable fact, I can at least try to help another person in this blighted place who might be in trouble. I just hope I'm not too late.

We stand there, staring at the door, neither of us quite ready to open it.

'Are you having second thoughts about doing this?' Lou whispers.

'Are you?'

'I asked you first.'

'I asked you second.'

We clamp our hands to our mouths to stop the nervous giggles from escaping.

Jesus Christ, Dev was spot on with his regression theory. We're like a couple of kids.

'Let's open it a fraction of an inch,' Lou says. 'We'll stay in here for a while, listening. If we hear anyone, we'll close it. If we don't . . .'

I take a deep breath. 'If we don't, we'll go in.'

34

Elle

Craig is blinking at her in confusion. He's still half asleep, but she has to tell him now. It's too important to wait. She turns up the radio while she speaks, and watches his face change from sleepy to incredulous as her words finally sink in.

'What do you mean, another way in? How? Where?' His voice is hoarse.

'Through a store cupboard in the gym. It's accessible from both sides.'

He stares at her angrily, as if it's her fault, and perhaps it is. She hasn't been thorough enough. She should have found it. 'So all this time we could have been—'

She nods.

'How the *fuck* did they find that?'

'No idea. They seemed to be deliberately looking for it. I saw them go into the gym and followed them in.'

Craig bites down on his lower lip. 'It's like history repeating itself. What is it with these damn women?'

'I told you Lou knows something.'

Craig puts his elbows on his knees and hangs his head in his hands. 'This could ruin everything. The boss is going to go *apeshit* when he finds out. We're so close now. So fucking close.'

She sits down on the old sofa and the springs dig into the backs of her thighs.

'You've got to stop them sniffing around,' he says.

'And how do you suggest I do that?'

'I don't know. But you'll think of something. You always do. We can't afford any cock-ups at this stage.'

35

Marlow

Now that we're actually doing this, the nerves have kicked in. I depress the handle as gently as I can and pull the door towards me, no more than an inch at first. I feel a puff of cold air on my wrist and face.

We wait, the two of us, ears strained for anything that might persuade us to shut the door, get out of this cupboard, and return to the familiarity of the gym. I'm almost hoping we change our minds anyway, but now that we've come this far, we should at least take a look.

The silence is oppressive, but still we wait. Lou pulls the door open another couple of inches and peers out. After a few minutes, we exchange a nod and I open the door just wide enough for us to slip through. I go first, closely followed by Lou.

I recognize this part of the pool building straight away. We've come out in the middle of the long corridor that leads from the main entrance – accessible from the playground – all the way to the double doors (now blocked off) that used to lead into the dance studio and gym. Like most buildings that have been abandoned for any length of time and left unheated, it smells of damp and stale air. And it's cold. So very cold.

We tread softly so that our shoes don't make a noise on the floor, and we don't talk to each other, not even in whispers, but communicate with facial expressions and gestures, subtle tilts of the head to indicate which direction we will walk in. Instinctively, I head for the changing rooms and the pool beyond. The door creaks as I open it, and we both freeze for what seems like ages before daring to continue. Adrenaline is coursing through my veins, and my heart is beating fast.

The communal changing room seems much smaller than I remember it, but it brings back so many memories: the awkwardness of wriggling out of my cold, wet swimming costume and drying off with a towel that never seemed quite large enough to cover all my bits; the difficulty of pulling my knickers and tights back on over damp thighs. On those rare occasions when I managed to get one of the few private cubicles, the relief was overwhelming.

Lou is already walking past the showers with their mildewed curtains, past the toilet stalls and through the little footbath (now empty, of course) that separates the changing rooms from the poolside. I follow her in, shuddering at the memory of bare feet on wet toilet floors.

We enter the main pool area and both gasp at the same time. There is something quite shocking about an empty swimming pool, especially a large one like this. It looks all wrong. Eerie and uninviting. Dangerous, even. Nonetheless, I really wish I'd brought my camera with me.

Lou is gazing up at the spectator area. 'I don't see any evidence of building materials or toolboxes, do you?' she says. It's the first time either of us has spoken, and even though her voice is low, I can still hear a faint echo.

'No.' I can't resist taking a couple of photos on my phone. Then I nod towards the steps up to the seats. 'Let's have a quick look up there, and then we'll search the rest of the building.'

This part of the pool is, unsurprisingly, empty, apart from a few pieces of litter under the seats. We make our way down to the poolside again and take one last look at the tiled, rectangular shell. It's so unsettling seeing it laid bare like this. It's unnatural, almost ghostly. My skin prickles.

'Let's get out of here,' I whisper. Lou nods and we retrace our steps through the empty footbath, past the toilet stalls, through the changing room, and out into the corridor again.

Further down is the 'staff only' section, which turns out to be a much smaller version of the main changing room.

There's a bench along one side and lockers opposite, two private cubicles, a toilet stall, and two showers. It's completely empty and of zero interest to anyone, surely.

'The only other room we passed was the pump room,' Lou says, as we walk back into the corridor. 'I don't know what I expected to see in here, but it's all a bit of an anti-climax, isn't it?'

Ignoring the warning notices on the pump-room door, we open it and step inside. Everywhere else in the building there are windows in the ceiling, but this room is windowless. Lou flicks the light switch, but it must be disconnected. We leave the door open so we can see what we're doing.

My whole body is tense now. There's something about this enclosed space that unnerves me even more than the gaping pool. It's probably because of the disturbing images that landed in my mind as we stepped inside. Blood on the floor. Maybe even a body.

But it's just a room full of tanks and pipes and cylinders.

'Is there anywhere else to look?' Lou says.

I shake my head. 'I don't think so. We've seen everything now. I think we should go.'

Lou nods and we turn to leave.

'Wait a sec,' I say. 'What's that?'

There is something glinting at me from under what I think is a filtration cylinder. I crouch down on all fours and stretch my hand underneath to get hold of whatever it is. My fingers touch what feels like a tiny piece of metal.

I pinch it between my thumb and forefinger and draw it out, recognizing it straight away. It's an Art Deco earring that matches the one I found on my first day here.

Lou gasps. 'That's Hayley's. This proves she was here.'

'And I've got the other one. I found it outside the entrance to the pool, when Rob was showing me round the day I arrived.'

I rake my hand under the tank to see if there's anything else under there. It's dusty and gritty, but then I feel something flat and plasticky. I sweep it out with my fingers and stare at it. It's a small see-through plastic bag with fine white powder inside.

Lou peers at it over my shoulder. 'Is that what I think it is?' she says.

'It certainly looks like it.' I glance up at her face. My mind races with possibilities. 'Do you know if Hayley was still using?'

Lou shakes her head. 'I don't think so. I mean, she was so . . . so well turned out, so *together*.'

'You mean, she didn't look like your average druggie.'

'No. Not at all.'

'But that's just it, Lou. There's no such thing as an average druggie. They're not all lying in shitholes with needles sticking out their arms. Some of them are doctors and lawyers and bankers.'

'I know that,' Lou says indignantly. 'I just don't think she was. She told me all about her past and how she was clean now. I believed her. That could have been there for ages.

This was a private school, wasn't it? There was probably all sorts going on.'

She's right. Everyone thinks the drug problems are going to be in 'sink' schools, but private schools are often the worst. The kids have money, for a start.

'But you're right, it *could* be hers,' Lou says. 'I'm beginning to think I don't know anything at all.'

She's not the only one.

'I wonder how she got in,' I say. 'She must have got hold of the key to the padlock somehow, or maybe . . . maybe she saw someone go in and decided to follow them. Unless she found the cupboard one day when she was sneaking about taking her photos.'

Lou shakes her head. 'She'd have told me if she had.'

'She didn't tell you everything though, did she? She didn't tell you about the Instagram account.'

Lou folds her arms across her chest and rocks herself backwards and forwards. 'But why would she be so stupid? Why would she put herself at risk like that?'

'We don't know for sure that anything's happened to her though, do we?' But even as I say these words, a little voice inside my head starts to question my logic, to hold it to account. The heart knows what the heart knows.

'No, we don't,' Lou says. 'But I've got a very bad feeling about all this.'

'Me too.'

I stare at the maze of pipework on the wall and a squarish patch of paintwork that looks slightly different from the rest. I'm just leaning forward to get a closer look when a sudden jangling noise makes us both flinch and stare at each other in alarm. Someone is unlocking the padlock on the main entrance.

Someone is coming in.

36

Marlow

I touch Lou's shoulder. 'Shut the door! Quick!'

As soon as it closes, we're plunged into darkness. I find the torch function on my phone and wave it in front of us.

'Get behind that big tank,' I hiss.

We edge forward, following the beam of light, and squeeze behind the filtration cylinder.

We crouch down on the floor, and I switch off the torch. Lou's breathing is loud and ragged in my ear. 'Stay calm,' I whisper, more for my own benefit than hers. My heart is pounding, and my chest feels as if it's being compressed. I clasp Lou's hand in mine and try to concentrate on breathing deeply.

The jangling noise has now been replaced by a heavy

scraping. The bolt on the main door to the complex is being drawn back. Lou stiffens beside me.

Why in God's name didn't we just leg it back into the cupboard as soon as we heard the padlock being unlocked? We could have been safely in the gym by now. Why did we even come here in the first place? It was insane. All I can hope is that it's Rob, back from work early and taking his Head Guardian duties a little too seriously.

It could be Harry, of course. Brampton was giving him a really hard time after my lie about seeing an intruder on site. Maybe he's come back to check on security. He might even have brought someone with him to install motion-sensor lights, or something like that.

I try to think of a believable reason why we might be here. I could make out it's because of the photo competition. I'll say I wanted to take shots of the empty pool and dragged Lou along with me for company. I've got the pictures on my phone to prove it. Then we'd say we heard someone coming in and hid in here because we know this area's out of bounds, and we didn't want to get into trouble.

I lean towards Lou and whisper in her ear: 'If we're found, leave the talking to me.'

Whoever has just let themselves into the pool building is now speaking, and I can tell straight away that it's neither Rob nor Harry. It's a much deeper male voice, and though it's too far away for me to hear the exact words, the tone is unmistakably angry. He must be speaking to someone on the phone.

He's getting nearer now, walking up this end of the

corridor. But as he approaches, I recognize the voice. It's James Brampton. Lou squeezes my hand. She hears it too.

I don't know whether to be relieved or scared. James Brampton owns this whole site and every building on it. It's an investment for him, worth millions of pounds. He's hired Guardian Angels Inc. to look after it for him, to keep it safe from squatters and asset-strippers, and thanks to me, he's just been told of a breach in security. He has every right to come here whenever he chooses.

But he's a busy man. A property developer. Didn't he say he had four more site visits to do today? Why would he come back so soon? And why, if he's paying the agency to look after security, is he wasting his precious time letting himself into empty swimming pools?

His footsteps stop. 'No can do,' he says. His voice is loud and echoey. He's right outside the pump-room door now; at least that's what it sounds like from in here. 'I need to close on this deal PDQ.'

He starts walking again. Sounds like he's pacing backwards and forwards. My dad used to do the same thing when he was talking business on the phone. 'You'll wear a hole in the carpet,' my mum used to complain.

'Have you dealt with our little *problem* yet?' There's a pause. 'Right. OK. I guess that's the only logical solution we have.' He sighs. A long, heavy sigh. 'I need to be 100 per cent sure she won't be causing us any more trouble.'

Lou's hold on my hand tightens and I know what she's thinking. *Hayley.*

'I don't want any more hold-ups, OK? There's too much at stake.'

His voice is lower now, but somehow more intimidating. 'I need to know I can rely on you. Because if I can't . . .' He leaves the threat hanging.

Lou has started to shake. I'm trembling too. I take both her hands in mine and squeeze them hard, all the while conscious of the sudden and ominous silence beyond the door. Has he heard us in here? Is he about to come in? But then I hear his footsteps start up again. He's going back the way he came. I exhale in relief.

A door swings open and then closes. His footsteps are getting fainter and fainter. He must have gone into the changing rooms, or through the other door that leads directly to the pool from the corridor. We can't take the risk that he's about to search the building and that sooner or later he'll come in here, even if it's just to put his head round the door.

'Get up,' I whisper. 'We have to get back in the cupboard, and we have to do it *now*.'

I open the door a fraction of an inch. It's silent out there. He hasn't left the building, but he's not in the corridor. Which means he's either by the pool or in the changing rooms.

'You go first. Check the coast is clear, then turn left and go through the first door opposite. That's the store cupboard. I'll close this door and then I'll be right behind you. Don't run, don't talk, just cross the corridor as fast and as quietly as you can.'

Lou nods.

'Let's do it.'

It probably takes us no more than five seconds to complete the manoeuvre, but it's the longest five seconds of my life, and even when we've made it into the cupboard, we're still in danger. We have to close the door and wheel the trolley back in front of it, knowing he might come out into the corridor at any time and hear us.

It isn't until we've made it back into the gym that we allow ourselves a minute to sag over our knees and catch our breath. I feel light-headed and shivery after the adrenaline rush. Cold sweat coats the back of my neck and forehead.

Lou turns to face me. 'What the hell do we do now?'

37

Marlow

We're sitting on the floor in my room, nursing mugs of black coffee and trying to make sense of what's just happened. We're both staring at the pair of Art Deco earrings in front of us, and the small packet of what looks like cocaine.

'Have you ever tried it?' Lou asks.

'I almost did, once. But then I chickened out at the last minute. What about you?'

'No. I took Molly once. And I've smoked a bit of weed. That's about it really.' She lets out a long, juddering sigh. 'I should have met her up here again, like she wanted me to.'

'It's pointless beating yourself up over it. You weren't to know she'd go there on her own. And we don't know for sure if anything's happened to her or not.'

I'm trying to be positive, but it's hard. Lou is right. Finding the second earring and the packet of cocaine in the pump room means something. I can feel it in my gut. Earrings like that fall out all the time. I've lost count of the number of times I've got home from somewhere and realized I'm only wearing one. But to lose both of them? And in the same part of the school? Surely that would only happen if there'd been a struggle of some sort. Which might explain the dried blood.

James Brampton coming back, and his aggressive, one-sided phone conversation, mean something too. He could have been talking about anyone or anything, but if the 'little problem' he referred to was Hayley . . .

Now that I recall them, his words sound even more ominous: *I guess that's the only logical solution we have. I need to be 100 per cent sure she won't be causing us any more trouble.*

'It's looking likely though, isn't it?' Lou says.

'Did you see that patch of slightly different-coloured paintwork behind all the pipes in the pump room?'

Lou shakes her head.

'There was definitely something off about it. If Brampton hadn't turned up when he did, I'd have had a closer look. Because if Hayley was in the pump room and her earring came off and rolled under the tank, then she must have had a very good reason to be crawling about near those pipes.'

'Maybe she found something and James Brampton caught her,' Lou says, her eyes widening in fear. 'What if this whole thing is to do with drug trafficking?'

Brampton's words come back to me with ominous clarity: *I need to close on this deal PDQ.*

'Do you think we should contact the agency?' Lou says. 'Or the police?'

'Yes, but then we'll have to admit to breaking into Hayley's room, although of course we didn't actually break in, did we? We used the key.'

'Yeah, but how did we get the key?' Lou says. 'And it's not just her room, it's the pool too. We've broken the rules in our licence agreement already. We could end up homeless. Mags'll never forgive me. She loves it here.'

'And even if we persuade Harry that Hayley might be in trouble, are the police really going to pursue a property guardian and former addict who's invented contact details on her application form and told Harry she's had a family emergency? They're just going to assume she's pissed off for her own reasons.'

Lou nods. 'And if we go to the police, I'll have to give a statement, and Mags might find out I was up here all those times with Hayley. And now with *you*.' She looks at her phone. 'Shit. She'll be finishing her shift in half an hour. I need to get back.'

I think of what Bryony said, about Mags letting slip that Lou sometimes has crushes on straight girls.

'Do you think it's possible she already knows?'

'I don't *think* so. I'm pretty sure I'd know if she did. She'd have been quizzing me about it. Why? What makes you say that?'

I pick up one of the earrings and roll it between my fingers.

'I just wondered, that's all.'

Lou stares at me. 'You think she might have said something to Hayley? Warned her off? Is that what you mean?'

'No, not at all. Although I guess if she did, that might explain why Hayley left without saying goodbye. But it wouldn't explain why her earring was in the pump room.'

Lou looks at her phone again. 'I've really got to go,' she says. She stands up and moves towards the door. 'So what *are* we going to do?'

'I think the first thing to do is speak to Harry, ask him a bit more about what Hayley actually said to him. I'll drop in tomorrow during my lunch hour. And now I come to think of it, we need to know whether she emailed him or went to the agency in person. Because if she went in person and he *saw* her, then all this worry is for nothing. Whereas if she emailed him . . .'

Lou's eyes widen as she catches my drift. 'If she emailed him, then it could have been someone else, using her phone.'

'Exactly. Right, you'd better go then. Give me your number, and I'll fill you in after I've spoken to Harry.'

Lou gives me a sheepish look. 'I'd rather you didn't call me, if you don't mind. Just in case Mags finds out.'

'Does she look at your phone then?'

'I think so. Sometimes.'

'You know, you really shouldn't—'

I don't finish the sentence because who am I to tell her

what she should or shouldn't do? I'm hardly an expert in romantic relationships, and even though I find it astonishing that Lou would tolerate that kind of behaviour, I don't really know anything about the two of them. Perhaps Mags has good reason to be suspicious. Or maybe Lou is a victim of her girlfriend's controlling behaviour. In which case, my heart goes out to her.

'Do you and Mags use the old toilets off the hall or the staff loo?'

Lou gives me a puzzled frown. 'The staff loo, of course. The others are rank. Why are you going on about toilets?'

I mime the act of writing on a door.

Lou cottons on at last and sticks her thumb in the air.

'The cubicle nearest the window,' I say, thanking my lucky stars I'm not in the kind of relationship where I'm on tenterhooks in case someone looks at my phone and gives me a hard time just for talking to a friend.

38

Rob

It is nine o'clock in the evening and Rob has been back at the school for three hours, sitting in the gloom of the office, going over and over the CCTV footage. Harry Kiernan sent him another email before he left work, informing him that an intruder was seen by the pool this morning and that James Brampton is on the warpath because of it. But so far, Rob has found no evidence of an intruder, although it is possible that someone *was* there in the brief period when the camera switched angles.

Rob looks beyond the computer screen into space, and blinks. Another urge is making itself known and pulling him away from his laborious task. Reluctantly, but with a familiar sense of resignation, he takes the small key out of his shirt pocket and unlocks the top drawer of his desk.

His hand closes round the set of classroom keys and he lifts them out, selecting the right one and grasps it between his thumb and first two fingers.

He will do it now, before he changes his mind.

It takes him all of five seconds to walk to Hayley's room. He must stop calling it that because it isn't her room any more. It isn't anyone's room now. He slips the key into the lock and lets himself in. His heart begins to judder like a tiny animal trapped in his chest. The room still smells of her, but it's fainter than before, and he wonders how long a scent can last in an enclosed space with no fresh air.

He wonders how . . . No. Nothing good will come of letting those thoughts in. It's too late for that.

Rob strokes Hayley's mattress and wishes things could have been different. Wishes he were a better man. A stronger man. He wants to go back in time and be braver. Stand up for what's right.

Things are spiralling out of control. All those clothes stuffed into bags, all those books and pens and cups and plates and make-up bags. All the myriad possessions and paraphernalia she kept in drawers and cupboards and arranged on shelves and tables, and which he, like the fool he was – like the fool he *is* – stuffed into black bin bags.

Where are they now, those bags? What has become of them? And what was it all for?

Rob stumbles out of the room, forgetting to listen at the door first to check that the coast is clear. A dreadful error, and one that he berates himself for making. Fortunately, no one is around, and he can lock the door and return to his room unseen. He is shaking now. Whole body shakes of guilt and remorse and terror.

This is what happens when rules are broken, he thinks. Order breaks down. But somewhere, at the very back of his mind, that vital piece of insight he's been trying so hard to grasp finally makes itself known.

Some rules *have* to be broken because they are the *wrong rules*. And that is where he has gone astray. That is where he has made a catastrophic mistake from which there is no coming back. Not now. Because he has failed to differentiate between the two types of rules: the good rules and the bad rules.

I'm at the cinema, about to watch a horror movie. Or 'black comedy slasher movie', as it's described. It'd better be good. I've got an extra-large box of popcorn wedged between my thighs, and I'm stuffing handful after handful into my mouth so fast bits keep coming out and falling on to my lap. I love popcorn. I can't get enough of it, especially the half-salted, half-sweet kind. I should have got two boxes.

The couple in the row in front of me keep turning round and giving me a 'look'. First her, then him. If they do it once more, I'm going to tell them to fuck off and mind their own business. The film hasn't even started yet, and there are other seats they could move to. Not as good as the ones they're in, but that's their problem, not mine. The people either side of me have already moved, which suits me down to the ground, because now I can put my coat on the chair next to me and make full use of both armrests.

While I'm waiting for the adverts to finish and the trailers to come on, I replay the events of the last few days in my mind. It's like my own internal movie. Marilyn DeVere-Cairns is definitely Boho Birdie. If anyone could make an empty old school look like a posh house, it's her. After all, this is the girl who messed around with boring photographs and turned them into so-called pieces of art.

Pieces of shit, more like.

She might be able to pull the wool over her dozy Instagram followers' eyes, but she can't fool me.

A lone man clutching a hot drink in a cardboard beaker has just come into the auditorium and spotted the empty seats either side of me. He's heading my way. As he gets closer, I pull a weird face at him, and he swerves off in a different direction at the last minute. Result.

I saw the look that passed over Marilyn's face when she first clapped eyes on me. It's the same look that man just gave me. A look of disgust. I'm glad she lost all her stupid artwork. I'm glad they all did. I'm not glad Lottie Lansdowne died though. That should never have happened. I'm not a complete monster.

I tip the box up and pour the last bits of popcorn into my open mouth. The woman in front turns round again and I belch loudly. She's only making it worse for herself by tutting like that.

I use the nail on my index finger to pick the popcorn husks out of my teeth.

Marilyn is making it worse for herself, too. I don't like liars.

39

Marlow

The following day, it's one thirty before I get a chance to leave the studio. I tell Lenny, my boss, that I've got a GP appointment and that I might be late back. He doesn't mind at all, even though I've been off for the last two days. In fact, he's surprised I even came in today. It probably helps that I haven't taken any sick leave the whole time I've been working here. I usually drag myself in even when I'm feeling like shit.

Guardian Angels Inc. is just off Borough High Street. I could walk it in less than half an hour, but I take the tube so I've got time to stop for coffee and a sandwich. When I turn up unannounced, the receptionist seems reluctant to tell Harry I'm here.

'Mr Kiernan is in a meeting at the moment,' she says. 'Can I give him a message?'

Her long hair has been carefully teased into immaculate waves, and her make-up is flawless. Big smoky eyes and vivid red lipstick to match her vivid red top. Her smile is fixed and fake.

I sit down on one of the chairs. 'I'd rather wait, if you don't mind.'

She looks irritated by this and starts to explain that in that case, I'm going to have a very long wait indeed as the meeting has only just started, but I cut her off mid-sentence with a breezy smile and an assurance that I really don't mind waiting.

A small muscle twitches in her left cheek and her smile begins to fade. Reluctantly, she picks up her phone and taps something into a small switchboard.

'A Marlow Cairns is in reception. She doesn't have an appointment, but she insists on seeing you.' I watch her face as she listens to his response. 'Yes, yes, I've already offered to do that, but she wants to wait for you.' She listens again. 'OK, I'll let her know.'

She replaces the receiver and looks me in the eye. The smile has disappeared. 'He said to go in, but you'll have to be quick.'

'Of course,' I say. 'The meeting.'

She doesn't even have the grace to blush.

Harry's office is as cluttered as I remember it being the last time I was here, which was when I first registered with the agency.

He gestures to a chair. 'S'cuse the mess,' he says. I'm pretty sure he said the same thing to me back then, too.

His phone rings and he picks it up, mouths 'sorry' to me as he does. 'Seb, I *literally* had my finger on speed dial. I'll be with you in ten. Yah, yah, no worries, bro.'

Harry is tall and slim, with dark-blond hair that keeps flopping over his eyes. There's an ease about him – a languor – that many people would find attractive, but not me. I met too many boys like Harry when I was growing up. And that's the trouble: even when they're fully grown men, they still act like boys.

He finishes the call and gives me a disarming smile, the sort that probably has some girls eating out of his hand. 'So, what brings you all the way here? I hope you're not going to do a Hayley on me and tell me you want to leave already.'

'No, I'm not. But Hayley *is* why I'm here.'

He raises his eyebrows in surprise.

'When you first offered me a room at the school, you said it would be one of the older ones in the Victorian building, where Hayley used to live. But apparently, according to Rob, that room has a leak and can't be inhabited until it's been fixed, so I'm in a room in one of the more modern blocks across the playground.'

Harry looks bored already, and I get the strong impression that he secretly despises people like me; people who agree to live in abandoned buildings, people so obviously less well off than he is, with his preppy clothes and air of entitlement. Even though, without us, his agency wouldn't make any money. I can't help wondering how he'd react if I told him I was a former pupil at McKinleys, and whether it would change his attitude towards me.

He stifles a yawn. 'And you've got a problem with that *because . . .?*'

I launch into the little speech I've been rehearsing in my head all the way here. 'It's not so much that I've got a problem with it – although I am disappointed – it's that when I was passing the room the other day, I couldn't resist unsticking a corner of the notice covering the window in the door, and I had a quick peek inside. It was raining heavily and yet the floor was completely dry.'

I fold my arms on the desk and lean forward, lowering my voice.

'I don't want to accuse Rob of making up the leak, but it is a bit weird, isn't it?' Harry screws up his nose and scratches his head. 'And another thing,' I say. 'It looks like Hayley's left some really good furniture behind.'

Harry sighs as if this whole thing is a complete waste of his time. 'So let me get this straight. What you're saying is that you want to move into that room and take advantage of all the things Hayley didn't have time to take with her?'

'No, that's not what I'm saying at all.'

He glances at his watch. 'So what *are* you saying?'

'I'm saying that I'm worried about Hayley. And so are quite a few of the others. She didn't actually tell anyone she was going, and she was quite friendly with them all. She's not responding to any of Bryony's text messages.

And Rob acted really strangely when I asked him about the room.'

Harry clears his throat. 'Marlow, I appreciate your concern for Hayley, but as I told you when the vacancy first became available, she left because of a family emergency. At least, that was the excuse she gave. Who knows if it's true or not? She didn't give me any notice at all, which means, in effect, that she broke the terms of her licence. She did mention the furniture and how she'd try to arrange to have it collected, but I'm afraid I told her that if she couldn't give me the required notice period and she couldn't clear the room when she left, she would not be allowed back on the premises and would have to forfeit her right to anything she left behind.'

He sighs. 'I know you probably think that's a bit heartless of me, but I do have a business to run. I'm not a fucking *storage* company. And people come and go all the time. That's why they like living in these sorts of places. They don't like to be too tied down. As for Rob acting strangely, all I can say is, he's, well . . . you've met him. But he's a reliable person to have keeping an eye on things. He follows procedure and he gets things done. I wish I could say the same for all my guardians.'

He sighs again. 'If you must know, I told Rob that he could either have the furniture himself if he could find a use for it, or pass it on to someone else. I don't know anything about a leak, whether he's made that up because he hasn't had time to get it moved or collected yet, and frankly, Marlow, I don't care. I've got enough on my plate at McKinleys right now, what with chalked messages appearing overnight and you seeing an intruder on the CCTV. You've met James Brampton. He's not the easiest of fellows to deal with.'

Harry frowns. I can see how he might find someone as intimidating and brusque as Brampton rather a challenge.

He leans forward and rests his arms on the desk. 'While there are plenty of good, honest people like yourself on our books, we also have our fair share of nightmares, let me tell you. People who trash perfectly good accommodation units, people who don't pay their rent and have to be evicted at our time and expense, and people who piss off at a moment's notice, like Hayley.'

He presses his lips together, as though he's deliberating over how much to tell me.

'I probably shouldn't say this, but this isn't the first time Hayley's let this agency down. She's on the flaky side, and she's a total fantasist. Reckoned she'd soon have enough money to put down a deposit on a flat, and all this property guardian "malarkey", as she called it, was just a stepping stone.' He laughs in one short, incredulous exhalation. 'Against my better judgement, I gave her another chance – my own stupid fault – and once again, I've got my fingers burnt. So when I come across someone like Rob Hornby, I do everything I can to hold on to them.'

He pushes his hair back from his face and it immediately flops down again.

'Was there anything else you wanted to discuss?'

'Yes,' I say. Harry's shoulders sag. 'I found one of her ear-rings by the swimming pool.'

Harry spreads his hands palms up, and lets his jaw drop open as if to say, *So what?*

'I think she might have been following someone in there, someone she saw from my window.'

Harry frowns. 'From *your* window? But how on earth do you know that?'

'Because I found some binoculars on the windowsill, and someone on site thinks they were hers. In fact, she told this person that she'd noticed some unusual activity near the pool and was going to investigate. The night before she left.'

Harry is sitting forward now, rapt. 'And you saw some-one there yesterday, didn't you? On the CCTV?'

'Yes.' It might have been a lie to excuse my presence in Rob's office, but it's worked to my advantage yet again.

'So let me get this straight. You think Hayley might have been monitoring something going on in the vicinity of the swimming pool, and that she went over there to investigate.' He drums his fingers on the desk. 'I bet it's one of those fucking memorial-garden campaigners.'

'Yes, and then the next day, she was gone. I'm worried that something might have happened to her, that she might have stumbled across something while being a responsible and vigilant guardian, and been harmed in the process.'

Harry considers this for a moment. 'There's only one problem with that theory,' he says. 'She managed to call me and tell me she was leaving the next morning. So she was obviously fine, wasn't she?'

'You mean, you actually spoke to her?'

He pulls a puzzled frown. 'Yes. How else would I know she wanted to leave?'

'And you're sure it was her you spoke to?'

'Dear God, Marlow, what *is* this?'

He leans down and opens a drawer to the right of his desk, takes out a buff-coloured folder, and starts shuffling through the papers inside. He finds what he is looking for and takes it out.

'But I tell you what, let's call her next-of-kin and make absolutely sure she's OK.' He looks at the address and frowns. 'Ah, they live in Melbourne. It'll be too late out there to call. Leave it with me, Marlow. I'll email them now and ask Suzy on reception to follow it up with a phone call first thing in the morning.'

He smiles. 'I'll let you know how we get on.'

I nod dumbly, knowing full well that Hayley gave the contact details for a cousin in Australia who is dead.

40

Marlow

I only have a short time to think about my meeting with Harry because when I get back to work, I'm fully occupied doing headshots for an actor. Then I have to edit them, which takes me a lot longer than it should.

Lenny leaves early, so I have to lock up the studio. It's the least I can do after taking a long lunch hour. By the time I'm on the bus back to McKinleys, it's getting dark, and I feel shattered. Even the two double espressos I made, using Lenny's all-singing, all-dancing coffee machine, aren't enough to cut through my fatigue. My eyes feel dry and gritty, and the bones in my face ache.

As the bus stops and starts in the Friday-evening traffic, I turn the conversation with Harry over and over in my head. He said that Hayley was a fantasist, and he's not wrong there. The Boho Birdie Instagram account is proof of that.

I take my phone out of my pocket and check, for what must be the hundredth time since Wednesday, to see if she's posted anything new, because if by some miracle she has, Lou and I can stop worrying about her.

But she hasn't, and all I can see behind my eyes is that solitary cut rose we saw yesterday in Lottie's garden. I scroll through the photos again. Maybe if I look hard enough, I'll find some vital clue. The missing piece in the puzzle that is Hayley's uncharacteristic disappearance.

But *is* it uncharacteristic? After all, I have no idea what Hayley was like as a person, and however much the other guardians think they knew about her, none of them were *that* close to her. Besides, nobody really knows what anyone is like.

I rest the side of my head against the window, my mind tying itself into knots trying to make sense of it all. A familiar figure is striding along the pavement in an Asda uniform, backpack slung over one shoulder. It looks like Craig, on his way to work. I peer at him through the glass and wonder if he'll catch sight of me, but then he swerves right and takes the stairs down into an underground toilet.

I'm about to start looking at my phone again, when the engine goes off and the driver climbs out of his cubicle. My heart sinks. This doesn't bode well. Sure enough, he tells us there's a problem and that we're all going to have to get off and wait for the next bus. There is a collective groan.

Why does this sort of thing only ever happen on the way home? It's Sod's fucking Law.

Reluctantly, and with varying degrees of huffing and puffing and moaning, we all get off and stand, miserably, at the bus stop. Craig emerges from the underground toilets, only this time, he's in a pair of jeans and a navy fleece, his uniform now presumably stuffed into his backpack. I consider stepping out and tapping him on the shoulder as he strides by, but I decide against it at the last minute and shrink back against a shop window, eyes on the pavement.

He's obviously up to something. If he wanted a night off work, wouldn't he call in sick rather than venture out in his uniform? And why get changed in an underground toilet? Perhaps he doesn't want Elle to know he's doing something else tonight. In which case, he won't want to talk to me.

Eventually, the other bus arrives, and we all file on. I manage to get a seat at the back and resume my obsession with Hayley's Instagram account. A new comment has appeared on the most recent picture. It was posted yesterday by someone calling themselves @lionhunter04. It says: *Don't play with me.*

Something about those four stark words gives me a very strange feeling. It's another threat, not dissimilar to the chalked message on the playground: *DON'T GET TOO COMFORTABLE.*

The bus is getting nearer and nearer the school, and suddenly all I can think of is that crazy woman in the tracksuit who ambushed me in the street. Did *she* post this message? I hope she's not lurking outside the gates. She's the very last person I want to see right now. I don't have the energy for another confrontation.

I stare out of the rain-soaked window and think of what Dev said to me on the phone. *Don't get involved in other people's shit.* He's absolutely right. The stupid thing is, not getting involved in other people's shit is something I normally pride myself on. That's why I liked living in the chapel so much, because I only had myself to worry about.

I check to see if he's responded to my message yet, but there's still nothing. Only those two blue ticks.

Thankfully, there's no sign of the strange woman when I get off the bus. I open the gate with my fob key, wishing I'd had the sense to grab something to eat on the way home as my stomach is now rumbling. The low whirring noise of the gate mechanism sounds vaguely ominous this evening – not exactly the homecoming vibe I crave. I climb the three stone steps up to the main entrance with a sinking feeling at having to go back to the sad, makeshift home that is always going to be my ex-maths classroom, whatever I end up doing to it. How has my life come to this? How have I allowed this to happen?

The corridor and hall are quiet and gloomy, and I'm anxious to get back to my room and call Dev. He can't keep ignoring me for ever. But then I remember I'm supposed to leave a message for Lou in the toilets. It's absurd having to do this instead of just being able to send her a quick WhatsApp or text message. There's no way I can condense my conversation with Harry into one pithy phrase. I'll just write M followed by my number. She can call me whenever she can, and I'll fill her in then. It'll be up to her if she keeps the number or not.

But as I'm crossing the hall, I notice that one of the honours boards on the wall opposite is very slightly askew. For some reason, it bothers me. I'm sure it wasn't like that the last time I looked over there. I've got an eye for how things hang, and I'm sure I would have noticed if it wasn't straight.

It's then that I catch sight of the date on the board and realize it's the one that includes my own year group. 2005–2007. A terrible sense of foreboding grips me. A sixth sense that something about it isn't right.

I stop and tilt my head to one side. I screw my eyes shut, then open them again. The light in here is dim and my eyes are tired, so maybe I'm just imagining that the lettering on the bottom line looks a little different from the rest.

But I'm right. It *is* different. The letters and numbers are the same size as all the others, and they've been painted the same shade of white, but they aren't the same. They aren't the same at all.

I step a little closer and can barely breathe for the shock of it. The plain *wrongness* of it. I stagger back, heart thumping, unable to believe my own eyes.

Because there, on the very last line, it says: '2007 CHARLOTTE LANSDOWNE BA (HONS) 1ST CENTRAL SAINT MARTINS'.

In 2007, Lottie had already been dead for three years.

41

Marlow

The room starts to spin. Who on earth would have done this? One of the students before the school closed down, perhaps? As a dare?

But this isn't some clumsy etching of the sort found on the backs of the doors in the girls' toilets, or carved into the wooden picnic tables in the playground. The letters and numbers might not be quite as professionally applied as the others, but they have been done with the utmost care and precision. It must have taken whoever did this a very long time.

I screw my eyes shut and count to three, hoping and praying that the entry won't be there when I open them, and that the whole thing will turn out to be a figment of my imagination. Seeing her name like this is beyond creepy. It's as if Lottie never died and is living another life, one in which she fulfilled her dreams.

I open my eyes again, and there it still is. Lottie's name and mythical achievement. Painted on to a wooden honours board under all those other McKinleys girls who earned first-class degrees or scholarships, or won a prestigious prize. Names I recognize because they were all girls in my year group.

Maybe it was done by one of the art students as some kind of tribute. Anyone who attended McKinleys after Lottie's death would have known all about her and how she died. It's recorded on a plaque in the memorial garden, and there will have been assemblies where it was mentioned on the anniversary of the fire. A tragedy like that weaves itself into a school's history, becomes part of its fabric.

Just as it has woven itself into *my* history, embedded itself in my psyche like scar tissue.

Moving closer, I trace the letters with my fingers. I must have passed this board so many times in the last five days. How on earth did I manage to miss it? If someone here knew Lottie, then there's every possibility they know me as well. My mouth goes dry. So why haven't they said anything? Besides, I'd recognize them too, wouldn't I? People change over the years, get older, but they don't change *that* much.

Something is bothering me. Something I can't put my finger on. Thoughts swirl in my head. A maelstrom of confusion. And fear.

I feel sick.

'Are you all right, Marlow?' says a man's voice from behind me.

I'm so disorientated by what I've just seen that, for a split second, I think it's Dev coming out of the kitchen with two ready meals on a tray, and my heart does a strange little flip. If ever I needed a friend bearing food – if ever I needed Dev – it's right now. But it's Nikhil's face that I see through the steam coming off the cartons. Of course it is. Dev wouldn't just turn up like that. How would he get in without a key? I must be going mad.

I force a smile. 'I'm fine, yes. Just admiring these old honours boards. We never had anything like this at my old school.' As ill as I feel, the lie still trips off my tongue.

'Mine neither,' Nikhil says. 'They are rather beautiful, aren't they? I hope the owner incorporates at least some of them into the new development. Mind you, if he's planning on turning that beautiful memorial garden into a car park, I don't hold out much hope for them, do you? He'll probably have them chopped up for firewood.'

Firewood. Firewood. The word echoes in my head.

He can't have spotted the extra name yet. If he had, he'd say so, wouldn't he? Especially since he's just mentioned the memorial garden.

'Right,' he says instead. 'I'd better be getting back with these, or Gilly will wonder where I am.'

I watch as he heads off with his tray, and though I briefly wonder if she's told him about her pregnancy dilemma yet, my own agitation soon squeezes all other thoughts aside. I remain rooted to the spot, compelled to stare at Lottie's name until the letters swim before my eyes.

'By the way,' Nikhil says, turning round and lowering his voice, 'a few of us are having a little party tomorrow night. It's my birthday, so if you'd like to join us in the drama studio any time after seven, you're very welcome. There'll be food and drink. No need to bring anything unless you want to.'

I give him a thumbs up. 'Thanks, Nik,' I say, wishing he'd just go so I can process this alone.

When my eyes snap open the next morning, I know I must have dropped off at some point, must have had snatches of oblivion here and there, but it feels as though I've been awake for the last eight hours, tossing and turning. My head is splitting and my body aches with exhaustion. It doesn't help that my call to Dev last night went straight to voicemail, although he did at least respond to my Whats-App with: *Still ludicrously busy. Catch up soon.*

I shouldn't feel so hurt, not when I've kept him at arm's length all this time. I can hardly expect him to drop every-thing whenever I call, especially when I know I've been late returning *his* calls in the past. Friendship isn't some-thing you can take for granted. You have to work at it, and I haven't. I've only got myself to blame. If I want Dev to be a part of my life, I need to start letting him in more.

And I will, if only he'd call me back.

When my phone rings a few minutes later, I snatch it

up, convinced it's him at last. But it isn't. It's Harry Kiernan's snooty receptionist, probably about to tell me what I already know – that Hayley's next-of-kin isn't responding. Not unless her late cousin has somehow managed to speak to them from beyond the grave.

'Miss Cairns?' she says, mispronouncing my name so that the first bit sounds like 'car' instead of 'care'. I can't be bothered to correct her. It's my turn to do a Saturday shift at the studio today, and I'm running late as it is.

'Speaking.'

'Mr Kiernan asked me to let you know that we've now been in touch with Hayley's next-of-kin, and all is well.'

There's a brief pause where presumably she's expecting me to say thank you, but I can't. She's lying. Lying through her teeth. She obviously couldn't be bothered to make the follow-up call. Unless Harry never even asked her to do it in the first place. I think of how bored he was by the whole thing, how uninterested in what I had to say. He probably told her to fob me off. If ever I needed proof that the agency doesn't give a shit about the welfare of their guardians, this is it. Just wait till I tell Lou.

But as I'm on my way over to the gym for a quick shower, I realize I forgot to leave her my number on the back of the toilet door. The shock of seeing Lottie's name on the honours board wiped it clean out of my mind. I just have to hope she's at Nikhil's birthday party this evening.

42

Marlow

When I finally get back from work, Rob is standing in the hall talking to Big Dave, who's still in his motorbike leathers. Dave swivels his head to look at me and smiles that big, warm smile of his I no longer trust. I had intended to go and look at the board again. I didn't have time this morning, but I'm not going to do it while those two are there, so I lift my hand in a wave and say hi, then head to my room to change.

At half past seven, I make my way over to the drama studio. Everyone except Craig is already here – I don't expect Rob has even been invited, seeing as parties are on his list of forbidden activities – and the drinks are flowing. Tea-lights are flickering from tables, and it's as much as I can do not to go round blowing them all out. Somehow I manage to hold myself together.

There's not going to be a fire. It's only a few tea-lights. Get a grip.

I planned not to drink anything, not with my fuzzy head, but now that I'm here and Nikhil is holding out a glass of prosecco, I find myself taking it.

'Thanks,' I say, and take the tiniest of sips. 'Happy Birthday, Nikhil.' I clink glasses with him.

'Thanks, Marlow. Glad you could come.' He waves his arm in the direction of a table. 'Nibbles over there. Sausage rolls and stuff.'

'And falafel,' Gilly calls out from the other side of the studio. She is talking to Elle and Mags, who both wave at me. I wave back. Gilly holds eye contact with me for a beat or two longer than she needs to. I think it's her way of warning me not to mention our discussion the other day on the stairs leading up to the bell-tower. I give her what I hope is a reassuring nod.

Lou is standing at the table, piling crisps on to a paper plate. I go over to join her, and while helping myself to food, I explain about forgetting to leave her a message and tell her what Harry said yesterday. Then I relate the receptionist's barefaced lie about speaking to Hayley's next-of-kin. Lou listens intently. I can tell she's keeping one eye on Mags the whole time. She obviously doesn't want her to know that the two of us are quite friendly now. With any luck we can talk more freely later, when everyone has had a few drinks.

I saunter over to Big Dave and Bryony, who are sitting on a couple of beanbags on the floor in front of the old whiteboard on wheels, grinning up at me. Bryony is leaning against Dave's massive shoulders, and he's massaging the side of her neck and nuzzling her cheek. They must have decided not to hide their relationship any more.

Bryony squidges up to one side of her beanbag and pats the space next to her. 'Come and sit with me,' she says. 'You look knackered.' Where my eyes feel gritty and tired, hers are shining and perfectly made up. I can't help noticing that her voice is already slightly slurred.

Out of the corner of my eye, I'm aware of Elle watching me with a quiet intensity. I'd like to go and talk to her instead, quiz her a little more on our strange conversation in the office when she warned me to keep my head down. But it's hard to avoid Bryony's offer of a seat without appearing rude, and I am pretty tired, so I sit down next to her. I might as well start with these two and see what, if anything, they know.

After a few minutes of chit-chat, Bryony reverts to form and starts slagging off Gilly.

'Poor Nikhil. Look at him. He's putting on a good show of being happy on his birthday, but you can tell she's driving him nuts. Look at her, sipping her apple juice like a martyr. Maybe if she slugged some wine back, she might actually enjoy herself. But no, she thinks she'll have more chance of conceiving if she's teetotal.'

Except she's already pregnant, I think. Not that I have any intention of telling Bryony that.

Bryony squeezes Dave's knee. '*We'll* never have that problem, will we, darling?'

I raise my eyebrows. 'How do you know that?'

The two of them share a smirk. 'Because I don't want babies and Dave's already had the snip.'

I glance over at Gilly, who has sidled a little nearer to us and is clearly eavesdropping on our conversation. Our eyes meet and the look on her face is priceless. Relief and joy in equal measures. I'm pleased for her, I really am. At least she won't ruin everything with Nikhil now by confessing her ill-advised fling. I watch her go back to him and slip her arm around his slender waist. Then I return my attention to Bryony and Dave. I need to test something out.

'Those honours boards in the hall,' I say, watching both their faces as closely as I can. No reaction so far, apart from a vague curiosity as to what I'm going to say next. 'Have you noticed anything strange about them?'

'Not that I can think of,' Dave says, bemused. 'Although I did wonder why they've been left behind. Seems a bit sad, doesn't it?'

'It doesn't surprise me in the least,' Bryony says. 'The school merged with an academy, didn't it? Relocated to a more modern site. Those sorts of things belong in the past. And it's a new school now, with a new name. Out with the old, in with the new.'

'Have *you* noticed something strange about them, then?' Dave asks.

I take another tiny sip of my Prosecco. 'As a matter of fact, I have. It kind of freaked me out, to be honest.'

Bryony scrabbles about and tries to sit up, but she can't seem to move and starts giggling instead. Dave hauls her up. 'This is what three glasses of Prosecco does to her on an empty stomach,' he says. 'She'll be a nightmare later.'

'Come on then, spill the beans,' she says. 'What's freaked you out?'

'One of the names is Charlotte Lansdowne.' My eyes flick from Bryony's face to Dave's and back again. Bryony's expression is completely blank. She doesn't appear to recognize the name, but Dave has. His eyes widen in surprise.

'Isn't that the name of the girl who died?'

Bryony suddenly cottons on. 'Oh my God, yeah! It's her garden they're trying to save, isn't it? What do you mean, she's one of the names? She can't be. They're all past students who graduated. She was in the sixth form when she died, wasn't she?'

'Her name is definitely on one of the boards,' I say. 'But it's in slightly different lettering from all the others.'

'Fucking hell! That's crazy! Do the others know about this?'

'I don't know.'

Bryony is scrabbling to sit up straight again. 'Hey, you lot, come and listen to this.'

It's not exactly how I envisaged the evening panning out. I'd rather have spoken to them all individually, or in small groups, but I suppose I should have guessed that Bryony might react like this, and at least it gets it over with in one fell swoop. The others all troop over.

'Tell them, Marlow. Tell them what you've just told us,' Bryony says.

Everyone is looking at me expectantly. Especially Elle, whose eyes appear abnormally wide, as if by blinking she might miss something.

'The name Charlotte Lansdowne has been painted on to one of the honours boards hanging up in the hall.'

'Only the girl who died in the fire,' Bryony chips in. 'Only the girl who couldn't possibly have graduated.'

'Are you sure about this?' Nikhil says. 'Is that what you were looking at last night? When I came out of the kitchen? I thought you seemed a bit odd. Why on earth didn't you say anything?'

'I . . . I don't know. I think I was still in shock.'

'I haven't noticed it,' Nikhil says. 'Are you sure?'

A chorus of 'I haven't noticed it either' reaches my ears.

'Of course I'm sure. I didn't believe it myself when I first saw it, but trust me, it's there.'

I look into their faces, and every one of them is either intrigued or disbelieving: Nikhil, Gilly, Mags and Lou.

But someone is missing. Elle.

My pulse quickens. Were those saucer-like eyes just now some kind of warning? A warning I didn't heed?

I look around the room. I didn't see her leave, but she definitely isn't here any more.

43

Marlow

'Why don't we take a look,' Nikhil says. 'Let's all go over there right now.'

'But Rob might come out and see us,' Gilly says. 'I don't want him thinking we're having a party without him.'

'But we *are* having a party without him,' Bryony says. 'And anyway, he won't know if we don't take our drinks with us. Help us up,' she says, holding her arms out to Nikhil, who pulls her to her feet. 'Anyone else coming?'

In the end, we all go, and I can't help noticing that apart from Rob, it's exactly the same group who walked round the site on Tuesday morning, checking for security breaches after the chalked message appeared. Craig and Elle were missing then, too. Craig had been on night duty, so he was asleep, and Elle was . . . I don't actually know where Elle was. She could have been in bed with him, or out somewhere. All I know is, she wasn't there then and she isn't here now. And yet she *was* with us, only a few minutes ago, drinking a glass of Prosecco and giving me sly looks.

We cross the playground in the dark – Bryony, Gilly and Mags up ahead, giggling and shushing and nudging each other like a bunch of schoolgirls, Dave and Nikhil following on behind, deep in conversation, while Lou and I bring up the rear.

'I've been thinking,' I say, in hushed tones. 'Maybe one of the memorial-garden campaigners did this.'

'But why would they go to the trouble of painting her name on an honours board?' Lou says. 'That's hardly going to make any difference to James Brampton's plans.'

She's right. None of it makes sense. 'Hang on. Didn't you say that you and Hayley saw a man in black go into a hut in the middle of the night and not come out again?'

'Yes, that's right.'

'Well, I saw a load of old honours boards stacked up in one of those huts when I did the early-morning perimeter walk on Monday. Maybe the reason you never saw him come out again wasn't because you missed him during the five minutes you were out of the room and Hayley fell asleep, but because he didn't come out at all. Painting on a board like that would take a long while, especially doing it in those cramped conditions.'

At last, my brain has started to work. That must be why

I didn't notice it before, because it's only just been returned to its rightful place. Whoever it was could have removed the original board with my year group's names, and replaced it with one of the old ones. Then, when the job was done, they swapped them round again.

Two minutes later, I'm standing in the hall in the exact same spot I stood last night, a sickening emptiness opening up inside me. The 2005–2007 honours board with Lottie's name has disappeared, and in its place is a much older one from the 1980s.

'So where is it then?' Bryony asks impatiently.

'It's . . . it's gone. It was here.' I point to the board in front of me. 'It was right here. I know it was. I saw it. With my own eyes.'

Mags clears her throat. 'You hadn't been . . . drinking, by any chance?' she says.

I spin round, indignant. 'No, I hadn't been drinking. Someone's moved it. It was here, I swear it!'

They're all looking at me as if I'm crazy. Even Lou is giving me a curious look, as if to say, *What the hell is all this about?* Dave and Nikhil are wandering up and down the length of the hall, scanning the other boards.

'It wasn't hanging straight. That's why I noticed it.'

I gaze up at the top of this one and see that it's perfectly aligned with all the others.

'This shouldn't be here, don't you see? It's too old. Look at the dates on the others. They're all much more recent. This one is out of place. Surely you can see that?'

'Do you think maybe you imagined it?' Dave says.

255

'Maybe it's because of the message on the playground on Tuesday and all our talk about the campaigners. The mind can play tricks on us sometimes, especially if we're tired.'

'It was here. I saw it. Maybe they've swapped it back again. Maybe it's back in the hut?'

'The hut?' Nikhil says. 'What are you talking about? And who is this "they" you're referring to?'

'The person or people who did this, of course. There's a stack of old honours boards in one of the huts. I saw them in there on my first perimeter walk.'

I'm aware of them exchanging looks now, as if I'm completely wacko. And I don't blame them. It sounds ridiculous. I'm embarrassing them. I'm embarrassing myself.

'If you don't mind me saying so,' Gilly says, 'you don't look very well, Marlow. You look really tired. Do you think perhaps—'

Hot tears of anger and frustration spring to my eyes. 'I'm not tired. I'm telling the truth. Last night, there was a board here with Lottie's name on it, and now it's gone. I'm going to look in that hut to see if it's there.'

'Lottie?' Bryony says, narrowing her eyes at me in confusion.

A flush crawls up my neck and into my cheeks. 'Charlotte, I mean. Charlotte Lansdowne.'

I march off, without waiting to see if anyone else is coming with me. Right now, I don't care whether they believe me or not. I need to know what's happened to that board. I need to know I'm not going mad, because despite my protestations, I *am* tired. I'm shattered, just as I was yesterday evening when I got off the bus. And I hardly slept at all last night. But I know what I saw. I couldn't have imagined it or dreamed it. It's impossible.

When I get to the hut, my heart is beating fast. I don't just feel humiliated, I feel scared. Because this is fucking weird. Either I'm losing my mind, or something very odd is happening here.

Something very odd indeed.

My fingers don't seem to work well enough to draw back the bolt. Lou helps me and now the two of us are standing in the hut, the others peering in over our shoulders. I shine my torch on the boards stacked up in front of me and pull each one towards me to check the dates, but they are all really old and dusty, some of them dating back to the 1930s. Lou helps me check them all over again. The 2005–2007 board is not here.

'Satisfied now?' Mags says. 'Come on, let's all go back in the warm and have another drink. I've got a theory about this.'

'What's that then?' I say.

'You sleepwalk, don't you?'

I'm about to say no, but I can't, because that's the excuse I gave her on Tuesday, when she caught me snooping around outside Hayley's room in the middle of the night.

'Ye-es,' I say.

'So maybe, just maybe, after your conversation with Nikhil, you went back to your room to bed, woke up later, and went over to the hall again in your sleep. Maybe you dreamt the whole thing.'

I want to tell her that's simply not possible. But then I'd have to admit I was lying about the sleepwalking. So I go along with her theory.

I don't really want to have another drink. Not now. But I do need some food. So I allow myself to be subsumed into the group again and gently teased as we make our way back to the drama studio. It isn't long before Dave is regaling me with sleepwalking jokes.

'What do you call a sleepwalking nun?' he says.

'I don't know, Dave. What do you call a sleepwalking nun?'

'A roamin' Catholic,' he says, to a chorus of laughter and groans.

'Say what you want about sleepwalkers,' Nikhil says. 'At least they always follow their dreams.'

Later, when the party is over and I'm returning to my room, I see Gilly and Nikhil standing in front of the pad-locked gate to the garden. Nikhil has his arm around Gilly's shoulders, and her head is tilted to one side and resting on his shoulder. Their voices are low and they're oblivious to my approach. Perhaps Gilly is finally telling him she's pregnant.

By the time I get back to my room, I've almost persuaded myself that perhaps I *did* imagine Lottie's name on that board, that I wasn't sleepwalking as such, but that my brain was so frazzled from the events of the last few days, it was indeed playing tricks on me. Lottie has been on my mind such a lot in the past week, it's hardly surprising. Every-where I go, I'm hit by flashes of memory. Flashes of guilt.

Because I'm still here and Lottie isn't.

Before I go to bed, I check to see if Dev's left me any messages, but he hasn't. I suppose his radio silence is a message in itself. I'm also compelled to check Boho Birdie's account again.

My instinct was right. Under the previous comment of *Don't play with me,* a fire emoji has now appeared.

My unease grows. What's that Rolling Stones lyric? Something about playing with fire. Is that what this lion hunter person means? Except now I see that it isn't @lionhunter04 after all – I misread it earlier. It's @*liar*hunter04.

Liar hunter. That sounds altogether more threatening. I go over to where I've left the stash of leaflets that crazy woman thrust into my hand and re-read the felt-tipped words scrawled on the one on top: *I know who you are.*

I swallow hard. If that woman is also behind this Liar Hunter persona, and she's labouring under the impression that *I'm* Boho Birdie, then it doesn't make a blind bit of difference that I'm not. Because in her eyes, *I'm* her target.

44

Elle

'He's going to try and kiss me soon. I know he is.'

Craig sniggers like a schoolboy. She wants to take him by the shoulders and shake the shit out of him. But what good would that do?

'What am I going to do if he does?' she says.

'He won't. He doesn't have the balls. Just keep stringing him along. Keep him keen.'

'Oh, he's keen all right.' Elle sighs. 'Tell me something, have you ever thought of giving it up?'

Craig stares at her. 'Giving it up? What are you talking about? Giving what up?'

'All this.' She waves her hands in the air. 'The tension. The worry. The deception. It's all so fucking squalid, isn't it? I don't know if I can do it any more.'

It's the first time she's ever spoken to him like this. Been completely honest and shown her vulnerability. It isn't what they do.

Craig's mouth hangs open. 'Are you mad? You're made for this life. Same as me.'

'Am I though?' She closes her eyes and inhales through her nostrils, holds the air in her lungs for a couple of seconds.

'Lena, Lena, Lena. Don't do this to me. Not now. I have to be able to rely on you.'

Elle gives a short, derisive laugh. 'I'm not the one using my real name. You want to be careful, you know. Walls and ears, remember?'

Craig leans forward. 'Seriously, are you saying you want out?'

'I think so, yes.'

'But not, like, right now. You mean, when this job's over.' He rakes his teeth over his bottom lip. 'We're so close now I can taste it.'

'Don't worry. I'm not about to leave you in the lurch. I'm just giving you the heads up.'

Craig reaches out to stroke her chin, and for once, she lets him.

'You've got him eating out of your hand,' he says. 'He's already told you so much.' He leans forward and for a moment, Elle thinks *he's* going to kiss her.

'You're one of the best police officers I know,' he whispers. 'It'd be a bloody waste if you jack it all in. Are you sure this is what you really want?'

Elle watches his face and knows what she's always known, deep down. The job doesn't excite her the same way it does him. He actually *enjoys* the risk of being undercover. The danger. He lives for the adrenaline. Closing in on the criminals. Tightening the net around them.

She used to like it, too. Getting tapped up for decoy jobs to snare paedos and sex offenders. Working with the teams who'd infiltrated their online communities. But if she's totally honest with herself, the more experienced she has become, the more frightened she is. It was bad enough buying wraps from small-time dealers knowing there was a surveillance team stationed near by to swoop in if things went wrong, but infiltrating criminal gangs and disrupting drug supply lines is something else.

Her parents would be terrified if they knew what she did. *She* is terrified, too. And although this job with Craig is safer than many she's done – she's only here in an intelligence-gathering capacity, mainly finding out how much that sad sap Rob Hornby actually knows – it could still get very nasty indeed if their cover is blown. Big guys who run their dirty money through legal business fronts are smart cookies. Experts at keeping their own hands clean. But that doesn't mean they don't have plenty of henchmen on the payroll.

Craig holds her gaze. 'At the end of the day,' he says, 'you need to do whatever makes you happy.'

She nods. She might hate living cheek by jowl with him like this, but however much he pisses her off, they're a team. They have each other's backs. Tears spring to her eyes, and for the first time in the three months they've been holed up together in this awful place, pretending to be a couple and carrying out covert surveillance work, she feels something for him. Not love – no way. And not lust, although right this minute she could probably . . .

No, she absolutely couldn't. She wouldn't. To give in at this late stage would be madness, and she'd regret it for sure. What she feels right now is a tenderness, of sorts. A tenderness, yes. For DS Grayson Walker. Who'd have thought?

45

Marlow

All night long, I thrash about in my bed, unable to sleep for more than the briefest of snatches. At one point, I find myself sitting bolt upright, surrounded by my former classmates. They're all sitting at their desks, pointing at me and laughing, as if to say, *What the hell are you doing in bed?* I blink the dream away and try to still my mind, but it's no good. I've reached the stage where I'm unable to differentiate between waking and sleeping, and my thoughts tumble over each other in a never-ending series of acrobatic manoeuvres that leave me exhausted and dizzy.

Faces and memories from the past loom out at me, interspersed with more recent events, both real and imagined: Miss Latham with her steel-grey bun and all-seeing, all-knowing eyes; Mrs Barrie's infernal algebraic equations spreading across the whiteboard all on their own; a solitary cut rose lying on freshly dug soil; and Lottie, always Lottie, just on the edge of my vision, engulfed in flames.

When I finally claw my way up to the surface and wake properly, I feel weak and fragile. Headachy with exhaustion. The light seeping through the slatted blinds at the window is grey and watery. It must be very early in the morning still. The sun has not yet risen.

All of a sudden, my body stiffens. My heart rate accelerates, and there's a familiar tingling sensation in my fingers and toes. That noise I can hear – a crackling, spitting noise. It sounds like . . . it sounds like fire. It's another dream fragment, it must be. Except this one doesn't merge into the next. It gets stronger and louder with each passing second.

I'm out of bed so fast my head is throbbing. A wave of nausea threatens to overwhelm me, but somehow I make it to the window. A thick cloud of dark grey smoke is mushrooming up above the playground. I'm seized with panic. Rooted to the spot. All I can do is stare, open-mouthed, my chest so tight I can't breathe. I feel light-headed. There's a loud, rhythmic whooshing in my ears. This can't be happening.

Within seconds, I hear raised voices. Shouts. Feet pounding on tarmac. Nikhil is running towards the smoke, dressing gown flapping. He is closely followed by Big Dave.

Gilly is shouting at the top of her voice. 'Be careful, Nik. Don't get too close.'

Within a few minutes, more of the guardians have appeared, Rob among them. Everyone is in a state of disarray – coats hastily pulled on over nightclothes, unlaced trainers on their feet.

I step back from the window, heart racing.

I hear Rob shouting something about a small Class A fire and yelling that a couple of buckets of water should do it. My knees tremble and give way.

I'm on the floor now, trying not to cough. My windows are closed and there's no smoke in this room, but there might as well be. I feel like my lungs have been crushed, like I can't get any more air into them, no matter how hard I try. It's a panic attack and I know it will pass, but right now it has me in its grip, and all I can do is ride it out. Stay huddled on the floor, trembling, till it subsides.

When my heart rate finally slows and my breathing becomes more manageable, I force myself to stand up and move back to the window. Someone has doused the fire with water, and I see now that it was never going to spread. It was contained in an old metal incinerator. There is no more smoke. No more crackling and spitting.

No more fire.

I need to go down there. They'll wonder where I am. I can't pretend I haven't heard the commotion.

By the time I get there, they are all standing in a semi-circle round the smouldering incinerator.

Mags turns to face me. 'Emergency over,' she says.

'They've gone too far now,' Dave says. 'And it's in pretty poor taste, lighting a fire right next to the spot where the girl they want to remember burnt to death. What's *wrong* with them?'

'This is the trouble whenever there's some kind of organized campaign,' Gilly says. 'Not everyone who joins is motivated by the same thing. Some people just like making trouble.'

'You're right,' Elle says. 'I doubt very much the girl's parents would approve of this kind of behaviour.'

No, they wouldn't.

I think of that fire emoji on the Boho Birdie account, coming so soon after the *Don't play with me* warning. Something tells me that this fire has nothing to do with the campaign. Something tells me this is personal.

It's a message for me. From her.

From @liarhunter04.

She's accusing me of lying. Of faking my life. But why would she start a fire in a . . . ?

I take a step back. Because now I see that it isn't an incinerator at all. It's an old metal dustbin. My heart hammers wildly. Bile rises at the back of my throat, an acidic burning sensation that turns into a bitter mouthful I'm forced to swallow back down. The fire that killed Lottie started in a bin. A different sort of bin altogether, but a bin nonetheless. That can't be a coincidence, can it?

My throat closes up as the flames of the original fire crackle and leap behind my eyes, and I'm right back in that moment, when we first realized she was missing. The sheer horror of it. The blinding, choking panic.

My vision starts to tunnel. This is all getting way out of hand. Hayley's disappearance. The locked room with the non-existent leak. The strange goings-on at the swimming pool. The chalked message on the playground. Lottie's name appearing on an honours board that's now vanished. The Instagram account that some lunatic thinks is mine. The campaigners. And now this. A fire in an old bin. Right next to Lottie's garden.

They can't all be connected, but right now it feels like they are.

Lou is staring at me, a worried expression on her face. Now Mags is staring too. She's stepping towards me, peering at me with concern.

The last thing I see is a tiny pinprick of light.

When I come round, I'm lying on the ground in the recovery position, and someone has put a coat over me.

'It's OK, Marlow. You just fainted,' Mags says. 'You're going to be fine. Lie still for a bit longer, until you feel strong enough to sit up. You probably got out of bed too fast. I felt dizzy myself a minute ago.'

'Me too,' Bryony says.

Back in my room, my head is still spinning, and I know there's no way I can go to work tomorrow. Not after this shock. There's no way I can stay here either.

I look around my messy room and all the things I still haven't unpacked. It's not like me to procrastinate. I should be getting it straight, making it look nice and homely. That is, after all, what I do best. Which must mean that on some deep level, I know it's not right.

The dread that's been churning in the pit of my stomach has now stilled, but somehow it's worse than before. It's turned into a heavy weight that sits inside me like a rock. I need to get away. Find a new place to live. A new home. This school is bad for my mental health. I should never have come back. It was a stupid, stupid decision. But then, I've made a few of those in my time.

With a sinking heart, I phone Lenny's mobile and tell him I'm sick. Again. That I need to take some time off. He's surprisingly cool about it. Says I should get myself properly better this time. Says I've looked peaky for days now. Good old Lenny.

I'm going to phone Dev next, and if he doesn't answer, I'm going to call him again. And again and again, until he answers. If ever I needed to hear his voice, it's right now. I need someone sane to talk to. Someone who can reassure me. Give me advice. Someone who can pile all my things in his van and drive me as far away from McKinleys as I can get.

And while we're driving, I'll do what I should have done ages ago and let him into my life. Tell him everything. Tell him who I really am. Marilyn DeVere-Cairns. He'll be shocked and hurt. He'll be angry too, angry that I've been deceiving him for so long. But it's the only way. He deserves to know the truth, and once he's heard about the fire and the guilt I've carried for so long, he'll understand why I'm the way I am. It's why I'm so paranoid all the time. Why I'm imagining Lottie's name on an honours board. Why I'm jumping to the most ridiculous conclusion that a fire in an old dustbin is some kind of coded message specifically for me.

Everything comes down to my own guilt.

From this moment on, I'll be honest with Dev. I'll be a proper friend.

I press call. I'll suggest we meet somewhere for lunch today. Then, if he can't help me move tomorrow or the day after, I'll find someone online who can. After all, Dev's already made a jokey comment about me only wanting him for his wheels. I need to prove him wrong about that.

46

Hayley

The pebbles shift under my body as I twist and writhe in desperation to escape, but it's futile. I use my tongue to form words behind my sealed lips. *Let me go. Just untie me and I'll disappear. I won't tell.*

But though the words sound intelligible in my head, to him they are just muffled noises and grunts, swallowed up by the distant roar of the sea. I plead with my eyes, and for a moment, I think I see something flicker in his pupils. Fleeting compassion. Hesitation. But then he turns away, and he doesn't look at my face again.

I've seen too much to be allowed to live. The hollow space behind the wall. The metal toolboxes stuffed to the gunwales with gear. I knew straight away this wasn't some small-time pusher. This is a serious operation. These guys don't fuck about. I'm nothing to them. Less than nothing. I'm a problem that needs to be dealt with, that's all.

He crouches down in front of me, and beyond the bulk of him is the sea, vast and glimmering in the moonlight. The tide is coming in, and I hear the grate of the pebbles as the waves draw them back, then fling them down again. But the water can't reach me here. I'm too far up the beach to drown, and besides, it's not the incoming tide that will take me tonight.

He tightens the tourniquet below the crook of my arm, and I close my eyes, wait for the cold sharp sting of the needle penetrating my vein. An intense chill rushes through my body like an icy wave, but then comes the sweetness. The sweetness and the warmth, spreading and spreading and spreading. The blissful warmth of not caring any more. No fear. No panic. No regrets. My thoughts are fading fast. I feel almost . . .

47

Marlow

Dev answers straight away. The temptation to let everything spill out in one go is overwhelming, but I mustn't do that over the phone. I need to see him face to face. I need to see his eyes while I'm talking to him.

'Hi stranger, do you fancy meeting me for lunch today?' There's a pause. 'My treat. There's a really good Indian round the corner.'

'There's a really good Indian right here,' he says. 'There always has been.'

I laugh. Thank God! For a minute there, I thought he was going to give me the brush-off.

'So, will you?' I say. 'Will you come over, or shall I meet you somewhere? I don't mind coming your way if you prefer.'

'I can't,' he says. 'Not today.'

I feel hollow with disappointment, but I can't always expect him to be at my beck and call. I need to be patient.

'Still busy ferrying kids to uni?'

'Yeah, work's been mental lately. But I should have called you. Sorry.'

'No worries. I guessed you were run off your feet. I really want to talk to you though. Are you free at all today? For a quick coffee maybe?'

Another pause. A longer one this time. Something's wrong. I know it is. He's holding something back.

'Dev?'

'There's something I need to tell you,' he says.

My stomach tightens. That doesn't sound good. That doesn't sound good at all. 'Yeah? What's that then?'

'I'm getting married.'

'What?' I can't believe my ears. Dev is getting married? That's the last thing I expected him to say. 'That's a bit quick, isn't it? I didn't even know you had a girlfriend.'

'It's . . . it's kind of an arranged marriage, but we both want it to happen. No one's forcing us into it. We're happy. I've been meaning to tell you for ages, but it never seemed to be the right time.'

'Wow. That's . . . that's *huge*.'

The silence between us lengthens. I rush to fill it.

'Congratulations. When's the wedding?'

'Oh, not till next year. There's lots of stuff to sort out first.'

'Yeah, yeah, course there is. Bloody hell, Dev. This is a

bit of a shock, to be honest. I wish you'd told me. I thought we were mates.'

'Sorry. Like I said, I *wanted* to tell you. I just couldn't find the right words. So, what was it you wanted to talk to me about?'

I take a breath. Looks like I'm going to have to say it over the phone, after all.

'Well, actually, I wanted to tell you how much I value our friendship.' I try to swallow, but there's a huge lump in my throat. 'You do know that, don't you?'

I hear him sigh – a hopeless kind of sigh – and tears spring to my eyes. I've left it too late. I'm losing him. But I *can't* lose him.

'This marriage thing, it doesn't mean we can't still see other, does it?' But I already know what he's going to say. I can feel it in the weighted silence.

'It's . . . it's complicated. I don't want Yasmin to get the wrong idea.'

'Yasmin. That's a nice name.'

He clears his throat awkwardly. 'Yeah, she's a nice girl. A nice woman, I mean.'

'Why would she get the wrong idea? We're friends, aren't we? You can't split up with a friend.'

'Actually, Marlow, you can. And the truth is, we've been mates rather than friends. You said it yourself, just now.'

'But that's exactly why I need to talk to you. I want to tell you things. Things I should have told you a long time ago. I couldn't find the right words either. Please, Dev, don't do this.'

'The decision's been made, Marlow. I'm marrying her.'

'I don't mean the wedding. I mean *us*. Don't do this to *us*. Don't cut me out of your life just because you're getting married. That's crazy.'

'I have to. Not just for Yasmin's sake, but for mine. Surely you know how much I wanted us to—' His voice falters. Tears are streaming down my face now. He doesn't need to finish the sentence.

It's over. I've lost the only real friend I've had since Lottie. And it's nobody's fault but my own.

'Dev, please. I don't want to beg you.'

'Then don't. It wouldn't work anyway. I've made up my mind. I'm sorry, Marlow, but you'll be fine. You always are.'

'No. Not this time I won't be. There's weird shit going on here, and I've got to get out.' I don't even know why I'm telling him this. It's pointless now. Although maybe some small part of me is clinging on to the hope that if I can just keep him talking, he'll change his mind and come over.

'Where will you go?'

'Thought I'd go and stay with my parents for a while.' I *was* hoping to crash at Dev's place and put my stuff in his spare room, but that's clearly off the cards now.

There's a pause. 'Thought you didn't get on with your parents.'

'I don't really, but, well, they are my parents. Maybe it's time I rebuilt a few bridges.'

'They're down in Devon, aren't they?'

'Erm, not any more. They're in France now.' I hold my

breath. It's the first time I've actually told him the truth about them.

'France? You never said. What they doing in France?'

I take a breath. 'They've retired there. Sold their house and bought an apartment.'

There's a pause while he takes in this information. 'You see, this is what I mean,' he says. 'Why didn't I know that? Why didn't you ever tell me? I've told you everything about my family.'

'I'm telling you now, aren't I?'

'It's too late, Marlow. It's too late.'

I'm on the street, outside the school gates. I'm in such a state I can't even remember putting my shoes on and leaving my room. Dev's words echo in my head. *It's too late, Marlow. It's too late.*

He's getting married. To a woman I've never even heard about. I can't believe he's been keeping something like that from me all this time.

Really? You can't believe that? Because you haven't kept anything from him, have you, Marlow?

I don't know where I'm going, but right now, I don't care. I feel numb inside. I'm putting one foot in front of the other on autopilot. I've lost my best friend. My *only* friend. And it's my own stupid fault. I've known for a long while that I was taking him for granted, but I carried on anyway. Didn't put the effort in when I should have done. And more than anything, friendships rely on honesty.

My eyes are blurred with tears, and I stumble over a loose paving slab I didn't even see, almost fall flat on my face. But now I'm walking again, striding out as blindly and carelessly as before.

It takes me a little while to realize where I am. It wasn't a conscious decision to come here, but somehow or other, I've ended up on Lottie's street. And there, a few houses down on the other side, is her parents' home. I don't even know if they still live there or not, because I haven't had the decency to keep in touch with them as I should have done.

I used to tell myself that they wouldn't want to see any of Lottie's friends because it would be too painful for them. What I really thought was that it would be too painful for *me*. Everything I've ever done has been a curious combination of self-protection and self-sabotage. It's why I don't let people in, why I don't allow myself to get close to them.

Because the last person I was close to was Lottie, and Lottie is dead.

When I saw that light shining from Angie's eye, I took it for a sign that I should come back to McKinleys and lay my ghosts to rest. But there's only ever been one ghost in my past, and that's Lottie.

I'm directly opposite her parents' house now, and I can hardly bring myself to look at it. All these years I've tried to tell myself a different story, and sometimes I even managed to believe it. Because the stupid, utterly reckless teenager who started that fire for her own selfish ends can't possibly have been me.

I'd convinced myself I could get away with it. A small,

contained fire that would either burn out straight away or be extinguished as soon as it was discovered. A fire in the large wire bin full of waste-paper that was directly under the shelf where Ms Thompson had put my sketchbook and some of my coursework. All because I didn't think my work was up to scratch.

It doesn't matter that I changed my mind literally the *second* after I'd flicked my lighter, that the thought of destroying all those weeks and months of hard work was suddenly too awful to contemplate. It doesn't matter because I *hadn't* put it out. In the midst of all that paper, a tiny ember must still have been burning away. Coming to my senses made no difference whatsoever. Because the fire *did* take hold. It burnt down the entire art studio, and Lottie with it.

Sometimes, I almost manage to convince myself that it's simply my guilt at telling Lottie how easy it was to get into the art pods that has made me concoct this dreadful story as a form of self-punishment.

But it *was* me. I started the fire.

I killed Lottie.

People I pass on the street are giving me curious, pitying looks, and I know I don't deserve their pity. I deserve this half-life I've chosen for myself. Lottie never got to live her life, so why should I get to live mine? And now I've lost Dev too. I've got nothing left. It doesn't matter that I didn't know Lottie was in the building. It doesn't matter that I only wanted to destroy my own work. None of it matters because the fact is, I chose to flick that lighter. I chose to start that fire.

The fire that will never go out in my head. The fire that will burn until the day I die, and – if there is a heaven and a hell – the fire that will burn me for eternity too.

I should never have come back – it's just made everything so much worse.

I stop walking and make a decision. I can't keep wallowing in self-pity and regret like this or I'll go mad. I have to keep going, keep doing things to stay sane. Keep moving. It's the only way.

I'll go back to my room and start searching online for a short-term storage unit that isn't too pricey, and a man with a van who can pick up me and my stuff ASAP. Then I'll swallow my stupid pride and call Mum and Dad. See if they'll lend me some money to go over to France and stay with them for a while, just until I've decided on my next steps.

There's something else I have to do as well. It might be too late to make it up to Dev, and there's no way I'll ever be able to make amends to Lottie or her family, but it's not too late to find out what's going on at McKinleys, and whether it's got anything to do with Hayley's disappearance.

And yet, even as I think this, I have the most awful feeling that maybe it's been too late for Hayley all along, and that I've been deluding myself that there's still a chance to save her. Melancholy swells inside me like a giant wave.

I keep thinking of that patch of slightly different-coloured paintwork behind all the pipes in the pump room. What better place to stash drugs than an abandoned old swimming pool that's due for demolition in less than a year? That would explain why Brampton was so over-the-top furious when I said I'd seen an intruder on the CCTV.

This is, after all, the man who wants to turn a dead girl's memorial garden into a car park for the sake of a couple of extra spaces. If Brampton *is* doing something illegal, the police need to know about it. Then maybe his property-development days will be over, and someone decent, with a heart and a conscience, can buy the site and keep Lottie's garden exactly as it is. If I leave here without at least *trying* to solve the puzzle, that'll be yet another thing weighing on my conscience and adding to my guilt.

Tomorrow is Monday. In the morning, when everyone's gone back to work, I'll take another look in that pool. I'll find out what's going on.

48

Marlow

As I climb the three stone steps leading up to the main entrance, I realize that it's exactly a week since I first arrived. I remember thinking at the time that something was a bit off about Dev on the drive over here. Now I know why. He was working out how to tell me he couldn't be friends with me any more.

The hall is as gloomy as it was last Sunday, maybe even gloomier. I pass the pigeonholes outside the office and notice something I missed earlier. Rob has printed out a label with my name on – M. Cairns – and stuck it below one of the slots. As if I belong here now. As if I'm staying.

That's odd. Something's been posted into my slot already, yet nobody except Dev and the agency knows I'm here. I haven't got round to changing my address on anything official.

When I draw out the small, square envelope with a first-class stamp in the corner and read what's handwritten on the front, my stomach drops. It's got my name on it. My *real* name. Marilyn DeVere-Cairns, followed by the name and address of the school. But nobody knows about that name. I haven't used it in years. I paid to have it legally changed as soon as I was eighteen because I hated it so much.

With a growing sense of trepidation, I prise open the envelope, and there, inside, is a plain white greetings card with a fire emoji on the front. My heart begins to thud as I open the card. There's nothing written inside. Nothing at all. It's completely blank.

I feel a stab of fear. My old name on the envelope coupled with the picture on the card is the only message I need. I think of that comment from @liarhunter04. *Don't play with me*, followed by the fire emoji, just like the one on this card.

My mouth goes dry. This must be from Liar Hunter, too. And now I know for sure that it's someone who was at school with me. Someone who knows what I did. Even the 04 in their name is a clue. Because that was the year it happened. That was the year of the fire. The year Lottie died. 2004.

Lou emerges from the kitchen and startles me. 'You've found it then,' she says. 'I meant to tell you, but what with the party last night and the fire this morning, I completely forgot. It was my turn to sort the post yesterday and I guessed it must be you.' She smirks. 'No wonder you didn't tell us your real name. Sounds like something out of *Downton Abbey*.'

I'm too much in shock to be embarrassed. I slide the card into my pocket. 'Yeah, I only really use it for my bank account and passport.' Another lie, because everything's in my new name now, but how else to explain this suddenly appearing? Can she hear the tremble in my voice? The fear?

But Lou just nods as if it's nothing. Because to her it *is* nothing. She has no idea what it means, me receiving this card. And the worst thing is, I can't confide in her, much as I'd like to. Because then I'd have to tell her *why* it's so frightening. I'd have to admit that I started the fire, and while I might have been ready to tell Dev, I've only just met Lou, and I've already made the decision to leave as soon as I can, so what would be the point in burdening her with my dreadful secret? And anyway, how do I know it'd be safe with her? I've known her for what, seven days?

'I'm glad I've bumped into you,' I say. 'I wanted to let you know I'm probably going to be leaving soon. I didn't want you to worry if I suddenly disappear too.'

Lou frowns. 'But you've only just arrived.'

'I know, but it's complicated.'

'Family emergency?' Lou says, arching her eyebrows.

'No. Not exactly. But it does involve seeing my parents again. I'm going to stay with them for a while. I need to sort my life out. Stop living like this. Not that there's anything wrong with being a property guardian,' I add, in case she thinks I'm criticizing her own choices.

'It is a bit shit though,' Lou says. 'I'd like a bit more permanence in my life, too.' She lowers her voice. 'All this business with Hayley and some of the things that have been happening here – I'm not surprised you want out.'

'I'm going to check that pump room one more time before I go,' I whisper.

Lou looks alarmed and beckons me into the kitchen again. 'No. Don't do that,' she says, as soon as we've closed the door behind us. 'If there's something dodgy going on here, we shouldn't get involved. I told Mags everything last night, after the party. About going up to your room with Hayley. Everything I told you.'

'Did you?'

'Yes. I saw your reaction when I wouldn't give you my number, and it made me think. I figured I owed it to Mags, and to myself, to be honest with her. I can't go through life worrying about what she's going to think all the time. It was a difficult conversation because I had to admit I kind of fancied Hayley, but it was the right thing to do. It made me realize how much I don't want to lose Mags. And her looking at my phone, well, it's my fault really. I've *made* her feel jealous. Sneaking around behind her back. Being evasive. I feel like our relationship has moved on to a new level now. Like we're more solid, you know?'

I nod. I know what she means because it's exactly what I wanted to do with Dev.

'Mags reckons we shouldn't get involved, and she's right.

If there's some kind of criminal activity going on here, *especially* if it's anything to do with Class A drugs, it could be really dangerous. People like that are ruthless. And it's like we said: the police aren't going to be interested in Hayley. Not with her past. They're stretched enough as it is.'

She moves towards the door. 'We're making plans to move on as well, as it happens. So please, Marlow, don't go back to the pool. It's not worth it.'

'OK. I won't.'

But I will, I know I will. Because I can't give up on Hayley just yet. And if Brampton is up to no good, I owe it to Lottie and her parents to find out the truth. If I can discredit him somehow and stop his development plans, then Lottie's garden will be safe. Preserving her memory – it's the very least I can do.

'Lou?' I say, as she turns to leave. She looks back at me over her shoulder. 'Promise you won't tell anyone about my name.'

She grins. 'Don't worry. Your secret's safe with me.'

When she's gone, I pull the card out of my pocket and examine it again. My secret isn't safe at all. Someone must have seen me light that fire.

49

Rob

It is late on Sunday night, almost midnight, and Rob is sitting in one of the old science labs, perched on a high stool in front of the bench at the back and breathing in the faint chemical smell that lingers even now. It is dark and cold in here, and he has finished his task. He doesn't quite know why he is still here, but something is pinning him to this stool. Some irresistible force. Perhaps it is the memory of those long nights when he first arrived on site, when he was the only one here.

Well, not quite the *only* one.

Rob thinks back to those nights with something like nostalgia. He was happy then. No, not happy, he thinks. That is the wrong word. Rob isn't sure whether he has ever been entirely happy. Happiness as a concept is somewhat alien to him. Contentment is probably more accurate, but even that isn't completely right. Sometimes Rob wonders whether there is any such thing as true contentment or true happiness. At best, these states of mind are fleeting. At worst, illusory.

The week before Guardian Angels Inc. took over the security arrangements at the school, someone had broken in via the windows of this very lab and spray-painted graffiti on the walls. Coarse, vulgar words that have now been painted over. They had started to deface one of the teak worktops too – the one in front of the whiteboard – but must have been frightened off by something.

Rob likes to think it was Lottie who scared them.

He runs his hands over the worktop he's sitting at now. He likes the smoothness of the hard wood, the feel of it on the soft palms of his hands. He likes the fact that generations of girls have sat at this very bench, conducting their experiments under the watchful eye of a science tutor. Pouring and mixing and measuring out solutions, setting up tripods over Bunsen burners, peering into conical flasks and making laborious notes.

He likes the fact that Lottie might once have sat here, and that his hands are touching the same worktop she touched. It's why he used to come here all the time after the school closed down. It's why he applied for a position here as soon as he saw one advertised on the Guardian Angels website.

After the break-in, the agency soon secured the site, but if someone was determined to get in, they would. Which is why there are now ten of them living here. An occupied school is less attractive to vandals than an empty one.

But Rob wishes they hadn't come. The others. He was managing perfectly well before they all turned up. He enjoyed the solitude. The peace. He enjoyed his nightly patrols. But most of all, he enjoyed the proximity to Lottie.

He still does enjoy this – of course he does – but it isn't quite the same any more. Not since the dreadful business with Hayley. He can sense Lottie's disappointment in him for what he has done, or rather, for what he has failed to do. He can sense her judgement. And she is right. He should have rescued Hayley somehow. He shouldn't have let that awful man get away with it.

But then, there are lots of things Rob has let him get away with. Lots of comings and goings he has turned a blind eye to.

He shifts position on the lab stool so that he is facing the honours board he has been working on for the past six months. Such a painstaking job, hand-painting her name and achievements. A real labour of love. He didn't think he'd be able to do it, and although it isn't as perfect as he would have liked, he is satisfied with the result. When he tried hanging it on Friday, to see how it looked, he was filled with an enormous sense of pride, even though it wasn't sitting straight on the wall. He didn't have time to rehang it before some of the others came back from work and interrupted him. But still, he only noticed one tiny flaw, which he has now put right. It is a fitting tribute to the girl he loved. The girl he will always love.

She didn't want him in life, but in death she is his, and his alone. Being near her like this is what makes him turn a blind eye to what has been going on under his nose. He cannot afford to lose his position here. It's his home. Lottie's presence is everywhere. He used to visit her grave in the churchyard a few streets away, but although her bones were there, she wasn't.

When the development is finished, Rob will make sure his name is first on the list for one of the planned single-bedroom dwellings. He has a considerable amount of money in his savings account, thanks to the generosity of his childless and adoring aunt. God rest her soul.

Although now, of course, there is Elle to consider. Elle has been showing interest in him, and he cannot deny the frisson of excitement this gives him in a very particular and private part of his body. For although Lottie will always be the girl of Rob's dreams – his number one love, high up on a pedestal above all others – Elle has one distinct advantage over her.

Elle is alive.

50

Elle

It is Monday morning. Elle drags the suitcase from under her bed and starts piling her clothes inside. Today will be her last day on site. Her last day pretending to be a property guardian.

Her last day living as Craig's girlfriend.

If all goes to plan – she can't even bring herself to contemplate what might happen if it doesn't – it will also be her last day as an undercover officer. She wishes it could be her last day on the force as well, but she'll have to work her notice. With any luck, it will be desk duties only from now on.

The chronic anxiety and stress she has been suffering for months is different today. Today, she is wired and fearful.

They can't afford to mess this one up. Not after all the hours she and Craig and the rest of the team have put in. The weeks and months of information gathering. The piecing together of connections and following trails. There is too much at stake to start bottling it now.

And yet, not for the first time, Elle wonders whether any of it will do any good, in the end. They might win a few battles, here and there. Remove a few key players. But they're never going to stop the trade in illegal drugs. Never going to stop the suffering and misery. The ruined lives.

This is why she needs to get out. Because she doesn't believe it's a job worth doing. Not any more. However many of these lowlifes they put away, more and more of them will spring up and take their place. It's an unwinnable war. A war that will never end.

Elle pushes her cynicism to the back of her mind. Today isn't the day for it. Right now, she's still a key member of this team, and she can't afford to lose focus.

She takes a few deep breaths and directs her attention to her feet on the floor. Grounds herself in the present moment. According to the intel the operational team have been gathering, their suspect has been using an encrypted messaging app to communicate with other members of the organized crime group. Today, at precisely 10.45 a.m., he will be meeting a wholesale dealer known only as J at the swimming pool and exchanging ten kilos of high-purity cocaine for cash. Cocaine imported from his contacts in Dubai. It is just one of several exchanges that he and his associates are believed to have made in the last two years.

Elle wanders over to the window and gazes out at the playing field. Her eyes stick on the section of fencing that will be removed shortly before the planned seizure, allowing her armed colleagues to enter the site and make their way into the old gymnasium and through the store cupboard into the pool, where they will, if their intel is correct and there are no last-minute timing changes, 'surprise' their man and his buyer mid-transaction.

Elle's involvement is now over. She has done what she was deployed to do and kept her eyes and ears open.

Elle returns to her suitcase and continues packing. The familiarity of the task soothes her frayed nerves. Craig will be here soon, and together they will wait for the raid to be over. His long hours of monitoring their suspect's nocturnal activities have also come to an end. Hours that have on occasion, he says, proved even more tedious than a night spent stacking shelves in Asda, because this one is clever and likes to conduct his nefarious business in broad daylight whenever he can. It is, Elle thinks, astonishing how much men in high-vis jackets and hard hats can get away with in plain sight.

Both she and Craig will stay in character when the police knock on their door to question them, and when they go to the station to give witness statements.

When it's all over, Elle will return to her flat in Plaistow and have the longest, most luxurious bath she's had in months. And while she's doing that, she will contemplate her future.

She can't wait.

51

Marlow

Monday morning is here at last. I did get to sleep. Eventually. Probably because I was so shattered after the emotional call with Mum and Dad, and then trawling through all those storage facility and man-with-a-van websites. Still, at least that gave me something to do. It distracted me from dwelling on the terrifying knowledge that for all these years, someone has known what I did. It's made me doubly determined to get out of here as soon as I can.

I've managed to find a reasonable lock-up unit that's big enough for all my stuff and paid the deposit online. Now I just need to confirm a suitable pick-up time with a van driver called Steve. He can do it this afternoon, thank God.

The sooner I'm out of here and on that train to France, the better.

The sooner I delete my Instagram account, the better, too. If this person, this Liar Hunter, knows who I am and thinks I'm masquerading as Boho Birdie, I don't want them finding my Marlow Cairns account as well, leaving threatening messages on there. I'm relieved I'm not on any other social media platforms.

Harry will be pissed off when I call him, but he's just going to have to deal with it. Lenny's going to be angry too, when he finds out I've gone to France. I might even get the sack, but maybe that'll give me the kick up the arse I need to sort my life out, once and for all.

I slip my phone into my pocket and my camera round my neck, because if I'm going to have a closer look at that wall in the pump room, I might as well take a few pictures of the empty swimming pool while I'm there. I can edit them while I'm in France and maybe enter that competition. Even if I can't find out what's happened to Hayley, I might as well get *something* out of my ill-fated week here. Sometimes you need to take a calculated risk to get a good photo. She who dares and all that.

Now that I've made arrangements to get out of here, I feel an enormous sense of relief, which tells me it's the right decision. It's not like leaving the chapel or some of the other interesting places I've lived in the past. This is different, because I should never have come here in the first place. I should have known it would end badly.

The only consolation I have is that whoever it is who sent me that card has never tried to make contact with me before. My name change will have helped with that, of course. So for whatever reason, they've kept their knowledge to themselves all this time, rather than telling someone else. It's only by some bizarre coincidence that they stumbled across Hayley's Boho Birdie account, recognized the school, and then saw me on the street and recognized *me*. It's that campaigner who gave me the flyers. It has to be her. But instead of telling someone, she's deliberately taunting me with her knowledge. Unsettling me.

I thought there was something about her that looked familiar, but then I dismissed it. Who the hell *is* she?

I try to remember all the girls in my class. Some of the names and faces spring readily to mind, but I know there are others I don't remember. Vague, shadowy figures at the furthest reaches of my mind. I wasn't one of the popular girls – not by a long chalk – but I wasn't completely on the periphery either. There were others who were a lot less popular than I was.

The memory lands like a little dart in my brain. There was a girl who really hated me. She took offence at my artwork for some reason. But then she hated everyone else, too. What was her name? Kat, that's it. Kat Morwood. Although we used to call her . . .

Oh God, we used to call her Fat Moron. How awful we were back then. How cruel. We never said it to her face though. At least, I don't *think* we did. She used to sit behind me in maths – in this very classroom. Sometimes I'd feel her eyes boring into the back of my neck, like some evil presence.

But the woman who gave me those flyers looked nothing like Kat Morwood. She was much thinner, and her face was completely different.

I close my eyes and try to picture her face, her eyes. That dark fleck in her iris. Didn't Kat have that too? Yes, yes, she did! Oh my God! It *was* her.

I sit with the knowledge, turning it over and over in my head, examining it from different angles. And suddenly it doesn't seem quite so scary any more. Kat Morwood was such a vicious, nasty person. Nobody had a good word to say about her. Not even the teachers. She was toxic through and through. Even if she told someone what she'd seen, who would believe her? Besides, it was eighteen years ago. The police and the fire investigators came to the conclusion that it was a tragic accident.

Something else occurs to me. She probably didn't see me at all. It would be just like Kat to make up something like that. She was so petty. So vengeful. Even so, I'm glad I won't be spending another night here now she's on the scene.

I lock up my room and go over to the hall. There's no one about when I slip under the rope barrier across the stairs and make my way up to the bell-tower, where there's a perfect view of the entrance to the swimming pool. Once at the top, I make sure there's no sign of any men in high-vis jackets. No sign of Harry Kiernan or James Brampton. No sign of Rob. The school is empty apart from myself and Craig, whose snoring I heard as I left Block C. If I'm going to do this, I need to do it *now*.

Five minutes later, I'm in the gym. Then I'm inside the store cupboard, facing the door on the other side that leads to the pool. Even though I know there's no one here except me, my heart is hammering. If Brampton *is* up to something, then Lou's right and this is dangerous. But he's not here right now, and it's only going to take me a couple of minutes to nip into the pool, check out that wall and take a few pictures.

I put my ear to the door and listen. Not a sound. I take off my shoes and open it gently. Then I slip out of the cup-board and into the empty corridor, walking as fast as I can in my socked feet, my camera bumping against my chest.

52

Marlow

The tiled floor is cold beneath my feet. I move swiftly along the corridor, feeling the tingle of goosebumps on my upper arms. My heart knocks in my chest.

Now that I'm doing this, the fear has kicked in, and for a moment, I consider turning back. Returning to the relative safety of the store cupboard. Once I'm back in my room, I can book the train tickets to Montpellier, wait for Steve and his van to arrive, and be on my way.

But I'm doing this for a good reason. I have to keep reminding myself of that. I'm doing this for Hayley – and for Lottie, in a roundabout way. And yes, if I'm honest, I'm doing it for myself too, because even though I'm unlikely to end up winning that competition, the empty pool is going to make such a great picture. I'm at the door to the changing room now anyway. The whole thing is only going to take a few minutes.

Inside, the air is even colder than it was in the corridor, and my socks are starting to feel damp. I sit down on one side of the wrap-around wooden benches and turn my camera on, adjust the settings. I take a few shots of the changing room and the lockers with their doors hanging open. But it's what's in the next section of the building that interests me most and draws me to it like a magnet.

I step in and then out of the square footbath on the other side, and once again, I'm standing at the poolside, staring out over the rectangular shell of the pool, all sharp edges and slopes. There is something strangely majestic about its emptiness. Something eerily beautiful.

I draw my camera to my right eye and start snapping away. Then I check the images on the LCD viewfinder and make some further adjustments.

As I'm moving around the pool taking my pictures, sometimes crouching, sometimes standing, once from the top row of the spectator area and then as close to the edge as I dare, I wonder what it is about this place I find so alluring. Maybe it's the same reason I'm drawn to all abandoned buildings: because they represent the impermanence of life. Seeing something that has been carefully designed and constructed for a specific purpose left to deteriorate slowly, to be degraded by neglect and the passing of time, resonates with me somewhere deep inside.

Empty buildings, and this pool in particular, symbolize what I have become. A ghost of my former self. An empty vessel. Someone who will always be on the outside look-ing in, taking pictures and wishing things were different. Wishing she could turn back the clock until none of it had happened and Lottie was still alive.

Back in the corridor, I'm almost at the cupboard when I find myself staring at the door to the pump room. I don't want to go in there again. I don't want to look at it for fear of what I might find. But I have to see what's going on with that wall.

The silence is thick. Apart from me, the place is deserted.

It won't take more than a minute.

I push the door open and go inside, squeezing past the filtration cylinder until I'm just inches from the wall. Now that I'm looking directly at it, I see that I was right. The cream-coloured paintwork on this whole section is subtly different. It's brighter than the rest, cleaner looking, which means that, for some strange reason, it's been repainted. I knock and the sound is hollow, but when I knock on either side it's a much duller sound.

I squat in front of the pipework and feel behind it where the wall meets the floor. This is where the patch is, and I see at once that someone has carefully stuck a piece of wallpaper there, painted the same colour as the wall. I press my fingers on the paper, and it bows in. There is nothing behind it, so I peel the paper back from one corner and see an opening not much bigger than my hand. It looks like someone has deliberately cut into the plasterboard.

Instinctively, I lower my head as far as I can get it with-out actually touching the floor. I can't see anything beyond the opening as it's dark in there, so I get my phone and shine the torch into it. The light falls on something metallic. I can't quite see what it is, so I bend down even further. My ear grazes the cold floor and I manage to break a bit more of the plasterboard off, but it's an awkward manoeuvre with my camera still hanging round my neck, so I unhook it and place it on the floor next to me.

My breath catches in the back of my throat as I get a better look inside the hole. It's a toolbox. One of those folding metal ones. I move my head to one side and see another one just like it. And another. And then another. Four metal toolboxes have been hidden in a cavity off the pump room of a disused school swimming pool. It certainly explains why the workmen Hayley and Lou saw coming in here with them left empty-handed. They must have smashed a hole in the wall, stashed them in the cavity, and then inserted a piece of plasterboard. Maybe they left this small hand-sized hole behind the pipework to make it quicker and easier to remove the board when they came back to retrieve the toolboxes.

If this is what I think it is, then this isn't the hidey-hole of a recreational user, or even a small-time drug dealer. This is a serious amount of gear, and I need to get the hell out of here right now.

But first, I need to take a few pictures, to prove what I've seen. It'll be quicker and easier to use my phone. When I'm satisfied that I've taken enough and that they've come out clearly, I get to my feet, pick up my camera and cross the pump room. I'm almost at the door when I hear something that makes my blood run cold.

It sounds like someone is crying. Distressed little whimpers. Whoever it is, they're getting closer and closer.

How the hell did they get in without me hearing them? Either they know about the store cupboard, or they were already here when I came in.

My mouth is so dry I can barely swallow. The door to the store cupboard is just a few paces away on the other side of the corridor, but I can't make a move yet because whoever it is will see me. The whimpers are becoming more frequent now and . . . deeper. It sounds like it might be a man. My mind spins. What in God's name is going on here? Who is it?

Suddenly, there is silence, and my heart almost stops. They must have noticed the open door to the pump room. Footsteps approach and I curse myself for still being here, for coming in at all. I should be in my room, making plans to leave this godawful place far behind me. It's yet another of my stupid, *stupid* decisions.

I don't know who this man is or why he's crying, but if he's responsible for what's hidden behind this wall and finds me here, my fingers covered in flakes of plasterboard, the gaping hole right behind me, I'm done for.

The door is moving now, being pushed open wider. My whole body is shaking.

Oh God. Is this what happened to Hayley?

53

Marlow

I see his shoes before I see *him*. Brown suede Hush Puppies. The relief I feel that it's Rob Hornby staring down at me, his face blotchy and tear-stained, and not the intimidating figure of James Brampton, or some nameless thug in a high-vis jacket and hard hat, is short-lived. Because Rob must be involved in all this, or why else would he be here? Why else would he be guarding this place so vigilantly?

Why else would he have lied to me about Hayley's room?

'You!' he says, accusingly. 'I told you never to come in here. How did you get in?'

His eyes stray to the wall behind me, and he recoils as if an invisible bullet has hit him in the stomach.

'What have you done?' He's whispering now, his face ashen with fear. 'You shouldn't have done that.'

Now he's grabbing me by my jumper and yanking me to my feet. My camera clatters to the floor. I try to resist him, to prise his fingers off and push him away from me, but he's too strong, and I find myself being propelled out of the room and down the corridor at speed, towards the main entrance.

'What are you doing? Get your hands off me!'

'Shut up,' he snaps. 'I'm trying to help you, don't you see? You have to hide. I can't stand by while another girl dies in this place.' My stomach lurches. So Hayley *is* dead. Oh my God. She's dead. She's *dead*. 'He'll be here any second,' Rob hisses. 'I won't be able to help you then.'

'Who? Who will be here?'

He shoves me into the staff changing room and into one of the toilet cubicles, pulling the door shut behind us.

'You have to stay here. Crouch on the toilet lid so your feet can't be seen. Keep quiet or he might find you.'

'But there's another way out.'

'No, there isn't.'

'There is, it's—'

But it's too late. It's too late to make him understand. The main door is opening. Now we're both trapped in this fucking toilet. Frantically, I get up on to the lid, but it's pointless. We can't both fit on here, and Rob's feet will be clearly visible in the gap under the door.

'What the fuck are you doing, Hornby? Why aren't you at work?'

I recognize Harry Kiernan's voice straight away, yet at the same time, I don't. There's a new quality to it. A harsh, aggressive tone I've never heard in all the years I've known him. Panic flares inside me. It can't be him who's behind all this, can it? Lazy, laid-back Harry Kiernan, with his floppy dark-blond hair and boy-band looks. Jesus Christ! Did he already know she was dead when I went to see him?

A look of terror flashes across Rob's face. The fear in his eyes is all the confirmation I need. I can smell Rob's sour breath in my face. He's frozen to the spot, still clutching my arms as I crouch on the toilet seat. Any second now, Harry will find us.

But then, something changes in Rob's face. It's as if someone has flicked a switch and changed his setting. The muscles tighten round his mouth and his eyes narrow. He releases his grip on my forearms, turns and walks out of the toilet, pushing the cubicle door closed behind him. I hear him walk out into the corridor.

'What the fuck are you—' Harry's response is interrupted by a dull thwacking sound. Rob must have punched him. I didn't think he'd have it in him. Now there's scuffling and grunting, the squeak of trainers scrabbling on the tiled floor. Another thwack, but this time followed by the sound of a body slumping down. Then silence.

Still crouched on the lid of the toilet, frozen with fear, and cursing myself for being stupid enough to waste time taking pictures of the pool when I should have gone straight to the pump room, got my photographic evidence and left, I wait for the fight to continue. But one of them is down and isn't getting up, and it doesn't take much to work out which one of them it is. Harry's so much stronger than Rob, clearly the more dominant of the two. That punch will have infuriated him. The sound of gaffer tape being ripped from a reel confirms my worst suspicions.

I'm crying now, my tears flowing freely. With Rob, I might have stood a chance. But with Harry . . . There's no way I'm getting out of this alive. Rob's words come back to me – *I can't stand by while another girl dies in this place* – and my body starts to shake.

The shock when the cubicle door swings open and it's Rob standing there in front of me is overwhelming. But I'm not safe yet. Nowhere near. He might have managed to knock Harry out, but for how long? And Rob's still up to his ears in all this. His eyes are wild, the pupils darting in all directions. Beads of sweat have sprung up on his forehead and upper lip.

When he speaks, his voice is high like a little boy's, and frightened. So very frightened. 'I . . . I don't know what to do.' He takes a step back, hugging himself and rocking backwards and forwards like a traumatized child.

I climb down off the toilet, my legs stiff from where they've been scrunched up under me. As I step out of the cubicle, I glimpse Harry's legs from the open door that leads into the corridor. Nerves thrum in my neck, my chest, my belly. He's been knocked out cold.

Rob is cringing by the bench in the changing room, his

eyes also glued to those legs. Sweat now coats his forehead and there are two spreading patches of it in the armpits of his T-shirt. All I want to do is get the hell out of here. Escape from whatever this is. But something holds me back. Stops me from sprinting out of this changing room. The knowledge, deep inside my gut, that making a run for it now will not end well.

'What's going on, Rob?' My voice sounds tinny and alien in the cold, empty space. 'You need to tell me what's going on.'

He looks at me, and something blazes in his eyes. Fear or fury, I can't tell which it is. The muscles in his forearms tighten and a shiver runs through me. What the hell have I walked into?

'Why should I trust you?' he says, and with that one question, I know he *wants* to trust me. This is my chance to get out of here. I have to take control of the situation before Harry comes round.

'Because I can see that, deep down, you're not like him.' I jerk my head towards those legs, still motionless on the floor. 'You're not a bad person.'

Rob's eyes are now trained on me, and I can sense he's as frightened as I am, but somehow that makes it worse, because he's on the edge. Unpredictable.

I take a deep breath to steady my nerves. 'Tell me your part in all this and I'll tell you what to do. We'll work it out. Together.'

Rob's face twitches. He runs a hand through his hair, kneads his fingers into the back of his neck. 'He thinks

I'm an idiot. Some simpleton he can boss around and manipulate.' He spits the words out.

'But you're not, are you? You're much more intelligent than him.'

Rob tilts his chin back. A small, proud gesture. A tacit agreement. 'It's just that, I . . . I don't always pick up on things. Tones of voices. Facial cues, that kind of thing. I . . . take people at their word. Always have.'

'I get it, Rob. I get it. Harry has underestimated you. We can sort this out, the two of us. But you've got to let me help you.'

He's pacing up and down the small square of the changing room like a caged animal, his arms still folded across his chest, his fingers digging into his arms.

'I didn't know what was happening at first. I thought he just wanted me to monitor the no-go areas. Make sure no one flouted the rules and broke in.' He rakes his hands through his hair again. 'Rules are important,' he says, anger spiking. 'Without rules, everything breaks down.'

'You're right,' I say, aware of the sudden change in his tone. The indignation. A fresh wave of alarm ripples through me. 'You're so right. Now tell me everything. I can't help you if I don't know what's happened.'

It's so cold in here it feels like a fridge, but Rob seems hardly aware of it with his T-shirt and bare arms. He's still pacing up and down. Still sweating profusely.

'I was the first one to live here. The only guardian on site for the first month.' I watch his Adam's apple jerk up and down as he swallows. 'I was the happiest I've ever been because I was . . .' He presses the fingers of both hands

309

across his mouth, and I wonder what else he isn't telling me. 'I could have carried on living here too, managing the place on my own, but Brampton insisted there needed to be more people on site. For security.'

He exhales slowly and deliberately, trying to calm himself down. Every few seconds he glances out of the door, his eyes like saucers. He gestures towards Harry's inert body and lets out a juddering sigh. 'I thought he was my friend and he relied on me. I . . . I *liked* that, and I didn't want to lose my place here. But then all this weird stuff started happening.'

'What kind of weird stuff?'

'Unplanned site visits. Things that weren't in the diary. CCTV footage being wiped before I'd had a chance to look at it. Harry said he'd already checked it, but that was *my* job. I knew if I started asking too many questions, he'd get rid of me, and I . . . I didn't want to leave. I *can't* leave. I won't.'

What is it he isn't telling me? I want to shake it out of him, but I daren't. Because Rob is on the edge of losing it, and right now, I'm in a very precarious position.

'Did he . . . did he kill Hayley?'

Rob breaks down. Tears are running in rivulets down his face. 'I think he must have done. He didn't even know I was there that time she came in. I crept away before he saw me.

'She . . . she wouldn't give up, you see. Kept trying to get inside. I saw her on the cameras. That's why I went in after her, to tell her to get out. She stole the keys from my office!'

His voice is indignant as he says this, as if the fact of her stealing the keys is a crime as serious as the drugs. No wonder Harry could twist him round his finger.

'But she'd already found the drugs when you got here.'

He nods. 'I followed her in, found her bag and phone in the changing rooms. Then I heard Harry. I didn't even know he was in there. She was pleading with him, and then . . .' He clamps his hand to his mouth, starts rocking again. 'I should have been braver. I should have tried to help her, but I couldn't move. I let him drag her away, and I did nothing to help her. Nothing!'

I stare at him, horrified, my mind awash with visions of poor Hayley being manhandled out of the building.

'Don't you see? If he'd seen me there, I'd have been in trouble too. Just like Hayley. Maybe not then and there, but sooner or later he'd have come for me.'

'So, what – you just carried on as if nothing had happened?'

He nods, not looking me in the face. 'He called me the next morning, told me she'd had to leave quickly – a family emergency, he said. I had no choice but to pretend I didn't know anything, carry on as normal, don't you see?'

Not really, Rob, no. But then I can't tell him that. His emotions are all over the place. I don't want to do anything to destabilize him even more.

'He might be the one lying out there, but he's still got me over a barrel. My fingerprints are all over her possessions. My DNA too. He made me pack them. Told me she'd collect them from the agency. I thought maybe . . . I

311

thought maybe he'd let her go after all. Warned her off or something. So I did what he asked, like the fool that I am. But I didn't put her phone in with her things. Something told me not to, so I hid it. He kept asking me if I'd found it in the room, and I said I hadn't.'

He dry-heaves into his hands. 'That's when I knew he must have done something with her. I'm in this up to my eyeballs, and he knows it. He knows it.'

I jerk my head towards the door. 'Is he . . . unconscious?'

'I think so.'

'But he's still breathing, right?'

Rob looks at me in horror. 'You think I've killed him?'

'No, no, I don't think that. But if you've knocked him out, he'll come round again, won't he? It's only a matter of time. And what are you going to do then?'

'I've tied him up.'

'But you can't keep him tied up for ever. We're going to have to call the police and let them know what's happened before anyone else turns up. He can't be working alone. Is Brampton involved in this too?'

'I don't know.' Rob is now wringing his hands. 'We can't call the police. They'll think I did it. They'll think I killed her. I've watched those programmes on TV. I know what will happen to me. I've been framed.'

'Please, Rob. You've got to trust me. I'm on your side.'

He exhales in one long, shuddering breath.

'We need to check on him.'

Rob puts his arm out to stop me from exiting the room before him. What little control he has over this situation is clearly important to him. He's not ready to hand it over yet, and if I want to keep him on side, I need to accept that. I need to go slow.

Once outside in the corridor, I kneel down next to Harry's head and check for a pulse. The relief when I feel one is short-lived. His eyelids are starting to twitch, and a barely audible moan escapes through the tape on his mouth. We don't have much time before he wakes up, and though Rob seems to have trussed him up fairly effectively, we can't keep him here like this.

'We have to call the police,' I say. 'You need to tell them what you've just told me.' I look up at his anxious face. 'We'll work out what to say to them, so they understand you aren't part of it.'

'But I *am* part of it. I knew something wasn't right, and I didn't do anything. I'm a terrible, terrible person.'

His face suddenly freezes. When I follow his gaze and see Harry's cold, grey eyes fixed on us, I recoil. This is the man who has almost certainly killed Hayley, and even though his hands and feet are tied and there's tape across his mouth, my insides turn to jelly. I have to be strong. I can't afford to lose it. Not when Rob is wavering like this.

'Let's get out of here now and lock him in, go back to the office and phone the police. It's the only way, Rob.'

But Rob is shaking his head. His face is deathly white. 'He'll spin it somehow so that I'm the one they'll put away. He's clever. He's . . . he's devious. I won't let you call the police. I won't! I have to stay here. I can't leave.'

He fixes me with a wild stare. 'I can't *ever* leave!'

54

Marlow

'But we have to call them,' I plead. 'Don't you see? It's the only way out of this.'

I tug at Rob's arm, but he shoves me away and starts dragging Harry's body into the changing room. Harry is now thrashing around like a fish on a hook. I can't stand it any longer. I have to get out of here while Rob's distracted. I'll go back to my room, grab my rucksack and whatever else I can get hold of, and leave. Leave it all behind. It's only *stuff*, after all. I can't get involved in this. It's a dangerous situation, and any hope I had about saving Hayley is gone.

But it's not too late to save myself.

I make a dash for the store cupboard, but suddenly Rob is right behind me. He drags me back into the changing room and closes the door behind us. He's gripping me by the wrist so tightly it hurts.

'This isn't going to work!' I say, desperately trying to shake him off. 'You're making it worse.'

His fingers tighten round my wrist. 'No! *You're* making it worse. You need to shut up for a minute and let me think. Let me *think*!'

I can hardly bear to look at Harry on the floor. He's stopped thrashing around now and his eyes are staring at me. Why did he come here today? There must have been a reason. For all I know, his associates will be here soon, and Rob and I will be collateral damage. God knows what these people are capable of. I have to try another tactic to get Rob to leave with me now and call the police.

Rob starts pacing again, in front of the closed changing-room door. Pacing and wringing his hands. 'I'm a terrible person,' he says again. 'I should have done something to stop this happening. I should have acted sooner.'

Suddenly, the solution is staring me in the face, and I know that I have to do it. It's the only way I can convince him I'm on his side and that I understand the predicament he's in.

'I'm a terrible person too,' I say, my voice little more than a whisper.

I'm not even sure he's heard me, he's so distracted by fear and panic. I raise my voice a fraction.

'I've also done something I'm ashamed of. Deeply, deeply ashamed of. Something I've never told another living soul.'

Rob stops pacing and stares at me. His body is still full

of tension, but at least he's listening. If I can just make him understand what it's like to live with guilt day in, day out, then maybe I can persuade him to do the right thing and talk to the police.

'I used to go to this school,' I say. A furrow appears on Rob's forehead. He wasn't expecting that, and nor was Harry, if the look in his eyes is anything to go by. 'I didn't want to take a room here at first, because it held too many bad memories, but I didn't have anywhere else to go and I thought it might be good for me, coming back. I thought it might help me come to terms with what happened. Come to terms with . . . with what I did.'

Rob's jaw is still tight with tension, but he's slowly becoming less distracted. I gesture to the bench, but he shakes his head. He's still too agitated to sit down, and maybe it's better not to. I can feel Harry's eyes boring into me from the floor, so I turn my back on him and focus all my attention on Rob, who's now working his thumb ferociously into the palm of his hand.

'I was studying for my A Levels: Art, English and History. But it was all about the art. I wanted to be a famous photographer.' I almost laugh. 'The naivety of youth, eh?' I give a rueful smile. 'I guess I knew deep down I wasn't going to get the grades I wanted, which meant I probably wouldn't get on to the degree course I wanted either. I kept hoping I'd pull it off at the last moment, but the more I tried to produce something good, the harder it became. I was too much of a perfectionist, you see.'

I perch on the edge of the bench and hold Rob's gaze.

'What I really wanted was to throw all my coursework away and start again, but I knew I wouldn't be allowed to do that, not at that late stage of the course. There wasn't enough time.'

I take a deep breath. 'It didn't help that one of my best friends was a seriously talented painter.'

Rob is blinking at me from behind his glasses.

'I mean, supremely talented. It's not that I was jealous of her; I wasn't. I didn't want to be a painter, I wanted to be a photographer, but I could see the level of work she was producing, and I knew mine didn't come close.'

Rob is gradually calming down. He's still working his thumb into the palm of his other hand, but more slowly now. Listening to me is having the desired effect. I carry on, but by now I'm doing this as much for my benefit as his. It's something I've needed to do for a very long time.

'I had this crazy fantasy that if I could just find a way for my coursework to be *damaged* somehow, I'd be given more time, or at least have a reason for not succeeding other than not being quite good enough. Sometimes I blame it on my parents, for putting me under so much pressure. Or the teachers and Miss Latham, for having such high expectations of all of us. Or the whole fucking education system. But I know that's just making excuses. There's no one to blame for what happened except me. I was a stupid little girl thinking only of her A Level grades and getting into the right art college.'

Rob is becoming stiller and stiller. He is clasping his hands in his lap, his back ramrod straight, and listening intently. I feel emboldened to go on, so I start to tell him what happened. Every last bit of it. I can hardly believe that I'm saying the words out loud, and not just to one person, but to two. Harry Kiernan might be tied up, but his ears are uncovered. He's listening too. He has no choice.

And now that I've started, I'm compelled to continue with it, to tell him – to tell *them* – every last, shameful thing. Just as I was compelled to come back to McKinleys against my better judgement, because some tiny, buried part of me must have known that it was the only way I'd ever start to ease the burden I've been carrying all these years. The burden that has ground me down into this lonely, nomadic existence. The burden that has alienated me from my parents and from myself, from the girl I used to be.

Rob is motionless now, and I know that I have his full attention. Maybe, just maybe, my pitiful tale will persuade him to do the right thing. So I recount the dreadful details of that hellish day, from start to finish. How I went to the toilet just before morning break and waited there till the bell rang, then slipped back into the empty studio. How on the way out, I poked a corner of my portfolio through one of the slats in the shelf, then casually flicked my lighter into the overflowing recycling bin underneath – the huge wire crate stuffed with paper and card that Ms Thompson never emptied till it was practically overflowing.

By now, my eyes are blurred with tears.

'But the second I saw that flame, I knew it was a mistake. I realized it wouldn't just be *my* work that got spoiled, it would be other people's too. And I thought of Miss Latham's face if I got caught, and my parents' faces when they found out what I'd done. I'd be expelled for sure, and my whole life would be ruined over one childish, selfish act.

'So I pulled it out straight away, the burning piece of paper.'

Rob's pink-rimmed eyes are still trained on my face, hanging on my every word.

'I dropped it on the floor and stamped on it hard. Then I stuffed what was left of it into my rucksack and snuck out of the building as fast as I could, went and stood on the far side of the playground, pretended to be eating something from my lunchbox.'

I feel Rob's eyes on my face, watching me as I speak. I'm crying now. Big fat tears sploshing down my cheeks and soaking into my neck. 'But the fire didn't go out. I must have set light to more than one piece of paper, and before long, the whole studio was on fire. The alarm was ringing and there was smoke everywhere. Thick, black smoke.'

Rob sits down on the bench opposite me. His arms are tightly folded across his chest, and he leans forward over his lap, his eyes fixed on mine. I'm getting through to him. He's totally absorbed in what I'm telling him.

'I was terrified. We all were. The teachers rounded us up and led us out of the school, on to the street. The fire engines arrived, and I was so scared they'd find out it was me. I still had the lighter in my pocket, and the burnt paper in my rucksack. I felt like everyone could see it was me who'd done it. That it was only a matter of time before I was hauled off to the police station.'

My breath judders in my throat. 'And then they took the registers.'

Tears are streaming down my face now. 'I had no idea anyone was upstairs in the art pods.'

'But someone was,' Rob says. His voice is calmer now, and so are his eyes. He is still and focused, and I remind myself why I'm doing this, why I'm sitting in a cold, damp changing room with him, Harry Kiernan trussed up on the floor beside us. I'm doing it to make him understand what it's like to live with a dark secret. How it ruins your entire life.

I take a deep breath. 'Yes. My best friend was up there.' My voice falters, but I force myself to go on, because I can't stop now. 'My best friend, who never did anything she wasn't supposed to. The awful thing was, I was the one who told her how easy it was to get in, and how Ms Thompson didn't always lock the door. I used to do it all the time instead of hanging about in the cold.'

I sniff back the tears. 'I remember her face when I first told her. She said, "You're crazy. Ms Thompson will give you detention if she catches you."'

I close my eyes and shake my head. 'She actually worried about things like that.'

'Because she understood the importance of rules,' Rob says.

'Yes, yes, exactly. Which is why I never for one second thought she'd try it herself. And I never for one second thought the fire was still burning when I left the studio.'

I hear the long, slow sound of Rob's exhaled breath as he absorbs what I'm telling him.

'I've kept this dreadful secret for so long, I've almost convinced myself it didn't happen, and that it's some peculiar form of survivor's guilt. Because how *could* it have happened? How *could* I have done something so unutterably wrong? It's not who I am. It's inconceivable.'

A muscle is twitching in Rob's left cheek. Listening to my confession is having an effect on him. It's making him realize that he's not the only one to have done something bad, something that has resulted in another person's death.

'So they were right, when they said it could have been deliberate,' he says, his voice measured and low.

I feel a spike of unease at this strange reaction. But then, Rob's brain works in a different way to other people's. He finds it hard to gauge emotions, so of course he's focusing on the facts. I'm going to have to try a little harder.

'Yes, but they were only half right, weren't they? Because I changed my mind. I put the fire out. At least, I thought I did. So it wasn't really deliberate.'

Rob frowns. 'But it was to start with. Your intention was to start a fire. So in that sense, it *was* deliberate.'

He's leaning back on the bench now, looking at me

through narrowed eyes. Harry starts thrashing about again, but he might as well not be there for all the attention Rob is giving him. Why isn't he worried about Harry any more? Why is he looking at me in that peculiar way? And why is he arguing with me over semantics, for Christ's sake?

Because that's the kind of person he is. You know this. Don't worry about it. Keep going.

I moisten my lips with my tongue and take a deep breath before continuing. 'My intention, at first, was to start a fire. But then I changed my mind. I didn't intend to burn the whole studio down. That was the *last* thing I wanted to happen. And I certainly didn't intend to—'

'To kill Lottie,' Rob says.

'No! No, of course not. That's what I'm trying to tell you. I'm trying to tell you how terrible it is living with guilt because of a stupid, stupid mistake. I'm trying to explain what—'

'But you *did* kill her,' he says. 'Your actions resulted in her death. Your actions resulted in an innocent girl dying.'

I stare at him, open-mouthed. I knew he'd be shocked. Horrified, even. But this cold, analytical summary of my heartfelt confession is something else.

I try again. 'Ye-es. Just like *your* actions have contributed to . . .' I glance at Harry, who appears to have given up struggling to free himself and is looking unusually calm for someone trussed up on the floor.

Rob gets to his feet, and there is something about the controlled way he does this that scares me. The colour is rising in his cheeks.

322

'You killed the most precious, beautiful girl in the world,' he says, his hands balled into fists at his side.

I stand up too, dread coiling in my gut like a snake. This isn't working. Why is he reacting like this?

'You killed my girlfriend,' he says. 'You killed the girl I loved.'

55

Marlow

No. No, no, no. This isn't happening. Lottie didn't have a boyfriend.

I'd have known if she had a boyfriend. She'd have told me. I'd have seen him. We were close. Always at each other's houses, always confiding in each other. She didn't have a boyfriend. Neither of us did.

My stomach churns as the memory seeps into my mind. The Valentine's card. The one we laughed at in the park. We both got one that year. Hers was really soppy, with a pressed flower inside. It was from the creepy son of one of her mother's friends, who kept loitering on the street outside her house and looking up at her bedroom. She told her dad eventually, and he went out and had a word with him. Sent him packing.

Robin. Oh my God. His name was Robin. She said he made her shudder.

I look at Rob's face, and it's as much as I can do not to shudder right now. He seems to have forgotten all about Harry lying on the floor behind us and the mess he's in. It's only me he's concerned with now. I can see it in his eyes. Those small, pink-rimmed eyes blinking at me furiously.

He takes a step towards me, and I instinctively take a step back. 'It was an accident,' I say. 'You've heard what I just said. I was Lottie's friend. I would never have hurt her. Never in a million years.'

He comes closer. 'But you *did* hurt her. You burnt her to death.'

He's right in my face now, forcing me to walk backwards, past the toilets and the showers and towards the little footbath that leads to the pool.

He grabs my wrist. 'Why didn't you admit what you'd done?'

'Because I was a wreck, don't you see? I was frightened, terrified of what might happen. Not just to me, but my parents too. It would have ruined their lives as well as mine. They'd have forever been known as the parents of the girl who set fire to her school and killed a pupil. I'd have had a criminal record – I might even have ended up in prison.'

I stumble back into the footbath and almost fall. He trips too, and I take the opportunity to wrench my hand away from his and break free. We're in the main pool area now, and my voice echoes in the void.

'I'm telling you all this for a reason, Rob. To make you understand you're not the only one who's done bad things.'

He rounds on me in an instant, grabbing both of my fore-arms, his fingers digging sharply into them. 'I haven't done bad things. I've stood by and let them happen, yes, but it isn't the same. It isn't the same at all. I didn't kill Hayley.'

'No, but you didn't try to save her either.'

No sooner are the words out of my mouth than I realize my mistake.

His voice, when it comes, is menacingly low. 'How dare you compare my situation to yours. You deliberately started a fire for your own selfish ends and killed my girlfriend in the process, and you've kept that secret for eighteen years!'

'But I've told you now, and I'll tell the police too. It's been hell trying to live with the guilt all this time. That's what I'm saying, Rob: we need to call the police now, before Harry's associates realize he's missing and come looking for him. He can't be working on his own.'

But it's as if Rob can't hear a single word I'm saying. His face is puce, and I'm acutely aware that in his rage he keeps forcing me to walk backwards and that we are now peril-ously close to the edge of the deep end of the pool.

It's in this precise moment that we hear the sound of running footsteps, followed by a sharp ripping sound. Oh my God! One of Harry's accomplices must have turned up and untied him. Now Harry is barking instructions. 'Get the fucking gear and get the hell out of here. Tell J there's been a last-minute change of plan. You, stay here with me. There'll be some cleaning up to do.'

My stomach plummets at this last sentence. 'Please, Rob, let me go. I know another way out. We can get into the

326

corridor through the other set of changing rooms and into the store cupboard. Come *on*.'

But Rob won't let go of my arms. He won't move. He's rooted to the side of the pool in fear and indecision. What's wrong with him? Can't he see what's going to happen if we don't get out of here?

And now it's too late. Harry is at the poolside in an instant. Rob drops my arms in shock, and I stagger back. Harry's eyes are small black bullets drilling into Rob's terror-stricken face. I watch, horrified, as he draws his shoulder back and delivers a punch so swift and savage, so unnervingly precise, that Rob doesn't stand a chance. Harry's knuckles smash into his cheekbone and Rob folds like a deckchair, teetering at the edge of the pool, arms flailing, eyes wide in panic. It's as if time has slowed, and though my instinct is to rush forward and pull him to safety, I'm unable to move. Unable to breathe.

Rob falls backwards into the empty pool, the thud of his body landing at the bottom immediately followed by an ominously loud crack as his skull connects with the unforgiving tiles. The noise galvanizes me into action. I turn to run away, but Harry grabs hold of my shoulders and pulls me back. It takes all my body strength to brace my legs and keep both of my feet on the floor. I don't think I can withstand it any longer, yet I know what's going to happen. He's going to swing me over the edge too. My socked feet slip and slide on the cold tiles in my desperation to get away from him, but there's no way I can. He's too strong for me.

Suddenly, there's a noise so loud and unexpected, so

booming and reverberant, that for a second I think there's been an explosion. It's the sound of doors being hoofed in and boots – what sounds like hundreds of them, an army of boots – pounding down on the tiled floor outside. For one frozen second, Harry and I lock eyes in shock, and then a swarm of armed police officers in riot gear charge through both sets of changing rooms at the same time, an eruption of noise and movement that makes Harry drop my hands and stagger back.

Resounding shouts of, 'Police! Get your hands in the air! Get your hands in the fucking air!' bounce around the cavernous space like pinballs ricocheting in a giant pinball machine. With nothing to absorb the sound but the hard, reflective surfaces of the pool, the noise is deafening. It's pandemonium. Waves of sensory chaos. Acoustics so disorienting and harsh, I can hardly stand up.

'Move away from the edge of the pool. Look at me!' shouts one of the officers. 'Walk towards me. Hands in the air!'

I do as he says, but as I step forward Harry lunges towards me, and in that instant I know exactly what he's going to do. He's going to try to hold me hostage as some kind of bargaining tool. I skitter sideways and hear a loud, crackling sound. Harry's within a hair's breadth of me when he drops like a stone. Three police officers surge forward as one, and as they crouch over Harry's body, I realize they've tasered him.

I sink to my knees. A wave of nausea engulfs me and I'm pouring with sweat. Now I'm heaving, vomit splashing on to the tiles at the side of the pool. More shouts and arrest warnings reach my ears from the staff changing room, and police officers are climbing down the metal ladders to the pool floor, like beetles scuttling into a pit.

One of them is squatting at my side talking to me, but I don't hear a word he's saying, and my voice doesn't seem to be working. I'm cold and clammy and shaking all over. I wipe my mouth with my hand and peer down into the gaping pool. Rob is lying inert at the bottom. He's on his back and blood has spread around his head, the bright redness of it vivid against the white of the tiles.

More police officers crouch next to him. 'Dead,' one of them says, his lone voice a sinister echo.

What happens next is a whirlwind. Paramedics. Police. People in crime-scene suits climbing in and out of the pool. Echoing voices drifting through from the corridor. More paramedics join the police still huddled with Harry at the side of the pool. Something is wrong. He should have come round by now. He must have cracked his head as he went down.

I can hardly bear to look as Rob's body is lifted out of the pool on a stretcher. I have been wrapped in one of those shiny silver blankets. Someone gets me a cup of water, but I can't take more than a sip without retching. Now Harry is on a stretcher too. It's hard to see him properly as there are so many people clustered round him, but it looks like his head is in some kind of helmet.

Later, in hospital, after I've been checked over and

pronounced medically fit for discharge, I am driven to the police station to give a statement. As I'm ushered down a corridor to an interview room, I catch sight of Elle in another room, talking to one of the officers. Our eyes meet briefly before I pass. I guess they're going to be talking to all of the guardians separately, to find out what each of us knew or witnessed.

As I sit down at a table and wait to be interviewed, it occurs to me that if Harry doesn't recover, we might never find out what happened to Hayley.

It makes me weep. I weep for the girl who took all those pictures of my old school and put them on Instagram, pretending it was her amazing renovation project. I weep for the girl who liked milky coffee and occasionally getting pissed with Bryony. I weep for the girl whose favourite ever book was *Rebecca*, and who took the time to polish the parquet floor in Mr Barker's old classroom. The girl who painted the old radiator brilliant white and hung voile panels at the window. The girl who used to do drugs because her father abused her. The girl who was kind enough to want to give Nikhil feedback on his screenplay and who would, almost certainly, have paid Bryony back the seventy pounds she owed her. The girl who, like me, was drawn to a puzzle and who made it her business to investigate.

The door of the interview room opens, and a police officer walks in and sits down opposite me. She asks me to tell her what I was doing in the swimming pool.

I take a deep breath and start to speak.

56

SOME WEEKS LATER

Marlow

The Montpellier Saint-Roch train is on time, and I'm one of the first in the queue – if you can call it that; it's more of a free-for-all – at the platform barrier in Hall 1 of the Gare de Lyon. It's a long journey and I've already been travelling all day, but I don't like flying. Besides, I've got plenty to think about, and if my thoughts become too much for me, I have a book to read and a Rubik's cube to solve.

My parents have told me I can stay with them as long as I like, and that I should think of their new apartment in France as my home. They also said that they were sorry for not understanding me when I was a teenager, for pushing me too hard. I was crying when they said that, and so were they. But they didn't know the real reason I was crying.

Confessions are always hard. That's why it took me so

long to tell the truth. For a while, I thought that maybe I never would. Some people keep their secrets for ever. They don't tell a living soul. If I hadn't come back to McKinleys, maybe I would have done the same thing. Because when you keep a secret for as long as I have, it gets seared into you. It burrows deep and stays there, embeds itself like a malignant tumour, destroying you from the inside out.

I sabotaged what could have been the best years of my life because of it, and would have gone on doing so. But this was a secret burning to come out. And now that I've said the words aloud, now that I've released them into the world, the healing process can finally begin. I can learn to forgive myself.

Life can be snuffed out at any second. I've always known that, ever since the day Lottie died. But seeing Rob lying dead in the bottom of that pool, and knowing that poor Hayley is lying dead somewhere too, really brought it home to me, made me realize how precious life is and how much time I've wasted.

When I told Rob what happened that day, I had no idea what the repercussions were going to be, and I didn't care. I was ready for them, whatever they turned out to be. Arson. Manslaughter. I just needed to tell someone. I needed to set the secret free and release its stranglehold on me. And as soon as I did, I felt purged. Expiated. For the first time in years, I felt free.

Until he exploded with rage, and then I felt scared. Terrified. I wanted to pluck the words I'd just spoken out of the air and swallow them whole. Put the secret back where it belonged. Deep, deep inside.

I didn't kill him though. Harry Kiernan did that. And he'd have killed me too if the police hadn't arrived when they did. They didn't tell me much, at the station. Only that they'd been monitoring Kiernan's activities for a long while, and that the investigation was ongoing.

The police saved my life. And although they don't know it, they saved my secret too. Rob's taken it to his grave and I'll take it to mine. Because honestly, who would it benefit if the truth came out now? Nothing will change. The fire will still have happened, and Lottie will still be dead. I'm not a bad person. I'm not. I changed my mind, didn't I? Realized the stupidity of my decision, the sheer reckless- ness of it. I was so, so sure I'd put it out.

But it didn't go out, and I've paid the price for that one terrible mistake ever since. I'll probably go on paying for it in one way or another, but at least I made that confes- sion. For a short period of time, two other people besides myself knew the truth.

It troubles me, of course it does, that one of them is still alive. When I asked, the police couldn't say what brain damage Harry might have sustained. But surely the longer he's in a coma, the slimmer his chances of a full recovery. Besides, what good would spilling my secret do him? He'll still be put away for trading in illegal drugs. That's all the police are going to be interested in. That and finding out what happened to poor Hayley.

I check the departures board one more time. It won't be long before I'm on that train. As I'm standing here, jostling for space among all these people, my phone rings. It's Lou. I'm so glad she made things right with Mags and finally agreed to take my number. It would have been such a shame to lose contact with her.

'Hi Marlow. Are you in Paris yet?'

'Yeah, just waiting for the train. How's it going?'

'Good, thanks. The new security agency let us move back in yesterday. They've asked me to be the new Head Guardian.'

'No way!'

She laughs. 'It won't be for long though. Mags and I are going to start looking for a decent flat soon.'

'That's great. And how are Gilly and Nikhil?'

'Well, apart from being in shock at what's happened, like we all are, they're totally made up about the baby. They're probably going to move in with Nikhil's parents for a while, just until they can find somewhere more suitable. Oh, and Bryony and Dave are still pawing each other in public. Honestly, it makes my stomach turn sometimes, the way they carry on.'

'I bet. They deserve each other, those two.'

'Elle and Craig have moved out though. In fact, they went pretty sharpish after the raid. Didn't even say goodbye. I popped into Asda the other night, to see if Craig was there. I never really took to him, to be honest, but Elle was nice. I wanted to see if she was OK, but he wasn't there and when I asked around, none of the staff seemed to know who he was. Bit weird, isn't it?'

'Yeah, that is a bit weird. Unless he worked at a different Asda. I've no idea where Elle worked. I never asked her.'

'I think she worked in an office somewhere. She never really said.'

'I hope the police find Hayley,' I say at last.

'Me too.'

'There's nothing more either of us could have done. You know that, don't you, Lou?'

I hear her sigh on the other end of the phone. 'Yeah,' she says.

'Right, I'd better go. The train's ready to board. Keep in touch, yeah?'

'I will,' Lou says.

And now the ticket barrier is open and we're all squeezing through. I hold up my phone to show the guard my ticket, and now I'm on the platform, borne along on a tide of fellow travellers. I'm on the move again. Because honestly, what else can I do? I have to keep going forward. Keep on with my life, however difficult that is sometimes, however much I despise myself. I have to live with the consequences of what I did to Lottie until the day I die.

That is my penance.

PLANS TO BUILD LUXURY HOUSING ON SITE OF FORMER PRIVATE SCHOOL NOW GOING AHEAD

The first phase of plans to build 25 homes on the site of the former McKinleys School for Girls is scheduled to begin in autumn 2024.

Brampton Developments bought the site in 2019, but progress has been delayed, owing first to the pandemic, and then to a local campaign to save the memorial garden dedicated to former pupil, Charlotte Lansdowne, who tragically died in a fire at the school in 2004. More recently, the company suffered a further setback when a significant amount of high-purity cocaine was seized from the building that housed the school's swimming pool. It is reported that the owner of the property guardian agency responsible for securing the site had been mixing legitimate business with illicit drugs-related activities. He was injured during the police raid and remains in a critical condition in hospital. Another unnamed man died on the premises during the raid.

The original Victorian part of the school will be retained and converted into luxury maisonettes, but the blocks erected in the 1960s and 70s will be demolished and new apartment blocks built in their place. There will be a mixture of one-, two- and three-bedroom homes available.

Speaking on behalf of Brampton Developments, planning agent Katie Isle confirmed that the owner of the company, James Brampton, has agreed to retain the memorial garden as a permanent feature of the new site. She said: 'Mr Brampton had already made the decision to respect the wishes of the family, even before this latest tragedy. It was the right thing to do in the circumstances – the only logical solution to what had become a highly contentious local debate.'

Former Head of McKinleys, Mary Latham, who retired shortly before the school merged with Bentley's Academy and relocated to a new site, has been an active participant in the campaign to save the garden. Latham reluctantly admitted that some of the more recent tactics, including graffiti on the perimeter fencing and trespassing on the site to lay flowers, were indeed carried out by campaigners, but were not condoned by the family and other core members. She was, however, at pains to refute any suggestion that the campaign was responsible for a fire started in a bin.

She said: 'McKinleys never really recovered from the tragic loss of Charlotte, or Lottie as she was called by her friends and family. I know I speak for the family, and everyone involved in the campaign, when I say that this guarantee from Brampton Developments means the world to us.'

I read the article again. So Mary Latham and her band of merry neighbours have successfully saved Lottie's garden. I tried to find Latham online yesterday, because I'd love to scare the shit out of her like she used to scare me, but apart from recent news reports about the campaign, and a handful of older articles about McKinleys and its history, there's diddly-squat. I can only imagine how scathing someone as punctilious as Latham is about social media. Silly old cow probably still handwrites letters and uses a landline.

I can't believe I managed to break in and light that fire the day before a major police raid. Talk about a close call. They must have been monitoring the place for months. It's a miracle I wasn't spotted. Mind you, I know that school like the back of my hand. That's what comes of being a heavy smoker from the age of fourteen. You need to scope out secret places for a crafty fag break.

When I first started smoking, I used to climb over the electricity sub-station at the far end of the playing field and drop down over the other side, on to the patch of private land covered in big red 'No Unauthorized Access' and yellow 'Danger of Death' signs. It's the obvious place to gain entry to the site. I'm amazed that Guardian Angels never considered it.

Another favourite was the little strip of land behind the caretaker's huts – and the bell-tower, of course, although that was a bit riskier because it was directly above Miss Latham's office.

But the best place by far was at the back of the art studio. Next to the staff toilet was a small storage room with a door that led out to a big bin for all the recyclables. It was basically a narrow, rectangular alleyway that no one except the cleaners and caretaker ever used, which made it ideal for smoking. I was very careful never to throw any dog-ends on the ground. I kept a little tobacco tin in my rucksack and used that instead.

Which is how, as I was returning through the classroom after a smoke, I came to see Marilyn's pathetic attempt at starting a fire. For a few seconds, I almost admired her. But the stupid little coward didn't have the guts to follow through with her plan. The panic on her face still brings a smile to my own all these years later. Not to mention her frenzied stamping.

I hung back and waited till she'd scurried off, then did what she was too scared to do, and re-lit it with my own lighter. Properly this time. I happened to have a couple of batteries in my pocket that I'd swiped from the science block earlier, so I dropped them in there too. There've been cases of exploding batteries causing house fires, so I figured if the flames took hold, the fire brigade would assume that's what had happened.

And by God, did those flames take hold. It was brilliant, seeing that place go up. And do you know what was even better? Watching Marilyn's face when it did. Serves the stupid bitch right for calling me a moron. For starting the nickname that made my time at McKinleys even worse than it already was.

Serves her fucking right.

Still, it was a shame about Lottie. I do feel bad about that, so I'm glad they've saved her garden. I really am.

Acknowledgements

I delivered this book a year later than planned. I was burnt out. I'm not sure what would have become of me if I'd pushed myself to meet the original deadline, so I'm very grateful to Sophie Hannah, who's not only a brilliant crime writer but a marvellous coach. Her words of wisdom gave me the courage to take control and say, 'No, I can't do it.' Sometimes you have to put yourself first and it takes another person to tell you what your heart already knows. Fortunately, I have an agent who always has my back and a very supportive publishing team. So thank you, Amanda Preston, Imogen Nelson and every single person at Transworld and LBA who works on my behalf.

Thanks also to my ever-growing circle of friends in the crime-writing community, for the lunches and the DMs and the WhatsApps, and to Graham Bartlett, who answers my police-related questions with patience and professionalism.

Any errors I have made in this department are entirely my own.

Special thanks also to a wonderful couple called Martin and Gillian Walker, whom I now regard as my own personal cheerleaders, and to all the readers who get in touch with me on social media. Your support means the world to me.

Thank you, Katie Isle (winner of one of my newsletter competitions), for the use of your name, although I'm sorry you had to wait until almost the end of the novel to see it!

Finally, thanks to Rashid for his ongoing love and support, and to the rest of my wonderful family, including my three beautiful grandchildren, Phoenix Heath, Milo Max and Theodora Moon, to whom this book is dedicated.

Lesley Kara is the *Sunday Times* bestselling author of *The Rumour, Who Did You Tell?*, *The Dare* and *The Apartment Upstairs*. *The Rumour* was the highest selling crime fiction debut of 2019 in the UK, and a Kindle No.1 bestseller. Lesley is an alumna of the Faber Academy 'Writing a Novel' course. She lives in Kent.

You can follow Lesley on Twitter @LesleyKara or visit her website at www.lesleykara.com